Richard Foreman is the author of numerous best-selling Kindle books, including *Augustus: Son of Rome* and the *Raffles* series of historical crime novellas. He is also the author of *Warsaw*, a literary novel set during the end of the Second World War. He lives in London.

PRAISE FOR RICHARD FOREMAN:

'*Augustus: Son of Rome* forges action and adventure with politics and philosophy. This superb story is drenched in both blood and wisdom - and puts Foreman on the map as the coming man of historical fiction' - Saul David, Author of the *Zulu Hart* series

'Classy, humorous and surprisingly touching tales of cricket, friendship and crime.' - David Blackburn, *The Spectator*

'A rattling good yarn, requiring only the minimum of suspension of belief, and leaves one eagerly anticipating the next instalment of the adventures of the team as they accompany the King to Harfleur' - Major Gordon Corrigan, author of *A Great and Glorious Adventure: A Military History of the Hundred Years War*

Also by Richard Foreman

Warsaw

A Hero of Our Time

The Complete Pat Hobby

Augustus: Son of Caesar

Raffles: The Complete Innings

Sword of Rome: The Complete Campaigns

Sword of Empire: The Complete Campaigns

AUGUSTUS:
SON OF ROME

RICHARD FOREMAN

ENDEAVOURINK

AN ENDEAVOUR INK PAPERBACK

First published by Endeavour Press
in 2012

This paperback edition published in 2017
by Endeavour Ink
Endeavour Ink is an imprint of Endeavour Press Ltd
Endeavour Press, 85-87 Borough High Steet,
London, SE1 1NH

ISBN 978-1-911445-25-8

Printed and bound in Great Britain by
Clays Ltd, St Ives plc

www.endeavourpress.com

1

The house was situated just outside of Apollonia, a Macedonian coastal town. But the architecture and character of the building were deliberately Roman. The expansive rectangular villa was of a single storey with few windows. The exterior was austere, but upon entering the house one would have been impressed by a picturesque atrium. Sunlight wafted down upon the feathery breeze illuminating much of the courtyard and the ornate mosaics which adorned the interior.

The famous owner of the house, who had still to visit his new property, had given a swift nod of assent to the blueprints and cost of the estate during a brief pause from which his intelligent eyes perused the map of some distant, supposedly barbaric land.

An unforgiving saffron sun, thankfully tempered by merciful coastal winds, bleached the coral-white walls of the house and baked the grasslands which encircled the property like an emerald moat. Upon a patch of this lawn sat two adolescents, conversing and playing with the brittle grass in their fingers.

The dusky skinned youths were similarly aged, but of dramatically differing builds.

The first boy, as lean as the poplar trunks in the background, was Rufus Salvidienus - the son of the quaestor for the region. His father, who considered himself as shrewd as he was ambitious, had encouraged his son to make friends with their auspicious new neighbours as soon as the family moved to the province. At first the aristocratic Rufus baulked at the idea of forcing a friendship. He believed that he might have to act subserviently to the youth with his great uncle's name, but little noble blood himself. But what at first was set as a politic task soon became an effortlessly enjoyable one.

With his sharp jaw and beak nose Rufus was often nicknamed 'the hawk' - a colourful title which at various times the boy and later man would be proud, teased and ashamed of. The youth's long glossy black hair, which he frequently fingered as if he were a courtesan, was also a source of ridicule and vanity to the patrician.

The second youth, broad shouldered - and broadly smiling - was one Marcus Vipsanius Agrippa.

Gusts of laughter could occasionally be heard from the two youngsters upon the lawn as they waited for their friend. The reason for his delay was due to yet another disagreement between son, mother and step-father. Again the adolescent, after trying to be reasonable, was near to throwing a tantrum about him not wanting to be accompanied by a personal bodyguard. The young master of the house eventually got his way and the family sat down to breakfast as if the argument had not taken place. The meandering conversation between the two waiting companions was eventually manipulated by Rufus towards the subject of politics - a subject that the youth was hopeful of making a career in one day. The innate Republican knew exactly what to say to stimulate and rile the ardent Caesarian and would-be centurion. It amused Salvidienus to antagonise the passionate Agrippa who, albeit being his friend, he duly considered to be his intellectual and social inferior.

"The Senate is Rome," Rufus pronounced, not without a modicum of conceit and self-appointed authority.

"What has the Senate ever done for the glory of Rome?" Marcus Agrippa replied, expressing a certain derision and even bewilderment in his tone.

"The Senate has tried to maintain that which is the glory of Rome - the Law."

"The Law is but a means to a senator's true end, self-interested profit and power. As he said the other day," Marcus Agrippa remarked as he motioned his head towards the house ("he" being their tardy friend), "justice goes to the highest bidder in Rome. He who can afford the most expensive advocate invariably wins the case. Truth has become tautologous."

"But too much has changed," exclaimed the son of the zealous optimate - quoting his father. At the same time a solemn looking Rufus Salvidienus also shook his head, in objection and pity, as if to stress the sincerity of his argument. The would-be senator had seen the technique used by an advocate during a visit to Rome a few years back.

"I would argue too little."

"Now you are just being contrary."

"No, I'm not."

And with that the two teenagers smiled and simultaneously launched what blades of grass they held in their hands at each other in playfulness. A short burst of laughter from them then echoed its way up the contoured slope and reached the ears of their companion, Gaius Octavius. For most of his teens Octavius had been a slight and sickly child, but the boy had owned the motivation to toughen himself up after spending some time on campaign with his great-uncle around a year ago. His face was tanned, but his skin and hair were still fairer than that of the two other Roman youths. His expression was sometimes broody, sometimes tranquil, and sometimes ironic - but as with now his usually serious mien could dramatically transform itself and his features could become amiable, engaging and not a little handsome.

His face was screwed up from squinting in the sunlight and from biting upon, and visibly enjoying, a crust of bread smeared in honey. Rufus and Marcus Agrippa shielded their eyes from the late morning sun as their companion descended upon them.

"Late again," issued Agrippa, sighing and comically rolling his eyes to his best friend.

"Up all night again? Were you reading, or just thinking about Briseis?" Salvidienus chipped in with a lewd expression plastered on his face. Briseis was a Greek servant girl within the household who Octavius had seduced and bedded a week before. Or rather one could argue that the alluring, experienced Briseis had seduced the lusty young Roman master of the house. The enamoured seducer had told his friends about the episode just to tell them, for they were his close companions, but perhaps more so he had recounted the experience in order to boast and make his friends feel jealous of him.

"Reading," Octavius replied with a wry smile, as well as a blush - lying slightly. For the most part however the conscientious student had been up all night - to the point where the dawn had eclipsed his lamp as a reading light - annotating notes from the texts that his part-time tutor, Cleanthes, had lent to his pupil from his private library. His ivory coloured tunic was clean, but plain and devoid of any ostentation or accessory, which marked out his family's status and wealth. There was a self-confidence, but not swagger, to his easy gait.

"Well I hope you also got some rest. Our Master said we are having a special lesson today," Marcus Agrippa said with relish in his eyes, excited as he was by the prospect of what their fencing teacher, an ex-legionary, had in store for their class this afternoon.

Salvidienus briefly smiled, trying but unable to share his pugilistic friend's attitude. He then got up, adjusting his tunic and smoothing his hair, to follow his classmate down the slope and out of the gates of the estate.

Octavius' initial reaction to the prospective lesson was one of feigned disinterest. He shrugged his shoulders and raised his eyebrow at his friend to affect being bored by, or above, such news. But when Agrippa's back was turned the wry smile disintegrated into an apprehensive frown. He realised the importance of the lessons, and there were times when Octavius tried to apply himself to the old legionary's instruction, but the thought regularly clouded the young Roman's mood that he was just not born to be a soldier. "You cannot put in what the Gods have left out," his step-father had once remarked. As a thing in itself this might not have worried the would-be philosopher, but the sense of failure troubled him because he imagined that it gave credence to the whispered arguments that Gaius Octavius was not a true Caesar.

2

A line of shrubbery, dotted with poisonous berries, fenced off the property from the neighbouring villas. Where the flanking estates housed gardens or pens for various livestock outside their villas though, there resided, at the front of Tiro Casca's modest property, a large circle - or "arena" as he called it - of sand and gravel. Rumour had it - rumours which the laconic proprietor neither confirmed nor denied - that the old Roman soldier had campaigned with both Pompey in Spain and Caesar in Long-Haired Gaul - and that he had killed more men than cholera. Some even reported that, before joining the army, Casca had been a famous gladiator who had won his freedom. Or rather, Crassus had bought it. His "war was now over" however. The ex-legionary, despite often pining for his beloved Rome, had retired to the Macedonian province, establishing a school for combat and athletics for the area's privileged Roman and Greek youth.

A receding crop of dusty brown hair, flecked with grey, crowned an ageing but still strong-jawed face. The grizzled soldier's skin was as leathery as the bloodied, cracked breastplate which Casca had proudly mounted upon his bedroom wall. His build was still stocky, with his arms, shoulders and legs as muscular and supple as a man half his fifty-five years of age. His ever expanding waistline however, forcing his belt to cut into his hips sometimes, betrayed the old soldier's fondness for red meat, washed down with undiluted red wine - which was as strong as it was sour. Like its vintner.

Having lost one of his front teeth in a battle some years ago, and chipping the other in a tavern brawl, there was a strange, almost comical sibilance to his voice - although people were fearful enough of the gnarled veteran not to comment about the minor affliction. Casca was an unapologetic disciplinarian, as well as an excellent teacher, and his students duly felt a mixture of fear and respect when in his presence. The fencing master was not without a sense of humour though, and his raucous cackle was unmistakable. But for the most part his demeanour was stern, as though Casca thought ill of everyone he encountered until they could prove him wrong. The scowling, former legionary breathed heavily through his nostrils, bushy with nose hair, almost snorting. He then addressed his class again for the day.

"So far I have taught you ladies basic swordsmanship. Today I'm going to teach you how to fight. If nothing else you'll learn how the two things are somewhat different animals."

Octavius had just recovered his breath. For the first half an hour of the session Casca had instructed Agrippa, who was a kind of prefect for the class, to have the pupils warm up. Stretching exercises were succeeded by a run. The scorching heat had sapped Octavius' body as much as the exertion. An all too brief interlude had followed in which the perpetually unimpressed tutor allowed his students to drink a ladle of warm water, each from the stone trough which was situated next to the house.

The twenty youths stood to attention in two rows of ten, wooden practise swords (tipped with padded leather) in their hands. Sweat trickled down Octavius' face, his temples seeming to be a magical font for the stuff, and his heart began to beat that much faster as he stood in the front rank. For a fleeting second after Casca had spoken, Octavius caught his intimidating tutor's eye - an act which usually presaged him picking out the student to take part in one of his training exercises. During which the pupil might suffer a bloodied nose or bruised ribs for the greater good of a martial education.

Casca noted the sheepish look on the pupil's face and, inwardly, he sighed. The ex-legionary, who had fought under his great-uncle, genuinely liked the boy. His affection for the intelligent youth however only accentuated his sense of disappointment. Casca could not fault the youth for his effort - and his intelligence made up for deficiencies in his lack of natural strength and skill - but Octavius would never make a good soldier or be a match for someone like Agrippa. It was with a heavy heart that he had to report upon Octavius' progress every month, if he could call it that, to Lucius Oppius. Oppius was a high-ranking centurion in the legion posted just outside of Apollonia. He was a veteran of Caesar's campaigns and was presently charged with the protection of the dictator's nephew. Lucius in turn reported on the youth to Cornelius Balbus, Caesar's private secretary.

Octavius couldn't help but observe Agrippa out of the corner of his eye. Marcus' hand gripped his practise sword and his brow was corrugated in determination. His muscular body, which already was no different from a fully-fledged soldier's, was taut in readiness. He was like a young lion about to pounce.

Agrippa gave off a slight grunt however, whilst Octavius quietly breathed a sigh of relief, as Casca proceeded to choose another five students to take part in his demonstration. The group was assorted, consisting of Romans and Greeks of varying abilities. Some, perhaps rightly so, were scared. Others wiped sweaty palms across their tunics to grip their weapons more tightly in preparation. They would do their best. The old soldier respected that.

"Now, using all that I have taught you and anything you ladies have taught yourselves, I want you to come at me at full speed." Casca used three training modes, slow, half, and full speed, depending upon his mood and the safety levels of the exercise. "Give no quarter, because I can assure you I won't be going easy on you," Tiro remarked and grinned, to the point where one could see the black hole of his mouth through the crooked gap in his teeth. For a second or two the students' attention was distracted by a brace of crows who cawed loudly and perched themselves on top of the tiled roof of the house, watching over the scene as if they had come to enjoy a show. Or pick over the entrails of any victims.

Even from around ten yards away, Octavius could hear the ex-legionary's scarred knuckles crack as he clasped the practise gladius. Cnaeus Tiberius, perhaps the only student in the class who could match Agrippa for strength and skill, took charge of his other four assailants. This was allowed; indeed Casca encouraged the use of teamwork and leadership. The son of one of the wealthiest merchants in the province, Cnaeus Tiberius directed, with a nod of his head and wave of his sword, for the other four to encircle their teacher as if they were hunters about to bring down a boar with their spears. He was certainly ready to give no quarter - he just hoped that his fellow students had the guts to do so too.

"Good, good," Casca remarked through narrowing eyes, impressed either with Tiberius' authority or the other four's willingness to work together. "But remember ladies, this is combat. Not swordplay."

Cnaeus subtly nodded to his two Greek classmates who were stationed behind their tutor to attack, conveying that he would try to simultaneously assail their target from the front. Casca smiled, anticipating the simple and obvious tactic. He swiftly turned to face the charging Greeks. Such was the huge arc of the Greek's swing, and the ex-soldier's strength, that he knocked the sword clean out of his first opponent's hand. Not having time to bring his weapon back in place to thrust at the second Greek, Casca merely made a fist and punched the youth square in the chest, flooring him. Sensing his attack, the fencing master swivelled to parry the efficient stroke from Tiberius. Sword clacked upon sword again as Cnaeus followed up his first attack with another well-balanced lunge. The student then took a couple of steps back from his tutor, as if he wanted to stop and admire his technique and have his master praise him also. Casca rightly did no such thing, not only because he was disappointed in Tiberius' predictable attack, but more so because his attention was directed towards the two students who were approaching him from both flanks. The first stupidly emitted an embarrassing battle-cry and held his sword aloft for too long. Before the spindly boy could bring his weapon bearing down on his opponent, Casca merely grabbed him by the wrist, to the hand which carried the imitation gladius; he then threw the youth around, as if he were a rag-doll, onto his fellow assailant who was charging at him from the opposite direction. The two students duly collided and collapsed into a heap on top of each other. One of them spluttered as he swallowed a mouthful of sand. It all happened quickly, yet Agrippa absorbed and admired the teacher's movements and control. Increasingly Marcus had come to believe that combat and warfare were sciences; one had to be deliberate, efficient. Methodical conditioning and foresight were as essential as numbers and the choice of terrain.

Cnaeus cursed his ineffectual unit underneath his breath. They reflected badly on him. Casca laughed, gleefully, sadistically, surveying the field of combat. The lad who had been punched in the stomach still groaned, prostrate, on the ground. His fellow Greek nursed a wooden gladius with a debilitating crack running through it. Tangled limbs, and bare behinds from hitched up skirts, sprang up from the ground where the final two assailants rested.

Octavius heard the crows on top of the roof caw again, as

if either laughing at the pathetic display or applauding the wily teacher.

Only Cnaeus Tiberius remained on his feet with a sword in his hand.

"C'mon. Don't fence, fight," the gruff master commanded.

The tutor was tested a little by his accomplished pupil's agility. His footwork was excellent. He was also pleased to witness the pluck of the lad who got up and fought on after being knocked down a couple of times, from the result of the old soldier fighting dirty and tripping his opponent. Casca was pleased to observe that Tiberius was not just a cliché-ridden bully and spoiled brat. He had some steel, as well as skill. At the end though, for all of Tiberius' ability with a gladius in his hand, he had not quite grasped the point of the lesson. Casca, soon after, closed the sparring session by disarming the lad, kicking the back of his legs and holding the point of the splintered sword to Tiberius' throat.

"Good, good Tiberius. But I am still looking for more. You're still fencing, not fighting. Who wants to try and surprise me then? Anyone? None of you other ladies want to dance?"

"Agrippa. I might've known you'd be up for some punishment. No sooner have the bruises disappeared from our last bout than you want me to paint some more on your body. You're either brave or stupid lad."

Agrippa merely raised a corner of his mouth in a half-smile as a reply. He then swung his sword around in his hand to loosen up his wrist whilst walking towards an opponent who he - and every other pupil in the class - had still to best. Rufus smirked and shook his head in bafflement that Agrippa would volunteer to face the sadistic veteran.

At first, pupil and teacher sized each other up and moved around in a circle together, but then they simultaneously locked horns. Agrippa rarely lunged or lost his composure in this initial exchange however, preferring to keep his distance, parrying Casca with energy saving wristy flicks of his birch wood gladius. Conscious of retaining a good defence, Agrippa also easily evaded the ex-soldier's sweeping leg, which had twice caught out Tiberius.

Octavius noted how the fencing master, for once, was breaking sweat also. He had watched Marcus observing the footwork and potential weaknesses in the tutor's technique. Agrippa had once remarked to his friend that Casca's tactic was always to counter-attack and let his opponent make a mistake.

"Again class, we have someone who can fence but can't fight. Your blood would be browning the sand if this was a battle right now," the goading teacher issued, wiping the perspiration away from his forehead. Whilst Casca was distracted with this little speech however, Agrippa subtly dug one of his open-toed sandals into the blanket of fine sand which covered the ground. In a further bid to distract and disorientate his opponent, the fresh faced student winked at the cantankerous veteran. And with that Agrippa flicked up the mound of sand he carried in his sandal into the eyes of the unsuspecting fencing master. Without hesitating, he thrust his sword and body in one movement towards the half-blinded Casca. The experienced combatant put his sword up however, and successfully blocked the incoming blow, with sword upon sword momentarily resting on each other like a hammer upon an anvil. But Agrippa was not finished fighting yet. Deploying the plan of attack that he had formulated beforehand, Agrippa made a fist with his spare hand and swiftly crouched and punched his half-blinded opponent in the groin. Casca roared in pain and stepped backwards, doubled up in acute torture. Before he even knew what was happening, the old soldier felt the rough edge of a wooden gladius upon his leathery neck.

Neither Agrippa, nor the rest of the class, knew what was coming next however, as they had yet to see their master bested. His opponent more than anyone was fearful - more scared now than at the beginning of the bout even - of what the egotistical teacher might do in response to being defeated. Breathless - and still somewhat in that certain agony and discomfort peculiar to man - Casca gazed up at his pupil and spoke.

"So you do know how to fight, as well as fence," he exclaimed, with a child-like expression on his face that Agrippa had not seen before. And with this remark and brief, private look between teacher and student, Agrippa too smiled and the tension went out of his still combat-ready body.

"I must teach you one final lesson now Agrippa," the tutor announced to the class in general, "After the heat of battle, one must learn to cool off." The doubled-over old soldier suddenly mustered all the speed and strength inside of him and picked his unprepared student up. Casca then carried Agrippa over his shoulder and dropped him into the trough of water by the house.

Laughter trumpeted out from every student within the watching class, bar the envious and resentful Tiberius. Agrippa took the joke in good spirit. A glow of pride also filled his heart as Casca offered him his hand in order to help him out of the trough. As he did so the teacher quietly remarked to his favourite pupil, "You will not just be fighting with legions one day lad - you will be leading them."

3

After instructing Agrippa to go inside and ask a servant to attend to him, Casca reverted back to his severe self and gave a lecture to the attentive class. "Viciousness, allied to intelligence, triumphs on the battlefield". He proceeded to run through various tactics - such as eye gorging, stamping and hamstringing - that would come in handy in a melee.

"If you have a helmet and your opponent doesn't, butt him... your shield should not just be used for defensive means. The umbo here protrudes for a reason - to ram into the pate of your opponent."

After the lecture the teacher arranged for a number of demonstrations, at half speed without actual contact, to illustrate the practicalities and effectiveness of fighting - as opposed to fencing. He closed the demonstration by dressing up one of the class in a Roman legionary's armour and discussing its weak points - and when and where to use the edge and point of the gladius upon such targets as the groin and neck. Upon asking if there were any questions a young Roman, he must have been no older than fifteen, wondered why they were being shown the weak spots in Roman armour, as opposed to those of their enemies?

"Romans shouldn't fight Romans," a corpulent and over privileged youth, one Ulpius Gabinus, remarked sententiously.

"They shouldn't, but unfortunately they do. And if you spent as much time learning your history, as you do eating Gabinus, you'd know that also," the veteran said with a practiced sneer, formed from half a lifetime of having to take orders from equally ignorant and pompous legates.

In the final hour or so of the lesson, Casca organised a small tournament, consisting of sword and shield bouts between classmates. Octavius won two but lost three of his contests, which was a disappointing but not unprecedented result for the diffident swordsman. Even Rufus bested him. The smug grin across the aristocrat's face smarted more than the bruise on his shoulder, which was also a reminder of his defeat. More so it preyed upon Octavius' mind that the result of the contest might find its way back to Oppius, who in return might report the poor display back to Caesar. A cloud of potent shame hung over the sensitive youth, imagining his uncle's disappointment. "Always be the best," Caesar had asserted to his nephew. He so desperately wanted for his great-uncle to be proud of him. He wanted to repay his faith in him - be worthy of the name.

Bored by the petering out of the action the crows eventually departed, cawing now in criticism at the lack of bloodshed. Shortly afterwards, peppered in dust and sweat-strewn, the students also scattered in various directions after their teacher called time on their demanding but rewarding lesson.

*

After class the three companions took shelter from the glaring afternoon sun. Passing through Rufus' father's estate the three youths rested their aching frames and sunburnt faces on a cool quilt of lush grass. A glade of willow trees, which Rufus' father cultivated in order that his slaves could produce baskets from them, provided a healthy measure of shade for their desired repose. The rippling sound of a dimpled rivulet trickled in the background and the faint but distinctive fragrance of lemon trees, from a neighbouring orchard, sang in the air to clothe the scene in further meditative pleasure.

Agrippa reclined on the verdure, practising his reflexes. With his eyes alert and the adrenaline still pumping, he regularly shot his hands up in the air in the attempt to catch the flies which dared to buzz over his head. He duly caught more than he missed, carefully keeping track of the score to see if he could beat his record, but eventually the young man grew tired of the game.

Salvidienus, with his fingers laced behind his head in order to protect his hair from the grass and soil, idly dreamed of a life in the Senate. He again listed, and charted, the 'course of honours' - the order and offices in which an ambitious politician might make his name in the capital. *Quaestor*: a junior rank, in which one could serve as a financial officer with the treasury or a clerk with the army responsible for the administration of supplies and plunder. *Aedile*: an officer charged with administration in Rome itself, the maintenance of its public buildings, streets and aqueducts. Rufus was suitably aware though that his time as an aedile would equally be concerned with staging the ludi Romani, the public games in the city. People today still talked about the games that Caesar put on during his tenure as an aedile. He too would win over the electorate through the spectacles he would arrange Rufus selfishly hoped that his father will have passed away by then so he could afford the gladiatorial contests and parade of exotic animals from his inheritance. After Aedile comes *Praetor* - one of the oldest and most revered offices in the state. As praetor Rufus could be elected to govern an entire army or province. He could sit as a magistrate in various criminal cases, possessing the power to either condemn or pardon. The sun shone through the leafy arbour as Rufus basked in the warm glow of the idea of *Consul* - and then *Pro Consul*. He would be the first Salvidienus to win the honour. Clients would lobby him with petitions. He would make his money, like Crassus, from property - not that Salvidienus would brook at accepting the odd bribe also to finance his honourable course. He would hold court at dinner parties, which would run on till late and turn into private orgies that he indulged. In his mind's eye a procession of beautiful girls and wives were paraded before him and he picked them out, as if plucking fruits from the bough, to be his lovers. And such would be his success, good reputation and popularity that he would have the pick of commands when proconsul - he would push back the frontiers of the Empire like Pompey the Great and write his name in the annals of Rome.

His eyelids felt as heavy as his limbs, but still Octavius squinted through them and lazily gazed up through a gap in the trees to take in the shimmering blue sky. He was momentarily distracted by a pair of pink finches darting about above him, the female teasingly evading the male in an aerial courtship dance. Eventually she would let herself be caught. Tufts of drifting white cloud parted and came together like giant lumps of wool. As if divinely inspired by Apollo, Octavius suddenly realised why he enjoyed nature so, and found himself at peace in the secluded bower. Nature did not have any opinion of him, or expect anything from him. He closed his eyes in an effort to remember the pleasant vista and reposeful feeling, so as to one day retrieve the memory when aggravated by less concordant scenes. Even this revelation, and the will to record it, became hazy however as the cusp of sleep wafted over him like a precious dream. But just as Octavius was about to pass over into the blissful realm, he was disturbed by a conversation which sprouted up and demanded his attention.

"Has your father said anything about you wanting to become a legionary?" Rufus, seemingly out of the blue, asked Agrippa.

"No, but I've still yet to tell him. He knows that I'm no farmer, though. Besides, I'll tell him that someone needs to keep Octavius out of trouble."

"I'd be more worried about you leading him into it. I have visions of you stepping out of the ranks, like you did today, and volunteering to take on the entire Parthian army. But your mind is made up; you definitely want to be a soldier?"

"Yes. Unlike you two, my family has yet to make a name for itself. I want the house of Agrippa to come out from underneath the shade of anonymity."

"Anonymity can sometimes be a blessing, as well as a curse, Marcus. And, like your virginity, once sacrificed you can never get it back again," Octavius mused, as much to himself perhaps as his companion.

"That's far from the best of your conceits. I'm convinced that most people would happily lose both sooner rather than later," Rufus replied.

"So when and where are you hoping to lose your anonymity, Rufus?"

"In the Senate, as an advocate. Sooner rather than later as well."

"You sound determined, Rufus. Why do you want to be an advocate, if you don't mind me asking?" Octavius inquired, mildly curious.

"I'm going to study to be an advocate so I never lose an argument with my friends. But seriously, look at our history. Advocates, senators, are the ones who are all powerful in Rome. What laws we don't make up, we can always interpret to our own devices. I'm joking, or at least half-joking. But the pen is mightier than the sword."

"So does that mean you'll be bringing a pen along to Casca's next sparring session then?" Agrippa posited, grinning at both his own witticism and also Rufus' self-important air.

Out of the corner of his eye Rufus saw Octavius smile also, and he felt that infrequent but familiar twinge of jealousy again that he wasn't as close to Octavius as Agrippa was. No matter what he did or said they would always have a special, closer relationship.

To silence these envious, sullen murmurings however, Rufus spoke and tried to continue the conversation.

"So what do you want to be, Octavius?"

Agrippa here propped himself up and turned to where his best friend lay. Surprisingly he had never asked Octavius such a question. And so too, Octavius had never confided in him as to what might be the answer, if indeed he had one. Being Caesar's nephew Gaius could surely have the pick of any career he wished, whether he chose to work his way up the political ladder, be given a foreign posting or commission in the army. Or he could afford to carry on with his studies, which he seemed to enjoy.

"I want to be...left in peace for an hour or two so I can take a nap," the evasive student answered, wryly smiling. Octavius enjoyed keeping people guessing, as though the whole of life was but a game in which he who could keep people guessing most, won. Or it was a cynical play, in which one acted out various parts to garner applause. "It is where you are placed at the end of the race that counts," his great-uncle had said with a boyish wink to him one time.

*

The sun arched overhead and lost some of its sting, to be replaced by a stodgy humidity. Octavius glanced at the sky, increasingly fomented and furrowing his brow. It would rain before he made it home. Three became two. Octavius and Agrippa had bid Rufus a farewell and the two remaining companions made their way home. Agrippa did not need to tell his friend to keep it between them when he spoke to Octavius about what Casca had said.

"And he should know. You should be rightly proud. I'd certainly want you on my side in a fight, Marcus." Octavius would later be gladdened by the realisation that he felt better, happier, for hearing this praise for his friend - as compared to the shallow vanity he felt at boasting about his bedding of Briseis.

"And I will be, against the Parthians. I meant what I said Gaius about wanting to come with you. Has your uncle said when he intends to join the army and disembark?"

Gaius, partly to impress Agrippa and partly to signify how much he trusted his friend, had confided in him earlier in the year. Caesar had written to Octavius and sketched out to his nephew the scope and intention of his newest - and most ambitious - campaign. After conquering the Parthians, and winning back the eagles that Crassus had lost, Caesar planned to march around the Black Sea and then onto the Caucasus. From there he would invade and subdue Scythia. The lands bordering Germany - and eventually Germany itself - would then be added to Caesar's conquests. He would write his name in the annals of Roman History again. Finally Caesar would return to Italy via Gaul, thus completing the circuit of his Empire, which would be bounded on all sides by the ocean. Pompey would finally live in Caesar's shadow. Perhaps more than the dictator even, Marcus Agrippa was champing at the bit to take part in the historic campaign.

Octavius' brow began to further crease as warm droplets of rain began to pelt down. A dreary shade of grey poured across the sky, like smoke. After a pause he finally answered his friend as to when they would depart.

"Soon, after the Ides."

4

When Octavius returned to the house the young master was handed a towel by one of the servants to dry himself off from the rain. There was a frantic and industrious atmosphere around the estate as slaves and a small retinue of soldiers busied themselves for the departure the next day. The axels to baggage carts were being greased with tallow. Food and presents were being packed. Clothes were folded. Rose petals were being scattered in order to perfume the carriage for the long journey. Atia and Octavius' step-father, Lucius Marcus Phillipus, were travelling back to Rome for business - and pleasure - in the morning. So as not to disturb his studies and military training Octavius had been asked to remain at home, a situation which the youth understood and complied with.

Octavius passed into the atrium and heard voices emanate from the triclinium. He tensed slightly as he heard Lucius Oppius' terse voice. A second later a brace of soldiers marched out of the room and brushed past him.

As if he had sensed his presence, Oppius stuck his head around the curtained door and glared at Octavius. The youth always felt a little intimidated under the stern centurion's gaze - as though he felt that he should be impressing the soldier, but wasn't. His compressed jaw was covered with stubble that was as abrasive as sandpaper. The careerist soldier, who might have been aged anywhere between thirty-five and forty-five, towered over most in terms of his height and build. Oppius was a keen rider and swimmer; furthermore, when not attending to the drilling and administration of the legion, the consummate centurion would spend his time in frequent fencing and combat practise. "The harder I practise, the luckier I get," Octavius had once overheard him drily state. His blue eyes were striking but ultimately cold, like two sapphires set within a marble statue. The only time when Octavius had witnessed the centurion enjoy himself was when he was in the company of his great-uncle or Mark Antony. Caesar was the only man who Oppius truly respected. Octavius could still recall the scene when his great-uncle asked one of his most trusted lieutenants why he wasn't married.

"Because I already have been - twice. The first nagged me that I always seemed distant. The second because I wasn't distant enough," Oppius replied - his tone being funnier for seeming all the more sincere.

Octavius ventured into the triclinium. Oppius had not said a word, nor did he communicate the request with his eyes, but somehow Octavius felt compelled to assent to the centurion's unspoken order to join them. It appeared that the soldier had been conversing with his mother and step-father, not that the taciturn officer ever uttered a word more than necessary. Even his step-father was intimidated, or confounded, by the manner of Oppius at times.

"Make sure you dry yourself off properly," Atia immediately remarked to her son. Her tone was cosseting, as if she wished to impress upon Lucius Oppius, and herself, how much she cared for her child - Caesar's nephew. Atia was the daughter of the First Man of Rome's sister, Julia. The elegant woman was approaching middle age but her former beauty and spirit could still very much be traced in her figure and bearing. Atia, confident, intelligent, and proud - in short, a Caesar, had first been married to Marcus Atius Balbus, a former praetor and governor of Macedonia. Due to his senatorial commitments and foreign postings, Octavius saw very little of his father as a young child. Balbus passed away before his son's fifth birthday. Octavius sadly could not claim to have truly known his father, but he was conscious of his achievements and reputation. He was a good man by all accounts, who had gleaned praise from Cicero no less. His mother also never spoke ill of his father, which was a further testament to his character, and for a time it had been a source of frustration and regret to Gaius that he had never got to know him. In his own eyes it did not bother Octavius that his father had not been born into true noble family. But a certain anxiety and irritation had crept into his thoughts of late in that it might prejudice him in other people's eyes. But a man should be judged on his merit, the idealistic youth believed.

"Leave him be, Atia," Phillipus announced, partly amused and partly critical of his wife's mollycoddling. His hair was now grey and his face a little wrinkled but there was still a healthy vigour in the senator's eyes. His expression was thoughtful, kind and trustworthy. It was an expression, unlike many a politician's, which mirrored his character. Atia's marriage to Phillipus had of course been politically motivated. Phillipus, the son of a former consul, was both an amiable and influential senator. As well as being intimate with Caesar and Pompey, Phillipus could also be seen to have had a foot in the opposing political camp - due to the fact that Cato had married Phillipus' daughter from a previous marriage. Indeed some argued that Caesar had ultimately chosen Phillipus over the rest of Atia's suitors because he felt, with his influence and relationship to Cato, that Atia and the boy would be safe if ever his own position became endangered. Marcus Phillipus' suit was not just the one favoured by Caesar however, for Atia too would have chosen the quietly virtuous older man as her husband. And a mutual fondness soon matured into something deeper, stronger. Love.

Octavius was fond of his step-father also. Marcus Phillipus embodied most of what was good about being Roman, Gaius believed. His step-father was brave, intelligent, superior, just.

"Now as you know Octavius, Marcus and I are leaving for Rome tomorrow. What you do not know however is that I received a letter from your great-uncle today," Atia announced and then paused.

The boy's heart skipped a beat and yet pounded a moment later. News from Rome. Would Caesar be here soon? Did he have some new honour to confer on him? Were there any words of praise for his great-nephew in the letter? Was he even in Caesar's thoughts?

"He has asked us that you be left in the care of Lucius Oppius while we are away," Marcus Phillipus remarked, finishing his wife's sentence. Caesar had 'asked' but the request was tantamount to an order. "I'm sure Caesar knows that you can look after yourself, Octavius. So too your mother and I will sleep easier, knowing that Lucius will be keeping an eye on you. I dare say though that you won't notice that he is even there."

"As long as he doesn't mind," Octavius replied, shrugging. The adolescent masked his feelings well. He was slightly hurt and resentful thinking that it was considered that he couldn't be trusted. It naturally nettled the youth to think that Caesar still thought of him as a child who needed looking after. But still his face did not, would not, betray his disappointment, a disappointment which was exacerbated by the fact that he wouldn't now be able to spend as many nights with Briseis, with Oppius keeping a hawkish eye upon him. He acted indifferently to the news. Yet later that evening, when Octavius reflected upon the situation, he realised that he was, or could be, genuinely indifferent to the minor change in events. There were far worse fates to endure than being in possession of a bodyguard. His existence was not an unhappy one he pondered, philosophically.

Bored by his mother's gossip as to who was marrying who in Rome, what spices were in fashion and what she should wear for her entry back into the city, Octavius excused himself. He bathed himself, declining the offer of a pug-faced serving woman to assist him, and then retreated into his room to catch up on his re-reading of Polybius and Catullus.

*

It was now late. Gaius yawned and put his book down. A breeze whistled through the gap beneath the door and wafted over the candle next to his bed. For half a minute or so the contemplative youth just sat transfixed, gazing at the wriggling flame. Buffeted. Straining. He admired how, no matter how much the breeze desired to extinguish the torch, the flame remained alight and always returned to its calm, beautiful form when the attacks subsided. The would-be stoic fancied, promised, that he too would be akin to the candlelight no matter how much fortune attempted to bend or break him. Octavius gently smiled at his own conceit and drifted off to sleep.

Maybe the dream was provoked by the drumming of the rain on the roof outside, but Octavius was plunged back into the sublime scene of the storm from a year ago. The ship was bound for Spain. A large wave arched over the creaking trireme as if it was a claw about to swot a gad-fly from the ocean's skin. Or as if they were caught in the jaws of an aquatic monster, which was foaming at the mouth. Oars littered the ocean like twigs within a brook. Octavius bumped and cut his head as he tried to negotiate his way onto the deck. Spotting the blood trickling from the youth's temple, Oppius immediately ceased reining in an untamed sail. Without warning, or a word said, he rushed up to the boy and checked the extent of his injury - and then resumed his task of fastening down the flapping sail. The wind ululated like a wolf, baying for blood. If it wasn't for the inky night the Spanish coast would have been in sight, but the mortal craft, at the mercy of Neptune, was a world away from safety. Timber bent and then splintered. Twice the land-legged young Gaius slipped upon the slick deck, but fell not. Water slapped Octavius across the face as a wave crashed into the side of the vessel. The sensation both enlivened and disorientated him to his peril. Voices also jabbed into his ears. Half were arguing to abandon ship, half were ordering to ride the storm out. Before Octavius even began to assess his best course of action, his mind was made up for him. Roscius, a hulking legionary - whom Octavius recognised as being part of Oppius' cohort - bellowed in his ears above the roaring storm to follow him.

The steely centurion but nodded his head to indicate to Octavius that he wished for the adolescent to clamber down the rope ladder into the lifeboat, which bobbed up and down on the churning ocean and continually knocked against the larger vessel. The commanding Oppius wore neither a look of worry on his face, nor did he try to give his young charge a comforting glance, as if to convey that everything would be alright. Octavius descended slowly into the small boat. Half a dozen sailors challenged Oppius and Roscius above him - complaining about commandeering the lifeboat. Either through violence, or the threat of it, the two soldiers soon out-argued the protesting mob.

On board the ship, and on land, Roscius had been a rock. His hard, weathered face was a paradigm of fearlessness and authority. Octavius almost gasped one time when the giant of a man made a couple of fists - likening the sight to seeing two boulders on the ends of his brawny arms. An expression of doubt and fright immediately overcame the stout legionary as soon as he placed a foot upon the puny lifeboat. The craft moved beneath his feet and Roscius nearly fell overboard. A serendipitous clap and rumble of thunder drowned out the curses which shot from the seasoned soldier's mouth. Oppius briefly smiled, witnessing the panic on his loyal friend's face. It was perhaps the first time Octavius had observed the professional, emotionless centurion do so. At the time of the crossing Oppius had been assigned to the protection of Octavius - upon the personal commission of Caesar himself - for less than a month. At first Gaius had been in awe of the Roman officer, admiring his physique and the air of authority which surrounded him. He was intrigued by the enigmatic officer. "Men want to be him and women want to be with him," his step-father had remarked. He soon grew even more intimidated and frightened by the centurion, however. After suffering monosyllabic replies, or having the soldier just walk away from him as if he wasn't there, Octavius stopped trying to engage his bodyguard. Phillipus also revealed to Octavius that Oppius had the ear of his great-uncle, and that he would doubtlessly be reporting his behaviour and progress back to Caesar. As a result the youth was conscious of what he had said and done in the presence of the centurion. In some ways he played the obedient child in front of the soldier, yet at other opportunities Octavius would do or say something to prove how much of a good Roman he was. But, after suffering the demoralising indifference of the soldier towards him on one too many occasion, Octavius eventually experienced fits of resentment where admiration once resided.

The centurion's smirk was fleeting however, and Oppius soon handed an oar to Roscius.

"Are you a strong swimmer, boy?" the officer then shouted at Octavius over the snarling wind. Such was the threatening tone of his voice that the pallid youth would have nodded in assertion even if the answer was no. Oppius ordered Roscius to abandon his greaves and breastplate, as he too dropped half of his uniform overboard. Sooner or later they would have to make a swim for it. It would be sooner rather than later as, not twenty yards from the ship, the lifeboat began to fill with water. Oppius instructed Octavius to try and bail out the pool of sea water forming at their feet using Roscius' large helmet.

The two powerful soldiers began to find some rhythm and Gaius even began to win the war against the incoming water.

"She's lying low in the water," Roscius huskily remarked to his officer, referring to their storm battered ship - his brow wrinkled in concern.

"It'll be lying even lower within the hour," Oppius replied matter-of-factly, seemingly unperturbed and resigned to the situation of losing both the craft and his men. Over the next few evenings though, a self-consciously sensitive and noble Octavius would recall the loss of life and try to honour the dead with generous and solemn thoughts. Caesar's great-nephew felt guilty because he reasoned that, if not for him, the men would not have even been out in the storm.

Before Octavius had a chance, however, to glance around to see how low the trireme was in the water, a hurtling wave, spurred on by a gust of wind, shunted into the side of the lifeboat. The three figures within the craft were tossed into the water like coins into a well. Disorientated. Frightened. At first Octavius was dragged deeper below as the water soaked and weighed down his tunic. His eyes and mind were a blur. It was as if someone had tied an anchor around his waist. But the adrenaline rush from his panic soon aided the strength Gaius needed to pull himself back up to the surface.

As his face broke through the skin of the sea and he gasped for air, Octavius woke up from his realistic nightmare, feeling now the same mixture of fear and exhilaration as he felt then, or rather just after the ordeal. Where the dream left off, his memory took over. Oppius had to perhaps worry more about Roscius than Octavius in terms of getting them to shore. He constantly swam back and forth between the two - with and against the tide - to encourage and watch over them as they made their way onto the secluded beach.

Heavy-limbed, shivering with cold and his muscles quivering with exhaustion, Octavius gulped in the air as he lay across the powdery sand. He had been delivered. Rain coughed upon his face. Darkness was legion. He sought but found not the silhouette of the doomed ship within the oily night. The lap of the incoming waves, which sometimes kissed his feet, made a shushing noise as if to demand silence. But all Gaius could hear was Roscius, short of breath too, lying beside him. Either he slept, or passed out, but the next thing Octavius recalled was Oppius - as if by magic - starting a fire. Not only did the small fire serve to dry them all off, but more importantly it acted as a beacon for those soldiers and slaves who had also bested the squall to make it to shore. The storm eventually abated. But they were still in danger. Having memorised the map during the crossing Gaius overheard Oppius confide in Roscius that they had landed upon a beach in enemy territory.

Octavius here decided however to switch off his memory, as if he were blowing out a candle. Not only did he want to be fresh for when his mother and Phillipus left the next morning, but he also wanted to be rested for his afternoon lesson with Cleanthes.

5

Morning. Spring again augured summer. It had been an unnaturally hot early March. Octavius sat out in the garden, eating a pomegranate, waiting for the moment when his mother and step-father would finally depart and he would say his farewells. He sat in the cooling shade close to the house, but the rising sun began to bathe more and more of the garden in its pristine light. The buxom flower beds, which bordered a large square carpet of grass, were erupting with colour - crisp red roses, glassy lilies, trumpeting bluebells. The fish pond, in which Marcus Phillipus vainly attempted to breed his beloved koi carp, seemed to sparkle with petals of golden light - appearing and vanishing on the surface of the turquoise water with hypnotic charm. The sound of a babbling fountain, in the shape of a curvaceous nereid with the water dribbling from out of her mouth, could irritate or placate the listener depending on their mood. Octavius smiled, remembering how when he first arrived at the house, he had practised his kissing technique in secret on the fountain, employing the excuse for himself and any potential watcher that he was merely quenching his thirst. Fortunately he had Briseis now for such things, Octavius reflected - grinning now to himself in a different way.

The pomegranate sweetened and freshened up his mouth, displacing the furry taste of sleep which had hung at the back of his tongue. The moreish smell of fresh bread also made its way around from the kitchen and enlivened the air. Perhaps because Cleanthes too baked his own bread, Octavius suddenly thought of his tutor and, as if now in the philosopher's company, a pensive expression shaped his features. Octavius suddenly appeared ten years older and troubled by things. It was at this ill-timed moment that Atia came out to speak to her son.

"What's wrong?" Atia remarked, crouching down beside her seated son and laying her fingers on his shoulder. Octavius loved his mother, and appreciated her consideration, but at this particular moment he would've preferred not to have been disturbed by her.

"I am fine, mother," Octavius replied and pursed his lips - preventing himself from uttering anything more.

"I never know these days whether you are looking sad, or just serious. But you never seem as happy as you once were," Atia posed. She knew by the tone of his voice and body language that he didn't want to be disturbed or confronted. Atia's maternal concern, and curiosity, made her want to force the issue. She was worried that her child was becoming too withdrawn. Perhaps it was this Cleanthes' influence. When he did speak to anyone nowadays he would often be glib or sarcastic, or quote philosophy to her to win an argument. She had increasingly grown frustrated and sad over the past year, feeling that Octavius was becoming too self-reliant and melancholy. Sometimes Atia melodramatically thought to herself that she didn't know her son anymore. She was becoming redundant in his life. He no longer got sick. She missed taking care of him. Intellectually and emotionally he had grown independent, superior even. As much as Phillipus had argued that it was a good thing that the youth had matured and changed, a doting Atia was not quite ready to say goodbye to her special boy yet.

"I am content, mother. Truly, you have no need to worry about me."

"You can always come to me, you know that? A problem shared is a problem halved," Atia remarked and smiled, as if Octavius were twelve years old again.

Still my sorrows would be double the next man's Octavius fancied, but he kept the conceit to himself. He also bit his tongue in response to the scorn he felt for his mother's sententiousness and unconsidered way of looking at life.

"No man is an island," Atia then added, briefly stroking her child's fair hair, gazing at him fondly, conveying that she understood whatever he was going through and that he could confide in her.

Octavius didn't say a word in reply, although he was tempted to argue the contrary. He thought how Cleanthes was independent, craving no man's flattery or counsel; he served no master, nor wanted for a servant. He inwardly smiled, recollecting the story Cleanthes told him about Diogenes. When Alexander the Great asked if he could do anything for the philosopher, Diogenes merely requested for the king to get out of his light.

"I know, mother," Octavius finally replied, sighing a little as he said so.

As only a woman can, Atia here changed the subject and mood as if nothing had come before.

"Now, how does your mother look?" she gaily announced, beaming and twirling before her son. Her dress was crisp and white, patterned and bordered in a shade of purple which had become associated with Caesar. The cut highlighted rather than revealed Atia's envied figure. Her hair was blonde, which had grown even fairer of late in the Greek sun, and was stylishly pinned on her head. Her slender, bronzed forearms were decorated by a couple of elegant gold bangles. Rouge reddened her cheeks and Egyptian kohl lined her fine blue eyes, but the make-up was in no way garishly employed by the naturally attractive woman.

"You look lovely mother, so much so that I'm worried your friends in Rome will begin to resent you out of jealousy."

"Friends are worth sacrificing for looking so beautiful," Marcus Phillipus similarly satirically expressed, entering the garden and smiling broadly. The elderly but red-blooded senator was still as attracted to his wife today as he had been on their wedding night. Phillipus was also happily not immune to the feelings of pride and satisfaction he felt by having such a sophisticated and admired wife by his side.

"Now you are teasing and confusing me as to whether you're being serious or not," Atia replied, radiating from the compliment and from having her family around her. Only Octavia, her daughter, was missing from the pretty and familial scene. But she hoped to soon see her also, and her husband, during their visit to Rome.

Atia cuddled up to her husband whilst still caressing her son's hair. Having so seldom been apart from her child over the years, it was an emotional enough occasion for the devoted mother to bring a tear to her eye. Partly because her playing with his hair had irritated him, Octavius got up to hug his mother.

"Now, you promise to write?" Atia half demanded, rather than requested.

"Only if you promise not to cry, mother. If nothing else it will ruin your make-up," Octavius replied, touched by his mother's love and silliness. Atia's response was to let out a laugh cum sob. She clasped her son close, as if he were still a baby, and wetly kissed him upon his cheek. Unseen by Atia, Octavius rolled his eyes and raised his eyebrows to his step-father, partly from embarrassment, and also to display how he was himself above such womanly sentiment as his daffy mother. Marcus Phillipus knowingly grinned and nodded his head at his step-son, pleased and approving of Octavius for indulging his mother so.

Octavius indulged his mother also by waving and remaining in sight of the litter until the Rome-bound party disappeared over the hilly horizon. He returned to the house and checked the rusting sundial in the courtyard. He still had a few hours to kill before his afternoon lesson with Cleanthes. As Octavius here thought of Briseis he felt a little ashamed and dejected as he remembered how Cleanthes had warned of such consuming passions and unbecoming behaviour. But nevertheless the philosophical youth was compelled to venture into the staff quarters of the house to seek out the pleasure-loving girl. Frustration and indignation heated his blood however, after being told that the mistress of the house had allowed Briseis some time off to visit her mother. Atia had suspected that something might be going on between the servant girl and her son, so out of precaution (telling herself that she was protecting both the girl and her son) she had sent the temptation away.

For the next hour or so Octavius lay on his bed, unable to read. Simmering. He was furious at his mother for ruining his fun, interfering. He was also troubled by the fact that her sending Briseis away meant that she had most likely discovered the extent of their relations, and he dreaded the scene of having to discuss the matter with her. But more so Octavius was annoyed with himself - that the servant girl's absence had made him burn with such emotion and affect his mood. It did not help that every time he closed his eyes he thought of her. Although she probably had little choice in the matter, Octavius now turned against the object of his ardency for leaving him. Why had she gone? She hadn't even tried to say goodbye to him. She was just a whore and he should treat her that way. His frustration was intensified by the fact that there were no other girls like Briseis in the household. Not only did Octavius duly want to relieve himself of his disappointment and stress - and forget about Briseis - but in the act of taking another girl he would also be getting his revenge on her, not to mention his overly possessive mother. Octavius slyly smiled at the prospect of turning defeat into a victory. But his dejection soon returned, restlessly bubbling his blood and thoughts alike.

The sullen young noble unfairly and irrationally snapped at a couple of slaves when getting ready to depart for his afternoon lesson. Partly because he wanted to be alone, Octavius decided to ignore the instructions of his mother and venture over to Cleanthes' house without an escort. He ordered one of the staff to tell Oppius that he would be making his own way to the tutor's house. The centurion would not be happy - and the slave might even suffer a beating for being somehow remiss, but such was the saturnine mood that Octavius was enmeshed in that he didn't much care for the consequences of his actions.

6

A wide-brimmed straw hat shaded his face in the midday sun. Octavius moistened his lips and as he did so, tasted the salt in the air. The journey would take a little longer, but he had decided to take the coastal path to his tutor's villa. As the solitary walker wended his way around a secluded bay, he couldn't help but be reminded of that similar, crescent shaped beach which he had landed upon that stormy evening.

The first thing Octavius remembered about the morning after was Roscius defending and deflecting jibes in relation to his aquatic prowess, or rather lack of.

"I come from Umbria. We have no need to be strong swimmers. When we do drown ourselves, it's in drink."

Perhaps it was from this morning onwards that Octavius noticed and liked the infantryman more. Roscius had been a soldier for most of his life, to the point where he knew nothing different. One campaign had blurred into another. The legionary held a vague dream of settling down one day on some land outside of Rome, but he was realistic enough to know that the idea was but a dream. The standard bearer was obedient in taking orders, yet could be left to think for himself in carrying them out. He was good-humoured yet disciplined; Octavius noted how the men respected, or feared, the giant of a soldier also. In battle he became a bear of a man. Yet Roscius was generous and patient with the inquisitive youth when Octavius near pestered him as to the life and details of soldiering. And also stories about Caesar. In return the illiterate legionary avidly listened to Octavius when he reported the feats of Odysseus, Achilles and Aeneas to him - sometimes quoting Homer from memory, word for word. So too Roscius was never far away from the boy when there was a hint of danger. Oppius had observed how the youth had taken to his friend - and so ordered Roscius to watch over the boy until they reached Caesar's camp.

For his own part, Oppius had little time for the privileged adolescent. He would do his duty by him - or rather Caesar - but that was all. Indeed a splinter of resentment towards the boy couldn't help but lodge in the centurion's heart as Oppius' task of babysitting had kept him from Caesar's side - and the rewards of a true campaign. He feared that, absent from the great dictator's side, he might miss out on worthwhile spoils and advancement. Campaigns, or deaths rather, provided promotions. There is always someone willing to stab you in the back and take your place, Lucius judged from experience. For a brief moment however, during the previous night, Oppius had been pleasantly surprised by the youth with his calm and courage under pressure; the boy had kept his head in the confusion and terror of the storm - and he had displayed hidden stamina in his swim to shore. But the sickly and over-studious boy would, at best, grow to be but the shadow of the man Caesar was. Although granting Octavius a modicum of respect for his display the night before, Oppius couldn't help but recall and compare the scene in Alexandria with his general. Whilst leading a sortie on a bridge in the city, Caesar and his cohort were suddenly counter-attacked. To save himself from capture Caesar daringly jumped off the bridge and into a boat. His men soon followed. Realising how the wounded needed space, he quickly ordered himself and his officers out of the small vessel. Oppius smiled, remembering the majestic sight of Caesar swimming two hundred yards to reach his fleet, holding his left hand out of the water to preserve some documents he was carrying, and clenching his purple cloak in his teeth to prevent his enemy from recovering it as a trophy.

There were around thirty survivors on the beach come morning. After the small reconnaissance and foraging party returned, Oppius took command of the bedraggled group (consisting of another centurion, a dozen legionaries and various other members of the cohort's retinue). Small cliques were forming, with the sound of the tide accompanied by murmurings of discontent. Some wanted to remain on the beach in the hope that a friendly vessel would sail by. Others wished to take their chances on their own, as a large group would attract attention and more likely be captured. But the focused centurion ordered that they break camp immediately. They would all make their way to Caesar's stronghold, which Oppius calculated was a three day march away.

"If we stay here, we die. What ships we spot will be enemy or pirate vessels. Storms on land I can steer us through. We have given our oaths to Caesar that we would deliver his nephew to him. Anyone that forsakes that oath will forsake their life."

"But how will we cross enemy territory?" a dissenting soldier, who was not a member of Oppius' own cohort, protested, taking it upon himself to speak what he thought was the majority opinion of the group.

"By not crossing me. I have time to *fight* anyone over this, but not argue," the centurion pronounced, with even the men who little knew of Oppius' reputation believing that he would make good his word - both in terms of leading them through the next few days and punishing anyone who opposed him. No one said a word later that afternoon when the dissenting soldier returned from a toilet break with a bruised eye and broken rib. Roscius came back with a sore hand.

"Be ready to leave by the time I've sharpened my sword. Anyone who lags behind will get left behind," the stone-faced soldier closed his brief address by stating.

Oppius' fellow centurion was no doubt disgruntled that he had assumed sole command, and a portion of the party were far from optimistic in regards to their fate, but nevertheless they broke camp and, much like now (as he stood and appreciated the Apollonian shore), Octavius gazed back down along the Spanish sands and thought to himself how beautiful nature was, as if created by the gods for our enjoyment and praise.

Not wishing to appear lacking, Octavius steeled and drove himself on whilst marching on that first day. Scouts were sent ahead and occasionally the group had to retreat into the woodland which flanked the dusty road on both sides, but for the most part the first day's march proved uneventful. From the bloodied and broken state of the soldiers, they observed it was clear to Oppius that the war was almost over in favour of Rome. Caesar had done it again.

Partly due to Octavius pushing himself to his physical limit, and having developed a slight chill from his swim, he grew weak and began to suffer shortness of breath as evening closed in. Without conveying the fact to the boy however, Roscius and Oppius had a pre-prepared signal, which Roscius would initiate, when he considered that Octavius needed to rest. At that point Oppius would allow the entire party to take a water break or catch their breath. He rolled his eyes or grunted slightly at having to organise his plans around the over-indulged youth, but nevertheless Oppius faltered not in doing his duty to the boy, or rather Caesar. Although it had been his intention to march throughout most of the evening, a brief word from Roscius made up his mind that the group should cessate their progress and sleep for an hour or so. With Oppius not permitting the group to light fires, arguing that it was "better to wake up shivering, than dead", Roscius sacrificed his cloak for the good-natured youth and used it as an extra blanket to keep the boy warm while he slept.

Later that evening, in the grey light of a swollen moon, Oppius and Roscius spoke about the day's events and the plan for the morrow.

"Will he be able to keep pace?" Oppius asked, fearing that he already knew the answer.

"Our pace? No. But the lad has done well. You should be pleased with him, impressed even," Roscius dared to say, in hope more than expectation of receiving a positive reaction from the hard-hearted centurion.

"You more than most of my friends know that I'm not easily impressed. I dare say necessity has also become the mother of invention for the boy to exert himself, rather than his mother exerting her need to be a necessity."

"You're too hard on the lad."

"He should thank me for it. Everyone else is far too easy on him. And he is nearly a man, not a boy. By the time I was his age I had killed - and more than once."

"And you're now old enough to know that's nothing to be proud of," Roscius replied, his expression momentarily pained as the veteran's heart recalled some of the best forgotten experiences of his own youth. Roscius fleetingly placed his hand on his brow, as if he felt a headache coming on, but then took a healthy swig from his fast emptying cup and regained his good humour.

"Would you want him standing by your side in a shield wall? That should be the question," Oppius asked.

"Not yet. But I'd certainly sit around and share a drink with him."

"But you'd drink with anyone."

"I know. Cheers." And with an affable smile upon Roscius' face, the two friends clinked cups and finished the last of the wine they had saved.

Despite nursing a hangover, Oppius made the aching-limbed party rouse with the dawn. They still had a lot of ground to cover. Again, scouts were sent ahead to reconnoitre the roads they intended to take. Oppius was now certain that Caesar had bested the enemy - the rebellious, Republican forces of Pompey's sons, Sextus and Gnaeus.

Perhaps even more so than yesterday, the day seemed uneventful to Octavius. It was now a matter of routine to stealthily retreat into the woods whenever a scout warned of a group of soldiers or natives approaching. At times Octavius even forgot his situation and his mind wandered. He noted how similar the landscape was to that of his family's estate in Velitrae, a small town just outside of Rome. The dry but fragrant air was the same. The wind rustled through the cypress trees in a familiar way. The crickets and thrushes spoke the same language. Even considering his bouts of illness and the loss of his father, Octavius' childhood in Velitrae had not been an unhappy one. In some ways his name had been a burden, but equally so the studious youth looked upon it as being something he should live up to. From as early as Octavius could remember it had been his heart's desire to please his great-uncle. And from his infrequent visits over the years and inspirational letters, Caesar was proud of his nephew. The gratification spurred the youth on the more to better himself, to study harder and be a good Roman. Octavius often couldn't help but fondly smile, remembering his privileged and fulfilling upbringing. But then a knowing and cautious expression would shape his features. Octavius was wise and pragmatic enough to focus on the future rather than dwell in the past.

The day was long. Dusk was short however. A deep mauve, which soon darkened to a bluish-black, combed itself across the sky. The firmament then grew hazier as a brash storm exploded in the air above them.

Octavius' feet grew even more leaden as the rain mulched the dirt road into mud. He might have even been pleased when one of the scouts returned and reported to Oppius that there was potential danger up ahead. They could now hide and find shelter. Rest.

A thin wisp of smoke spiralled upwards from a small house on the side of the road. Coarse laughter, as well as the smell of roasted venison, emanated from the dwelling. The second scout, who had remained with the house (and who had smeared himself in mud, camouflaged himself in branches, climbed a tree and assessed the enemy from close quarters), reported to Oppius that the enemy soldiers in the house numbered a dozen. He had also yet to notice a picket stationed up the road.

"I think we deserve that shelter and a hot meal more than they do men, eh?" Oppius said, wolfishly grinning to the soldiers who nodded in agreement, their eyes alert with the happy anticipation of both the fight and food. Oppius drew a quick sketch with a stick on some soft ground of the target. Four men, armed with javelins, would first attack in pairs through the two windows of the house. As soon as they struck however, Oppius, along with six other men from his legion, would come through the entrance to the cottage.

"Lose anything from your belt that isn't necessary. You'll need to be free to manoeuvre and react quickly once we're inside the house. Surprise is on our side and will do half the job. Immobilise rather than kill to begin with. Make every hit, cut, count. Roscius, I want you to remain here with Octavius. Regardless of what happens, I want you both to keep out of sight."

No word or movement was wasted. Octavius was frightened and excited as he watched Oppius and his band of brothers stealthily move through the woodland and approach the cottage. His chest swelled with the pride that he was in the presence of the best soldiers in the world, Roman legionaries. Out of the corner of his eye he noticed an anxious looking Roscius nervously biting his lip. He well knew that Oppius would succeed - and he understood how he needed to take care of Caesar's nephew - but it still felt strange being absent from his centurion's side in a fight. The water annoyingly collected and then heavily dripped down on his face from the leaves above, but Octavius, still wide-eyed, sucked in the scene.

The sound of the hissing shower was broken by the grunt of a legionary throwing his first javelin. The noise was quickly succeeded by a cacophony of confusing roars and agonising screams. Roscius grabbed the youth's shoulder, as if to hold him back, whilst in reality the action was taken to remind him why he had to remain back from the fight.

Oppius soon returned however, his face spotted with blood and crumbs of flesh - which were soon washed away in the drizzle. His arm however, up to his elbow, was dark crimson -

and his sword was streaked with gore. He offered his standard bearer a brief nod to convey that everything and everyone was fine. Octavius heard the desperate protests and pleadings of an enemy prisoner in the background, but they were soon silenced. The brief blood-curdling scream which sliced through the night and into Octavius' ears turned his stomach, but still the youth was eager to witness the sight of the carnage in the house. Oppius frustrated this desire though and ordered that Roscius and he remain where they were until sentries were posted and the house was cleaned up.

Fed and warmed by the room's crackling fire, Octavius still found it difficult to sleep. His feverish imagination played tricks on his mind. The owl's hoot was amplified to a howl. The scuttling of a spider became a rat, with teeth as big as a hare's. The sound of the sentry's patrol outside was turned into the enemy approaching the house. As the Romans had ambushed the Spanish, Octavius imagined how they too could be assailed at any moment. He feared waking suddenly in the night to see a swarthy barbarian over him, with a blade at his throat, and thus was prevented from swiftly drifting off to sleep. Eventually however exhaustion got the better of his febrile thoughts and Octavius finally slipped into a quilted slumber.

7

A gassy stench, similar to that of the refuge which sometimes built up when neglected from outside his own house, wafted up Octavius' nostrils as he went inland in the direction of his tutor's villa.

"Far more than my rumoured misanthropy, the inhospitable smell of the marshes keeps prospective visitors away," Cleanthes had once wryly remarked to his pupil. "I also can't help but have affection for the marshes, as their location and aesthetic saved me a welcome sum of money when purchasing the land."

Octavius scrunched up his features in disgust at the foul smell, and swept his hand in front of his face to brush away the cluster of flying insects swirling around him. He quickly ventured forward, however, along the squelching path, knowing full-well that he would soon come out into a quite different setting.

As the nauseating odour of the marshes had suddenly descended on Octavius like a noxious rain cloud, so too did the kaleidoscope of fragrances and colour strike his senses as he entered his tutor's garden through a half-concealed entrance. The menthol crispness of fresh mint and rosemary, as well as various other herbs, cleared out his nose immediately.

The faint sound of rustling, accompanied by the frequent metallic snap of a pair of garden shears, reverberated in the air. Octavius gazed, admiringly and amusedly, at his teacher whilst his back was turned to him. He was wearing a belted careworn cream gown made of a coarse material over an equally shabby tunic. His figure and movements were robust and senses alert though as, either through hearing or even smelling his pupil, Cleanthes ceased pruning his clematis and turned to Octavius.

Although he had been tutoring now for half of his adult life, Cleanthes considered himself to be an eternal student, rather than a teacher. His green eyes sparkled at seeing his accomplished pupil. There was an air of philosophical calm about the wistful gardener yet at the same time one sensed a restless mind at work: observing, collating, concluding, disregarding. His jade eyes shone brightly, but his skin was sallow and marked - both through pox scars and also insect bites. His dark brown hair and beard were also as unkempt as his clothes, shining with a film of grease.

Cleanthes was born in Athens. His father had been stable master to a series of Roman administrators. Such was his service to one of the ruling governors during his tenure upon the estate that the quaestor granted the stable master his freedom. Cleanthes' father, taking out a loan, quickly prospered as a horse trader, providing cavalry horses to the Roman army during its conflict with Mithridates. Wanting to give his son the kind of education that had been denied to him, Cleanthes' father enrolled his son in the finest academies and hired the most expensive tutors to teach his only child. And initially his investment paid off. Cleanthes proved to be a gifted pupil, proficient in logic, rhetoric and the practical sciences. When the feted student completed his studies he was courted by a number of wealthy patrons who offered the tutor various sums of money and gifts to join their particular household in a bid to out-do their neighbours. Initially Cleanthes declined. The attraction of spurning these incentives - and affecting an air of incorruptibility and intellectual independence - soon waned however, especially when his policy of rejection caused patrons to increase their offers.

Although it did not happen overnight, a certain dissoluteness and rebellious streak eventually instilled itself in the young sophist's life. Drink and women displaced his scholarly interests. Having tasted the pleasures of Athens, the moneyed young man even ventured to visit Rome to satiate his circadian appetites. The conceited academic told himself that his new way of life, centred among the taverns and brothels, was a philosophical experiment - for how can one know true virtue unless one has experienced vice? His dissolute reputation soon preceded him however, and his employment dried up.

Despondency and impoverishment followed hard. His father all but disowned him. An aged gardener, who worked outside of Athens, took him on. Cleanthes learned a trade and eventually freed himself from those vices which had eaten away at so much of the rest of his life - partly because he just couldn't afford his former lifestyle anymore. A year or so later his father died. He left his only son with a modest inheritance. Desiring a fresh start, Cleanthes moved to Apollonia and purchased the client list and equipment of a gardener there. He worked hard and supplemented his income, in order to buy some land and build a house, by privately tutoring a few select pupils. Within five years Cleanthes had earned enough money to settle into semi-retirement. He produced most of the food he needed himself and sold off any surplus at the market. He studied horticulture and occasionally still tutored the odd pupil who he believed had potential.

On the recommendation of Atticus, Cicero's trusted and learned friend, to Marcus Phillipus, Octavius was interviewed one day by the reclusive, but respected, tutor. Cleanthes was impressed by the youth and his willingness to learn - and it was a source of pleasure more than a task when Octavius visited him every week now. Such was the youth's progress that, in certain areas of epistemology and ethics, he had little left to learn. Cleanthes was impressed, yet a little saddened, by the young man's nihilistic thinking. Octavius had argued how there was no sovereign rationale for any course of action. "Meaning can be negated, or made to seem relative." It was one's will, or emotions - one's personality - which ultimately stimulated action. "Ideals are frippery, or afterthoughts that seemingly justify one's purpose. We put them on and take them off again like garments, according to the weather or whims. All is vanity." Octavius here briefly uncoupled his chain of thought. He half-smiled and shrugged, and then remarked, "Philosophers can and do argue themselves to death. Is it not soldiers, men of action - Alexanders, Sullas, Caesars - who rule and shape the world?" Upon another occasion recently, Cleanthes was struck by how much further reading his student must have been doing, unprompted by the tutor. Debating the theory of knowledge Octavius suddenly quoted Timons, "That honey is sweet I refuse to assert; that it appears sweet, I fully grant ... And how do we know what is sweet? What is sweetness? - We can infer, but we can never know ... Philosophy is but the sum of meaningless words ... Words, words, words." As superior as Octavius could feel in arguing such things, these conclusions would often dissatisfy the once idealistic student. Life should not be so annulled. Occasionally however such conclusions and theses would liberate the young nihilist: "If nothing is for certain, then everything is possible."

"You're late Octavius, again. The opening and closing of my tulips keeps better time."

"Fortunately or not, they do not have half of Polybius to read before they rise."

"You are beginning to have an answer for everything."

"I have had a good teacher."

"Or maybe your lateness furnished you with plenty of time to prepare an excuse. Whether you consider it a reward or punishment, I'd have you read the other half of Polybius to make up for your tardiness."

Octavius smiled and nodded his head slightly, assenting to his teacher's instruction, acknowledging his wit and apologising for his misdemeanour all in one gesture.

*

By now there were very few formal aspects to Octavius' lessons. For the most part Cleanthes just talked to his pupil and answered his questions, as one might converse with a familiar, older acquaintance. Whilst doing so Cleanthes often tended to his garden, infecting his student with an interest in horticulture and botany. Towards the end of the afternoon, as was his custom, Octavius turned the conversation towards Rome. He enjoyed his tutor's insights and witticisms in regards to the city's history, as well as its current statesmen and policies.

"When Caesar crossed the Rubicon, that now bloody river, Rome, as well as Caesar, crossed a point of no return. Or perhaps it was Gracchus who brought us here, or Sulla even. But Rome is fated to be seen as a prize that's won, rather than a master which must be served," Cleanthes remarked, his tone neither critical nor lauding Caesar, as he tied back some wayward vines on his plants with twine. "One can mourn the idea of the Republic, but not the reality. There were too many personalities, but not enough characters. Money spoke in the Forum, rather than principles. Vetoes were issued for petty reasons, such as who was sleeping with whose wife. Tribunes became demagogues or thugs, serving themselves rather than the electorate. People went hungry whilst others glutted themselves during extravagant feasts. The social and economic divides between rich and poor grew too pronounced - and everything tumbled into the chasm which was created by the divide. Soldiers were given broken promises. The

Republic, Senate, was only consistent in its themes of greed and hypocrisy. Marians fought Sullans and vice versa, long after both men were dead. There were too many parasites bleeding Rome dry. 'Tis an unweeded garden," Cleanthes wryly posited, as he stretched down and plucked a couple of weeds out of the black soil of his vegetable patch.

"Men's ambitions and their desire to make a profit are among the most frequent causes of deliberate acts of injustice. People who lay out sums of money to secure office get into the habit, not unnaturally, of looking for something in return," Octavius enjoined, with a tinge of both sadness and anger in his tone, making reference perhaps to the corruption of the ability to collect taxes for Rome going to the highest bidder. Cleanthes nodded in agreement, and also in appreciation, of his student quoting Aristotle in his argument.

"But yet whilst terminally ill, the Republic is not quite dead yet. The Senate might have been won with the sword, but your great uncle's victory must be maintained by him unsheathing his wits and knowing when to compromise. Caesar will not be able to cut off the heads of all his enemies, for he will unleash a hydra by doing so. Should he unfairly vanquish an enemy, then two will stand in his place," Cleanthes warned, briefly pausing to watch a spider spin his web across his blackberry bush - smiling in anticipation and revenge, in that the web would catch some of the irksome insects which plagued him of an evening whilst he slept.

"Why do you not go to Rome? You could make a name for

yourself. I could write to my uncle," the student asked his teacher, after a short pause.

"Thank you for the offer Octavius, but success would be the ruin of me," the tutor replied, his green eyes glimmering with a private joke as if he were quoting someone else.

"You could be the new Cicero."

"I'm not sure whether Marcus Tullius would be flattered by that or not. I reckon the ex-consul feels that he has some life in him yet, before he's replaced."

"Did you ever meet Cicero when you went to Rome?"

"Our meeting was brief, but memorable on my part. We met at a party thrown by a friend of mine. Cicero was the guest of honour, a position which he felt quite happy and comfortable with I dare say. He dressed smartly, but not ostentatiously - much like you, Gaius. He was neither old nor young when I encountered him, though there was definitely more vigour in his intellect than in his body. For a while I but observed the famous ex-consul. He was a great conversationalist, enjoying listening as well as speaking, albeit I dare say his favourite pastime was to act modestly when listening to people praise him. He could be vain, but self-effacing; critical, but forgiving. I couldn't help but be impressed by his naturally good, or assiduously trained, memory. He seemed to know everyone's name and business at the gathering, charming each guest equally with the attention he bestowed upon them. I finally drank enough wine to summon up the courage to approach him. He put me at ease immediately. We talked briefly about philosophy, with Cicero picking holes in his own writings. He also described a Cynic as being "but an ill-dressed and impoverished Stoic". He was openly satirical about his fellow senators, and the more powerful the patrician, the crueller the barb. He also instructed me a little about the art of oratory, principally by advising me of what not to do. "Just as lame men ride on horseback because they cannot walk, so too our new crops of orators shout because they cannot speak," he posited. My true claim to fame however, in regards to Cicero, is that I had the honour of witnessing him compose an original epigram in my presence. I commented upon how fine the port was. He paused briefly, with a good-humoured smile upon his face, and remarked, or rather I should say composed the following:

'There is nothing more to this life
Than some cheap port and a good wife.
But a cheap wife and some good port
Is a life too I cannot fault.'

I smiled as much at the witticism as upon seeing the great Cicero a little drunk. In some ways he is still the First Man of Rome and I know Cicero would be flattered to hear you say that. But even Caesar remarked that he should have won greater laurels than that of Rome's Generals, for rather than expand its territories, Cicero has expanded Rome's genius. Many men have tried to be the voice of Rome over the years, but Cicero has I warrant more of a claim now than most, for in his speeches and writings he has revolutionised its vocabulary and articulated its ideals. It's still important to let the old consul be heard, but of equal importance is not to listen sometimes," Cleanthes said in a hushed, confidential voice, as though someone else might be listening.

"What about Cato? Did you ever encounter him?"

"No. Unfortunately, or fortunately, I didn't ever have the opportunity to meet Cato. I still quite haven't worked him out. But not even the greatest philosopher in the world - which the Senator might have once argued was himself - could rightly discern when Cato was displaying virtue, or vanity."

"And Pompey the Great?"

"He spent half his life making his name - and the other half failing to live up to it. But now I am giving you witticisms rather than answers, Gaius. And that is no laughing matter," the whimsical teacher remarked, amusing himself rather than his pupil now.

8

Octavius ventured back home. It was now late afternoon but dusk was resting on the horizon to take the sting out of the vermillion sun. The baked dirt track meandered, as too did the young man's thoughts idly wander - sifting and remembering his recent conversations with Cleanthes. The subject of Cicero (the "Greek-Roman" as his tutor described him) in particular coloured his thoughts. He half-smiled again, recalling his tutor's judgement of him.

"Cicero is fond of saying that he is dedicated to truth, which is why he has admitted in the past that he is nothing but an actor."

Yet, for all of the satire and barbed comments surrounding the ex-consul, both Cleanthes and Caesar had spoken well of Cicero. Octavius remembered how Caesar had even given his copy of 'On The Nature Of The Gods' to him - and for a month or so he immersed himself in Cicero's dialogues and philosophy. The adolescent couldn't help but admire and be inspired by some of his teachings, and equally so his elegant writing style, which impressed upon the intellect and heart alike. Octavius had read his works avidly and repeatedly. Night time had been illuminated by his polished prose and enlightening instruction. Many a time had he hoped to be in Rome with Caesar and introduced to the legendary statesman. Yet always Cicero had been away, or Caesar had been busy.

"I am one of those people who can more easily see why something is false than why it is true ... If conscience goes, then everything collapses around it ... Philosophy is a physician for souls, taking away the burden of empty troubles, setting us free from desires, vanquishing fears ... There is nothing so absurd but some philosopher has said it."

As much as his step-father, or Caesar even, Cicero had influenced his education and character Octavius suddenly thought, surprising himself a little by the realisation.

The student was wrenched from his reveries however, on hearing the increasing tamp of horse hooves upon the road ahead. His heart began to canter also in ominous trepidation. Even when young Octavius couldn't help but be conscious of the potential dangers and enemies he might incur in being Caesar's nephew. As either a target for ransoming, or a source of bloody revenge, he was fair game for the many opponents of Caesar. And Octavius was still young; he still became unnerved by the introduction of a furtive looking stranger, lively footsteps across the gravel pathway in the dead of night, and the sound of a potential raiding party of horsemen or pirates. Childhood nightmares, consisting of him waking up and having his throat slit, or being hunted down by a band of bloodthirsty cavalry, had not receded completely.

The sound of the four horses, sixteen hooves, drummed upon the ground to create one continuous, violent roar. The ox bow curve of the trail meant that Octavius was blind to the approaching group of horsemen. Surrounded by a cloud of dust the snorting horses careered around the corner. Octavius recognised the Roman uniform and the man leading the quartet immediately. His tense body justly uncoiled itself when he spied Roscius. The legionary, slightly ungainly on top of his chestnut mare, shouted out an order to stop to his men. Octavius remained where he stood upon the side of the road, affecting a state of calm insouciance in marked contrast to the breathless horsemen. The imposing legionary, cursing his charge (and also himself), clumsily wheeled his horse around and trotted back towards the wayward youth.

Roscius' bristled face conveyed relief and then stern authority. He was thankful of locating the boy quickly.

"You shouldn't be travelling alone, Octavius. More importantly, you shouldn't be upsetting Oppius," Roscius remarked, torn between wishing to rebuke the young master of the house, and finding his daring and defiance amusing. For all of the years he had known his centurion, through winning over his men and campaigning on four corners of the map, it was a teenager who now proved to be his most challenging antagonist.

Octavius but half heard the advice and warnings of Roscius, partly distracted as he was by the memory of a similar scene. Fear had also been happily and swiftly succeeded by relief back then as a group of ominous sounding horsemen approached their shipwrecked party in Spain. It had been the morning after the attack on the cottage. The woodlands had thinned out and the group marched through dusty plains and farmland. A couple of distant plumes of smoke animated the pale skies from where Pompeians, or Caesar, had instigated a scorched earth policy. The party was weary with each member, bar the tireless lead centurion, harbouring a suspicion that they were perhaps lost. Oppius heard the doom-laden noise first, fearing that his scouts up ahead had been lost to the prospective enemy horsemen. With an absence of forest cover to retreat into, Oppius quickly, but far from desperately, ordered the party to form square - the cohort's defensive formation to combat a cavalry attack. A square was efficiently formed, betraying years of practise and drilling. Shields were interlocked. Spears then protruded out from the fence of large, curved scutums like the spines on the hide of a porcupine - upon which not even the most daring, or stupid, horse would ride onto. A half a dozen men - including Oppius, Roscius and Octavius - occupied the centre of the square. Oppius was thankful - and praised Fortuna under his breath - that he had a trio of archers next to him. Roman confidence, with a shard of a threat, imbued his tone as the centurion advised the party that if they held their defensive positions and made their arrows and javelins count, they had nothing to fear.

"We will be fighting an already defeated army. They won't even need an excuse to flee, but I'd like to give them one all the same," Oppius exclaimed in order to ease some of the tension etched in the faces around him.

Octavius stood close behind the battle-ready Roscius. His mouth was dry, with both thirst and fright. His legs, which not five minutes before had felt stiff from marching, now felt loose - to the point where he thought that they would give way if he ran. A natural sense of dread sent a shudder down his spine, to a degree where the youth felt that an actual serpent could be slithering up and down his back. He shivered, yet sweated in the heat.

The thunderous tumult of hooves grew closer, louder. Octavius darted a quick look at Oppius and even he wiped the perspiration from his brow and gripped his javelin with apprehension. Out of the corner of his other eye Octavius was briefly distracted by the sight of an archer's bicep bulge as he nocked an arrow and drew the drawstring back on his bow in readiness.

The bright scarlet plume on the Roman cavalry officer's helmet shone all the more starkly in the sepia-tinged landscape. The collective sigh of relief, or deliverance even, from the shipwrecked party was palpable as the decurion and his patrol saluted their fellow Caesarians. Believers and non-believers alike gave praise to Victoria, Jove, or some other indistinct deity.

The decurion, having encountered Oppius' scout, had galloped towards the party upon hearing that Caesar's nephew was with the group. After the battle Caesar had been looking forward to seeing the boy - yet over the last day or so he had grown anxious as to the reason why he hadn't reached them already. Knowing how much Caesar favoured the youth, the decurion was keen to treat the boy well. He made sure to warmly, yet deferentially, greet the dictator's nephew. Octavius was all too aware of the cavalry officer's flattery also upon saying how brave and tough he was to have survived the shipwreck and marched so far, so quickly. Although Octavius replied that everyone was to be praised for equalling the feat he duly separated himself from the hardship of the group by accepting the decurion's offer to ride with him as they escorted everyone back to the camp.

Octavius' privileged position also afforded him the opportunity to catch-up on the latest news as the cavalry officer reported upon the success of the campaign to Oppius. Gnaeus Pompeius was dead, killed whilst fleeing. Sextus was still believed to be commanding his troops in Cordoba, but he could well now be retreating and heading for the coast. The key battle had been at Munda, on a slope outside of the hill town. Caesar had tried to draw the enemy down from the higher ground but Gnaeus Pompey, learning from his father's mistake at Pharsalus, refused to give up his advantage and remained resolute. Caesar would have to come to him.

And so Caesar's legions, outnumbered yet more experienced than their opponents, moved up the slope towards Pompey's forces. They wavered yet broke not under a shower of javelins. Many of his men were already fatigued from the long march to reach the enemy. Perhaps this was one battle too many for even the indomitable Tenth Legion, Caesar's loyal favourite which had followed him across Gaul, Germania, Britannia and to Pharsalus and Egypt. His army wasn't retreating, but the momentum of his advance had faltered. At best the battle hung in the balance.

Caesar acted. He suddenly dismounted and charged through his own battle lines, grabbing a shield from a mesmerised legionary. The General then imperiously stood out in front of his army, his scarlet cloak billowing in the wind. To attract the attention of his men - and enforce the fact that it was indeed Caesar who stood before them - he removed his burnished helmet.

At the very least the front ranks were distracted from their burgeoning fears and the gruesome sight of so many of their fallen comrades bloodily strewn around them.

"Aren't you ashamed to let your general be beaten by mere boys?" Caesar opened with, waving a dismissive hand towards an enemy army filled with raw, teenage recruits. A storm of anger and defiance was worn in the imperator's usually gregarious and handsome brow.

"Only victory will bring peace to Rome and these lands. Defeat will bring more than dishonour. If we win that hill then we shall not only win the spoils of war, but also our freedom and the right to return home. But if we fail here, this will be the end of my life - and the end of more than just your careers."

Pride, fury and resolution began to transform the visages of the officers and legionaries around Caesar. Centurions ordered men to form ranks again. The familiar, rousing sound of swords and spears drumming upon shields began to reverberate down the line. The ever-alert general also heard the sound however of orders and movement behind him, from the enemy, as a section of their front rank released a volley of javelins - aimed at the commander. The deadly missiles spewed into the air, clouding out the blue sky, screaming with violence. Agile for his age - and fearless from so many victorious campaigns - Caesar (or 'Fortune's son', as some of his friends and enemies had called him over the years) evaded some of the whistling darts, whilst angling his shield to deflect the others. Still the hordes of spears arched over the hillside and stabbed down upon the general to the point where the sight of Caesar disappeared in the rainstorm of missiles. Both sides knew - cut off the head, the body will fall. Even the veterans of the Tenth held their breath in anticipatory fear - and so too the rest of the legions instinctively realised that if Caesar fell their cause, livelihoods, were lost. His fate was inexplicably, yet tangibly, linked to theirs. They were one. A collective sigh of relief succeeded the baited quiet. Caesar, his splintered shield resembling a pin cushion, lived. Perhaps the gods truly did favour their undefeated general. Perhaps Caesar was even a god himself. A cheer, part triumphal, part goading towards their enemy, went up.

"It looks like their aim is as steady as their hearts. Well, what are you waiting for?!" And, to the thunderous roar of the stirred-up ranks, Caesar drew his sword and proceeded to stride up the slope towards Pompey's formations, as if he were prepared to fight the enemy on his own. But Caesar would be far from alone. Even before a riled centurion bellowed and punctured the air with a rousing "Onward!" many of the men had already commenced to surge forward, a rippling tide of steel and nerve. The ground rumbled. Men flocked around their valorous general, forming a protective wall of shields around him. The thought that they had nearly just lost him redoubled their efforts to protect their commander in chief - and fight for him. Yet Caesar had no intention to remain behind a shield wall and survey the battle from a distance. He would stay at the vanguard of his beloved Tenth Legion, spurring them on. His sword was as bloodied as any man's in the ensuing fight. Rear ranks on both sides pushed the forward ranks on, the roars of the former often drowning out the wails of the latter.

For a time the battle remained at a stalemate, with Death alone reigning supreme. Charon, the ferryman, would be busy by nightfall. Bloodily, steadily, Caesar and his Tenth Legion began to inch their way forward up the hill, diminishing Pompey's left wing. Pompey, realising the danger - and fearing that history was about to repeat itself (it had been Caesar's veteran Tenth Legion which had broken his father's left flank at Pharsalus) ordered his cavalry over from his own right wing to bolster his wavering left. Caesar, upon being informed of the opposing general's move, promptly told one of his staff officers to seek out his own cavalry commander, Nonius Asprenas. The order relayed was for Asprenas to attack the enemy's left wing, preying upon the withdrawal and weakening of Pompey's forces there.

The young, inexperienced recruits however, which populated Gnaeus Pompey's centre, mistook their general's troop movement for a retreat. Confusion fed upon itself. Like men jumping from a sinking ship the resolve of the virginal soldiers dissolved. Men fled - in their thousands - dropping weapons, either running towards Munda or out into the expansive Spanish plains behind them. The retreat was soon transformed into a rout. Caesar's cavalry cut down hundreds, like farmhands scything down wheat. A few of Pompey's men fought on, like Pompey the Great's veteran Fourteenth Legion - fighting to the death rather than surrendering. But Caesar had remained undefeated in his final battle. The civil war, after five long years, was all but over.

After the decurion's summary of the battle, Oppius questioned the cavalry officer as to who had survived, or who had been lost, in the engagement - concerned as he was for old comrades and his chances of advancement. Octavius, however, lost interest in the exchange and became occupied with his own thoughts. As gripped as the youth had been by the account, he also felt awe-struck by Caesar's dramatic heroism - and anxious that he was now about to be confronted by him again. As egotistical as the accomplished teenager had become over the last couple of years, he naturally felt small, inadequate, as he placed himself before Caesar.

A wave of admiration, other-worldliness and intimidation, ran through him even upon just whispering the name. Caesar was dictator, pontifex maximus, the conqueror of Gaul, Germania and Pompey. He had won more battles - and pushed back the frontiers of the Empire - more than any other Roman. Writer. Great orator. Winner of the corona civica. Indeed Octavius realised that he perhaps had a deeper and firmer relationship with the idea of Caesar, rather than with the actual man. As well as being quite daunted by the prospect of being summoned by Caesar, Octavius felt a certain privilege in that, whereas kings and other great men would bow and call him Caesar, he could call him his great-uncle. At the same time though, Octavius could be acutely aware that, rather than being his own person, his existence only inherited any value through being Caesar's nephew. But why had he been now summoned by his great-uncle, Caesar? Had the last five years changed him? Octavius smiled when recalling the affection and generosity his uncle had once bestowed on him after the twelve year old boy had composed the oration at Caesar's mother's funeral. Caesar had wept at his words. The following morning Octavius woke to the gift of being presented with half a dozen books that his uncle had recommended him to read the evening before, as the two of them, alone, had spoken about literature and "being a Caesar" on the balcony of his villa. "Always be the best," his uncle had stated. Those words had been a spur, and burden, to the sickly boy ever since. Octavius' fond, reflective expression soon returned to a more serious, anxious form. Years of campaigning, a war which had torn the world in two, must have taken its toll. Stories of executions had replaced stories remarking upon Caesar's clemency. He had heard the gossip of how Caesar had been seduced by a young Egyptian queen. The dictator had even erected a statue made from gold, dedicated to his decadent mistress, inside the Temple Of Venus. It was sacrilege. What the young, stoical Roman first considered untrue eventually became unjustifiable, un-Roman.

*

Whilst in Munda the weary teenager had accepted the offer to ride on the back of a horse towards the army camp, Octavius politely here declined Roscius' invitation to ride on the back of his mount in order to reach home sooner - and placate Oppius. He would walk. Despite his fatigue and eagerness to return home Octavius, to flaunt the fact that he considered himself free from the authority of the domineering centurion, occasionally slowed himself down and stopped altogether on his way back to the house, whether to take in a view or examine a specimen of plant life. But it wasn't the flint-faced, reproving figure of Oppius who greeted Gaius Octavius when he returned home. It was someone rather different, in every way.

9

Briseis. The lone demure figure of the eighteen year old servant girl standing outside of the front of the house captured Octavius' attention immediately, like thunder or sunshine. Roscius, and the small group of horsemen flanking him, took their leave of the young master of the house after they had passed through the gates of the estate. She cocked her head a little, slyly smiling as he approached - as though she knew and appreciated what the lusty youth was thinking. Her almond eyes narrowed and smiled, as sultry as the heat. Octavius tried to conceal his pleasure at seeing the girl, but for once his marble expression was fractured and his feelings, desires, poured through the cracks. They walked towards each other, a certain humorous (giggly, flirtatious) expression lining their semblances. Octavius removed his sun hat and ran his hand through his golden hair to straighten it out. Her honey skin glowed in the blush of dusk; she prettily tucked a couple of strands of her long, sable hair out of her eyes and behind her ears. Her dress was cream-coloured, made from Egyptian cotton; the perspiration from her previous labours caused the material to cling to her alluring figure (her round, pert breasts, contoured waist and strong, supple thighs). In order to make herself pretty for her young master, and to stress how the servant considered herself above a slave, Briseis adorned herself with jewellery - a necklace strung together with some semi-precious amethyst stones, which shimmered with the azure of the ocean. Bright copper bangles decorated her wrists. The serving girl had also borrowed a delicate gold chain, which she had stolen from her mother's room at home, which she wore as an anklet to help direct attention to her feet and shapely calves. Briseis' mother had herself used the trinket, a gift from a lover, many years before. Before, when Briseis had tried to wear jewellery, Atia had chastised the serving girl, ordering her to remove "every last cheap bauble" and to not get ideas above her station again. But the jealous old woman wasn't here anymore. Briseis would have Octavius to herself for once. Briseis' mother, Helena, was at first both a little confused and upset in response to her daughter's request to return to her duties having been given time off - but her daughter's performance of displaying a sense of duty and a work ethic eclipsed any suspicions or doubts she owned in regards to her motives.

Helena had herself been a slave who had obtained her freedom. Or rather the master of the house had conveniently bestowed it upon her out of precaution from his wife finding out about his affair with the kitchen girl. Once free, Briseis' mother sold herself as a prostitute. At first Helena resented the arrival of the unwanted Briseis, but she duly brought the girl up on her own. Her father could have been any number of men, none of which she could dare compromise. She found time to earn a good living as mistress to various Roman officers and bureaucrats. As her beauty waned - and her trade dried up - Helena increasingly sacrificed her own time and energies for her daughter. She saved some money in order that her daughter would not have to lead the life that she had. She would try and give Briseis the right education - so she could marry and become a lady. But Helena was not an alchemist - and one cannot fashion gold from brass. The first tutor she had, the teenage girl seduced. The second attempted to seduce her. The next couple of tutors — women - gave up on the wilful, ignorant girl. And so, to teach her a lesson so to speak, Helena had sent her daughter off to work as a servant - in hope that in discovering how desultory the work was she would prefer to return to her studies and embrace her mother's ambitions for her. Yet Briseis cultivated ambition more than her mother could have fancied. She would be a Caesar's concubine - was that not better than a life of being a wife to any other man?

The fatigue that Octavius had experienced - and the anxiety he felt at having to encounter a rankled Oppius - evaporated as soon as he entered the gates to the estate. The centurion wasn't even a memory anymore. Desire now consumed his heart...as well as other organs. Briseis had returned for no other reason but him. Octavius had hoped that he'd performed well as a lover, but did this not prove it? Yet, in quieter moments, Octavius also hoped that he was stimulating the girl not just through the act of sex, but rather he desired to touch her heart and instil in the girl the kind of finer feelings that he felt for her. He could not remember who had made the first advance between them. Initially they shared but clandestine glances. More than anyone else it was Briseis who Octavius would request to perform an errand for him. She laughed at his jokes. Her Latin was poor and so he used Greek, improving it as he did so. Indeed Octavius began to ask Cleanthes how he could improve his vocabulary - and what did Greek girls like? The former amorous tutor duly advised his pupil, half amused by the smitten student and half concerned for him. Love can be a sickness, as well as a salve he warned. Coy glances over the dinner table soon became more open and coquettish on the girl's part. She often brushed past him; her dress would be unbuttoned a little to reveal the promise of her perspiring bosom as she leaned over and re-filled his water jug. He tried to engage her intellectually. He would quote Euripides. He mentioned how beautiful her name was - and was she named after the Briseis of the Iliad, the woman who captured the heart of Achilles? Her reply was to shrug disinterestedly, cutting off Octavius' intended speech about Homer and the power of poetry before he even began. Yet he happily dropped the subject, captivated by the enticing smile upon her moist, pink lips.

He soon veritably lived for her laugh, and Octavius was but a shadow of himself when out of her company. They got into the routine of Briseis bringing the young master some light supper to his room of an early evening. She gazed at him with wonder and seduction as Octavius recounted some of the deeds and sayings of his great-uncle. Briseis, for her part, would tell him how other servants mistreated her, or confess how she worried for her future and that she did not want to marry someone she didn't love. Or the girl would ask him how she should wear her hair, or if a new piece of jewellery looked nice. One evening, when Atia and Marcus Phillipus were staying the weekend on a neighbouring estate, the serving girl stole a jug of wine to bring it to Octavius with his meal. They drank it together. His aspect glowed with drunkenness and desire. After a bout of giggling about nothing in particular, Briseis suddenly got up from the bed which they were sitting upon and twirled in front of the virginal youth.

"Oh, I forgot. Do you like? I just bought it?" the girl said excitedly, showing off both her new dress and the sweet-smelling figure inside of it. Briseis tantalisingly hitched up the skirt of the russet coloured garment to reveal a sun-kissed leg.

Octavius was too dumbstruck, awed, shy, possessed to reply. Before he had a chance however to give in to the temptation to reach out and touch the dress, or rather drunkenly paw its wearer, Briseis twirled once more, lost her balance and fell upon the Roman. He caught her by her hips as she fell towards him upon the bed, yet also he clutched her towards him - and Briseis fell willingly into his arms. Her soft thigh nestled itself into his groin. Her hands were pressed either side of his head, her scented hair falling around his flushed face. For a brief moment there was a pause, but then their lips mutually met. They kissed tentatively at first, then seductively - and then hungrily. The bed creaked a little. The flame upon the candle wriggled. The aromatic smell of the girl's hands, from where she had been working in the kitchen with spices, filled the air. For half a minute or so an aroused, awakened Octavius groped and felt every part of the girl's lithe body, which he had yearned to touch for so long. Briseis soon took control however - she grabbed his hands, entwining her spidery fingers in his. She kissed him softly and slowly, briefly sucking on his bottom lip as she withdrew. By now, without him noticing it - but yet Octavius appreciated it all the same - Briseis had straddled herself over her young master. The nubile but experienced woman pulled her skirt up so it was bunched around her waist, her thighs bare and bronze in the candlelight. With one hand she undid the buttons of her dress, provocatively slipping each side off her smooth shoulders to let the dress fall and reveal her round, hardening breasts. Octavius gazed up at her, adoringly, absorbing and admiring Briseis as if she were a goddess who had sparked a fire within him. His erotic dreams of her were coming true. On another night he might've even wept with happiness at the scene.

They made love when possible after that revelatory evening, although no matter how many times Octavius took Briseis, or vice versa, it was never enough for the youth. Satisfaction only fed his appetite. Sometimes the servant girl almost had to fight her young lover off as she refused to allow stolen kisses to transform themselves into something more time and energy consuming. And partly she denied Octavius to tease him - and increase his anticipation, as well as her power over him.

10

Rome.

The moon slipped behind a brown-grey cloud but still his lean, bony face shone pale in the glossy night. On more than one occasion his senatorial companion for the evening thought that Cassius Longinus looked like a ghost, such was his bloodless pallor. The milky radiance of the moonlight was displaced by the orange glow of torches as a quartet of former lictors, who had served two optimate consuls, illuminated the meeting between the two conspiratorial statesmen.

It was the dead of night, even the stars appeared sleepy. The two men stood atop Capitoline Hill, under the adamantine gaze of Lucius Iunius Brutus. The sword was unsheathed in the hand of the statue, symbolic of the legendary figure's duty to forever defend the Republic. He had even executed his own two sons for conspiring against the state. Marcus Brutus thought it was a cheap, transparent trick for Cassius to arrange for them to meet before his ancestor's statue, but more than once of late he had himself traversed up the hill and stood before the famed Roman who had vanquished Tarquin the Proud - a despotic King - and established the Republic. Neither of the two men mentioned the graffiti that had been inscribed upon part of the plinth. '*O that we had you now, Brutus.*' '*Would that Brutus was alive.*' The descendant of the first consul did not need to read the phrases again, for it seemed now they were carved, or branded, upon his conscience. Cassius however did not need to scan and mention the graffiti because he had been the author behind the inscriptions; so too Cassius had been behind the anonymous letters sent to the praetor's house, calling on him to defend the Republic. '*Brutus, are you asleep?*' '*You are no true Brutus.*' In the past the spiteful practical joker had employed the use of similar anonymous letters to cause mischief. Cassius had revealed to fellow senators that their wives were having affairs, or alternatively he had blackmailed and extorted money out of his victims to help him pay off his debts. Or sometimes he composed various missives just to amuse his black humour. Yet now Cassius could tell himself that his deceptions were ultimately honourable, to the extent even that he could and should be forgiven for all his previous misdemeanours.

An acrid smell filled Brutus' nostrils as Cassius' breath misted up in front of him in the gelid air. For a moment Brutus fleetingly fancied that the smell came directly from the source of the man's bitter heart. More than from any Republican principle Brutus knew only too well that Cassius' motives were borne from ambition and a personal sense of vengeance against Caesar. It still rankled Cassius that Caesar had confiscated his pride of lions which he had intended to display during Rome's Public

Games. So too Brutus himself had been involved in provoking Cassius, yet was not Caesar also responsible for that episode? Both men had been competing for the Praetorship of Rome. The dictator finally summoned both candidates to stand before him, his judgement being thus, "Cassius has the stronger case, but we must give Brutus the first Praetorship." It was not a love of Republicanism which had eventually prompted Cassius to heal his rift with Brutus, but rather it was his hatred for Caesar and his need to recruit Brutus to his cause. Whilst Brutus resented the idea of dictatorship, Cassius resented the dictator.

"Soon Caesar will join his army; or rather I should call them hired mercenaries, for they serve him rather than Rome. Once ensconced with his legions he will prove untouchable. We must strike at the heart of his despotism in the Forum, the home of the Republic. And we must act soon. After the Ides I warrant that it is his intention to leave for Apollonia to collect his precious whelp of a nephew and march on to subdue the Parthians."

Brutus here briefly thought of Octavius. He had met him on a couple of occasions and was justly impressed with the youth. At first he seemed shy, or rather observant, as he positioned himself in a corner of the room. When Caesar introduced his nephew to Brutus though he found the teenager to be confident, well-read and witty. Brutus hoped however that Octavius was not susceptible to certain other, darker, Caesarian traits.

"Agreed. The Forum it is," Brutus replied, with perhaps as much resignation as resolution entwined in his voice.

Marcus Brutus was a man of few words but yet when he spoke

people listened. And whatever he said, he meant. The loose folds of his woollen toga could not disguise his muscular build. His face was squarish, strong and handsome - if a little humourless. Pompey once joked that Brutus had even come out of the womb with the demeanour and seriousness of a forty-three-year-old. Yet Brutus was not without a sense of humour, contrary to what some of his detractors might have sniped - but the need to laugh, smile and flatter were of secondary importance to the judicious Roman.

Cassius smiled - his white teeth momentarily flashing in the darkness - and clasped a fraternal hand upon his fellow conspirator's shoulder. As much as Cassius was central to the plot, he knew that he needed Brutus, his reputation and name, as a figurehead. Finally Cassius dared to call the priggish but influential senator a "libertore", a freedom fighter.

"You represent both the old and hopefully new Rome my friend. The people look to other praetors for public doles, spectacles and gladiatorial shows but they look to you to deliver them from tyranny."

"Should we include Cicero?" Brutus asked, all but ignoring Cassius' rehearsed flattery.

"No. The new man is now an old man. Even if I thought he could keep his mouth shut before the deed, I dare say he would be unbearable should we succeed. He would doubtless try to propagate the argument that he was the saviour of Rome again - and that we should honour him with a triumph for delivering the Republic. No, Cicero has become weak, foolish. He's become as garrulous as Nestor. He either lives in the past or dreams of fantastical futures that only he can orchestrate. Did you also catch the story of how he cried like a baby after hearing about his daughter's death?"

Brutus declined to respond, but he judged that it was not weakness which had made Cicero weep so for the estimable Tullia, but love. And love bred strength. He briefly thought of the strength he gained from Porcia and fondly smiled to himself (albeit Cassius believed his companion was smirking at his jibes). But no, Cicero could not wholly be trusted, Brutus concluded. Despite being opposed to the idea of dictatorship, there was a strange bond between Caesar and Cicero - and the personal could affect the political. Brutus respected the ex-consul, perhaps as much as his former mentor Cato, but Cicero would want to seek a compromise. For Brutus there could be none. His reasoning, or rather logical syllogism was thus: Monarchy is bad. Caesar desires to be King. Therefore, Caesar is bad.

"My concern is rather with Antony," Cassius issued.

"No. Our cause is to kill a man who would make himself a King, not murder one of his subjects who could redeem himself and become a good citizen and servant of Rome. Mark Antony may have proved himself to be corrupt, incompetent and a bully - but he isn't a tyrant. The purity of our cause would be tainted with his blood on our hands. History must judge us as liberators, not murderers," Brutus replied.

"You underestimate how much trouble he could cause."

"And you overestimate him, Cassius. He's little more than a

drunk and a letch. Once we have done the deed, as you say, we will send him off to some distant battlefield, where he belongs. I would stake my honour on posterity not remembering Mark Antony."

"But he is Caesar's right arm."

"And he can do no more than Caesar's arm, when Caesar's head is off. Our cause is justice Cassius, not revenge or ire," Brutus calmly, but firmly, charged.

The wind suddenly howled, congealing the air even more. Cassius drew his toga tighter to his lean body - trapping the warm air between his skin and the silk laden material. He stamped his feet to quicken his ice-ridden blood. He glanced at his companion to see him register the cold also, but Brutus remained unperturbed by the sudden drop in temperature. Cassius believed that his fellow conspirator was equally chilled however - but that he was either too proud or affected to admit it.

"Lepidus too will serve Rome rather than Caesar when he is removed. He is a soldier, and soldiers follow orders," Brutus confidently remarked in reference to Rome's Master of the Horse, whose troops were posted just outside the city.

"And what about the people? His reforms have purchased their love. They could riot," Cassius warned.

"You say the people love Caesar. But the people also loved Gracchus and Marius and Clodius and Pompey. They love anyone who puts on a show for them and doles out corn. They are as constant, yet changeable, as the weather," Brutus issued; his tone imbued with a certain amount of disdain for 'the people', who he was intending to liberate and, as a praetor, had vowed to serve. "I will address the people afterwards. You saw their reaction at Lupercalia. For all of their wishes to put their demagogue up on a pedestal, they will be grateful for us toppling Caesar when they are told the truth."

Cassius nodded in agreement, but shared not his friend's confidence.

*

Brutus, along with his torch bearers, descended the hill alone. Cassius walked off in the opposite direction, deflecting the question as to where he was heading. Brutus marched, as if still on campaign with a legion, and every now and then the former lictors trotted a couple of steps to keep up with their master.

Even from half-way down the hill the senator could still see a fair amount of the city below him, white and grey in the moonlight. From left to right he scanned the Campus Martius and the phalanx of tents, ordered like its own city. The meandering Tiber, like liquid jade, flowed and glistened in the background. Brutus briefly remembered how Caesar, when he had been his mother's lover, had taught him to swim in the river one summer. Always his thoughts turned back to Julius. Compelled. Condemned.

The gardens of Lucullus possessed an air of colour and vitality even in the distance, in the dark. Maybe the pleasure-loving ex-consul had been right to retire from the political circus of Rome and the Senate. But this idle fancy of the Roman praetor was ultimately rootless. Duty was the highest pleasure.

The Forum, Senate House and Sacred Way remained bold and divine even in silhouette for the devout Republican as they stood before him. Yet, whereas he once strode up the Sacrae Via filled with the pride of achieving his ambition of becoming a Senator, Brutus of late felt repulsed and righteously indignant during his time spent, wasted, in the Forum. It was a farce to think that the Republic was still just that. It was fast becoming a royal court, filled with cronies and profligates.

A patternless group of dimly burning oil lamps littered a large part of the landscape, where the masses resided. A fire from a house, which thankfully seemed to be under control, illuminated the less scenic and less celebrated quarter of the city, the Subura. Caesar had once lived there. Was that why he could sympathise with the people so? The flames flickered out into the void like a serpent's tongue tasting the air, and lit up the wooden and red clay roofs of the surrounding jerry-built tenement blocks which stood, or rather leant, like a blot upon the landscape. Each room would be crammed with more than one family, often immigrants, with little or no access to running water or other basic amenities. Sooner or later the building would collapse or be consumed in a fire, if disease did not kill off the tenants first. When would Rome finally have its own official fire brigade and all-encompassing sewer and aqueduct system? The Senate would not pay for it and the people couldn't. As much concern and compassion as Brutus felt for some of his fellow citizens - indigent, trapped - the Roman aristocrat could also feel a strain of contempt and snobbery towards "the great unwashed", as Cicero called them, slavish to demagogues like Caesar and parasitic by nature.

It was so late that Brutus barely encountered a soul during his walk home. Even the nocturnal thugs and low-lives had drunk themselves into a stupor by now, or were in the arms of some poxed harlot within one of the city's sordid brothels. Despite pondering Rome's splendour, depravity, history and various odours (of stale wine, exotic spices, sweat, ordure, musty perfumes, damp and smoke) Brutus returned to looking inwards and was again absorbed by his thoughts.

His footsteps across the stone streets sounded like a sculptor chipping away at a block of marble, as Brutus chipped away again at why his personal feelings should not influence his sense of duty. Personal feelings, and self-serving motives, were certainly influencing many of his co-conspirators. Some were former Caesarians who felt resentful towards the dictator for overlooking them and advancing their rivals. Some craved revenge for fallen comrades and family members that Julius had vanquished in the Civil War. Others were offended and rebellious due to Caesar's undemocratic reforms, which favoured the people over the plutocrats; the once all powerful oligarchs were now being taxed on their extravagant lifestyles and their wealth distributed to the poor. Their dignitas was being insulted, their authoritas undermined.

Brutus smiled, thinking about Caesar's brio when announcing his reforms and remembering the confounded looks upon certain faces as they heard the revolutionary proclamations. Yet whereas personal feelings and self-serving motives spurred Cassius on, if Brutus considered his personal feelings towards Caesar then perhaps he would be dying for him now rather than plotting to kill his friend and sometime surrogate father. More than any other enemy soldier it had been Brutus who Caesar had sought out in order to spare his life after the Battle of Pharsalus. Caesar trusted him. Brutus experienced the shame again, as if he were in the room once more, when Caesar, not two weeks ago, dismissed the suggestion that there was a conspiracy against him - and that Brutus had somehow been implicated in the plot. Julius merely smiled confidently, paternally, at his adviser. He remarked, whilst laying a hand on his body, that "Brutus will wait for this skin of mine," - not only implying that Brutus was worthy to take his place, but that if he did so he would act honourably. In many ways Julius was worth a thousand squabbling, corrupt senators. And that same day hadn't he himself renounced any monarchical ambitions, replying to a supplicant who called him a king that "he was Caesar, not king?"

Thunder growled in the background, seemingly undecided as to whether it should unleash itself or not. Rain began to spot his toga but Brutus reached his house before the downpour commenced in earnest. He entered quietly, not wishing to disturb his wife. He had been an inconsiderate enough husband of late. With a brief nod of his head Marcus Brutus dismissed his man-servants and thanked them for their service for the evening. He retained one of their torches however and, retreating into the triclinium, lit a brazier and sat with his head in his hands before it. Tired. Tortured.

Brutus momentarily lifted a corner of his mouth, straining it upwards as if a weight dangled from his face, as he caught the pleasant fragrance in the air. Porcia had scented the coals with his favourite aromatic oil. The praetor again thought how he would be lost without her.

The flames flickered - dancing in the air to the rhythmic drumming of the swirling rain upon the tiled roof - and created hypnotic shadows along the plaster wall behind. Brutus scrunched up his crop of black hair in his hands. He suddenly got up, strode over to a low pine table next to the end of the couch and poured himself a large measure of wine. The sediment was heavy at the bottom of the jug from where he usually didn't touch the intoxicating vintage. He winced slightly at the taste of the first mouthful but then adjusted himself to the flavour. It was impossible to discern whether the troubled figure was drinking to find his resolve, or lose himself.

After a couple more cups Brutus, with a wistful drowsiness in his expression, half-smiled as he recalled how much the present scene resembled that of when Caesar crossed the Rubicon, and he had to choose between his friend and Pompey. Reason had overruled his personal feelings then; despite his attachment to Caesar - and his resentment of Pompey for being involved in his father's death. But yet, like now, Brutus served the Republic, not any one man. The debt he owed Caesar for sparing his life should not overrule his debt, duty, to Rome. He again mournfully, angrily, weighed up the case against Caesar in his mind.

Although there had once been three hundred senators - and now there were over eight hundred - power had increasingly become conferred upon one man. He had even dared to proclaim himself Dictator for Life. Caesar was a King in all but name. Officials were no longer elected, but personally chosen by Caesar - he bestowed offices like favours - and in return his supplicants would support his radical reforms. Statues had been commissioned - and placed in the company of images of the gods. Brutus sneered in contempt at the egoist as he remembered his near blasphemous comments, attacking the state and constitution that his heroic ancestor had helped establish. Caesar had dismissively called the Republic "a mere name without a substance" in front of everyone.

And then there was the would-be coronation at Lupercalia. Mid-February. Ironically the festival was in part a celebration of the renewal of civic order, but Brutus' sense of irony was eventually replaced with indignation. The day owned a religious and ritual significance. Young noblemen would dress up in animal skins. Carrying small leather thongs they would proceed to chase women around the city who were childless - and then gently whip them across the hand, or more indecorous areas. Many desired to be caught, believing in the superstition that the touch of the whip would increase fertility. Caesar presided over the rite, sitting on top of a gilded throne. He wore a lavish purple toga and red boots, similar to those worn by the legendary monarchs of the past. Mark Antony was also there. Although a little too old for such sport - and it was a blight on the honour of the Consulship which he held - he also dressed himself up in the ceremonial goatskin loin cloth and joined in the ritual, half-drunk and debauched from the night before. Brutus thought he looked ridiculous and was at first as contemptuous as he was confused as to why Mark Antony was taking part in the far from august festivities. One couldn't help but notice also how Antony gave certain girls a kiss on the hand that he had first struck, intending no doubt to increase their fertility through less superstitious means in the near future. As well as a whip however, the consul produced a diadem and a wreath when he approached the rostra on which Caesar surveyed the crowds before him. It was here that Cassius gave Brutus his first knowing, conspiratorial look.

"The people offer this to you through me," Antony grandly announced whilst lifting the golden wreath aloft. A small section of the crowd cheered enthusiastically, as if on cue. Their enthusiasm however proved to be far from infectious. Yet Antony was but one of the actors performing in the regal drama. If not for the sacrilege and malign ambition involved, Brutus might have deemed the display a mere pantomime act.

"Jupiter alone is King of the Romans," Caesar replied, refusing the wreath in a grandiose manner. A genuine wave of applause and love here erupted, drowning out those who called for the people's hero to accept the crown. Facing away from him, Marcus found it hard to discern Julius' expression - but for a moment or two he thought he saw him wryly smile. Perhaps he knew that it was the people's love - and power - which were important to him, not the ornaments of a crown and title. And Brutus truly believed that Julius loved the people in return. He had done so much for them - and not just from the cynical motives of ambition and the vanity of a legacy. His clemency was sincere, his reforms were progressive and his generosity was not a smokescreen.

Mark Antony, either desiring the spotlight or merely obeying pre-arranged stage direction, attempted however to bestow the crown on Caesar again. Boos and jeers though accompanied the mock coronation - and this time it was Brutus who permitted himself a discreet smile in favour of the people. Rome did not want a King, but yet Caesar here perhaps mistook their displeasure as a rejection of him. Mark Antony, either too drunk or obtuse, misjudged his performance - and his audience. He insisted on playing his part. Although seemingly not part of the script Caesar wrestled the wreath from his clownish lieutenant and tossed it aside. A few cheers here punctured the boos, but the damage was done.

The official record stored in the archive for the Lupercalia read *'Caesar offered the kingship: Caesar was unwilling.'*

Rome must not become a monarchy Brutus again told himself, his face ploughed with determination. There was an almost religious fervour in his aspect. The removal of Caesar would be tantamount to a ritual killing, a purge. He could not compromise his ideals. If he sacrificed his idealism, that which sets Man apart from the beasts, then Man, Rome, was not worth saving. Marcus Brutus would rather die than live ignobly. "I love the name honour more than fear death," he had once proudly exclaimed to Cassius, unwittingly plagiarising the line from a play that he had seen over a year ago.

Brutus' eyelids soon weighed as heavy upon him as his mood. Drowsiness swiftly succeeded his fervent resolution, dovetailing almost within the blink of an eye. His brow throbbed from the wine and the heat, which pounded out from the roaring brazier. His head swayed and drooped as if set upon a pivot, as if sleep were about to draw a veil over his evening. A gust of cold air feathered his flushed cheek however. The door creaked open.

Porcia entered. She walked a little gingerly at first but then, realising that her husband was aware of her presence, regained her natural poise and graceful gait. Despite his fatigue Brutus awoke to his wife immediately, revitalised. Her black hair cascaded down her elegant shoulders and back like liquid ebony. Her eyes were dark, but warm - and a little red and puffy from sleeplessness. Her face was feminine without being coquettish. She wore a sky-blue linen gown which stretched down to her ankles but revealed her slender arms and fine, ivory hands and fingers. Her features were aristocratic and intelligent, an inheritance from her father Cato, but yet as soon as she gazed at her husband her countenance softened and expressed devotion. Only after moving out of the half-light did Brutus notice the pale, almost translucent hue, to her skin. He felt an immediate mixture of both pity towards his wife and anger directed at himself for being so distant over the past month. But yet he could not burden her with his own anxieties. He loved her too much. And if she was party to the plot then she would be in mortal peril. Porcia smiled a little falteringly. She then wordlessly cuddled up to her husband, slotting her contoured body into his; his tautness lessened as she stroked his hair and kissed him upon the cheek. Either from the strain, or his love for his wife, Brutus was close to tears. She nestled her head against his muscular shoulder. Torrents of rain still splintered the air in the background. They both simultaneously looked up and furrowed their brows in slight apprehension at the storm growing stronger. Out of the corner of his sight Brutus observed his wife briefly close her eyes - either in sorrow or wincing in actual pain - before resting her head on his shoulder. Caesar was not to blame for this anguish. He was. Brutus burned with impotence and guilt, his feelings unleashed like Cerberus, yet muzzled.

"Are you not coming to bed? What's wrong?" Porcia asked. Although she had ached to ask this question before, she had not relented until now.

"Nothing."

"Nothing can come from nothing Marcus," she replied, both wittily and ruefully.

"Telling you would only make me worry for you my love, and thus increase my worries still. I will take care of things. I promise that everything will be alright," Brutus remarked with unconvincing reassurance.

"For better or for worse, remember? I would share your worries, as well as your love Marcus," she expressed whilst removing her head from his side and raising herself to look her husband in the eye.

He loved her. She was beautiful. Porcia was much younger than her husband but her good sense and wit belied the maturity of a woman twice her age. She first cupped his sorrowful face in her satin hands and then tenderly, almost maternally, stroked his cheek. He strangely never noticed it himself but others remarked how much Porcia resembled her aunt, Brutus' mother. Yet his wife had loved him more unconditionally than his mother. Whilst growing up Servilia had been more concerned with playing mistress to Crassus and Caesar, than she had been, with being a mother to her son. Only when she finally lost her looks and the patronage of certain men of power dried up (Crassus had died in battle and Caesar now had his Egyptian consort) had Servilia turned her attention to her son and her ambitions for him.

"You have not been yourself lately," Porcia said, concerned. Probing.

"Aye, I have been more subject than citizen," Brutus replied, ruefully and wittily.

The thoughtful young woman paused before speaking, as if either mustering the courage for what needed to be said or pausing to remember her lines like an actress.

"Marcus, I am Cato's daughter, and I gave myself to you not just to share your bed and board, but to be a true partner in your joys and suffering. I have no reproach to make, but what proof can I give you of my love, if you forbid me to share the kind of trouble that demands a loyal friend to confide, and keep your suffering to yourself? I know that men think women's nature too weak to be entrusted with secrets, but surely a good upbringing and the company of honourable men can do much to strengthen us, and at least Porcia can claim that she is the daughter of Cato and the wife of Brutus. I did not know before how either of these blessings could help me, but now I have put myself to the test and find that I can conquer pain."

As her father had suffered from a surfeit of conceit, Porcia too was not immune to a strain of Cato's pride and self-consciousness. Thankfully however the daughter did not inherit from her father his frigidity and haughtiness. Indeed more so than conceit one may have argued that Porcia suffered rather from an excess of sensibility, which was heightened all the more by the trappings of youth and her bookish education.

For a moment Brutus was confused as to the content - and portent - of his wife's remarks. He merely looked quizzically into her mahogany eyes. Confusion blurred into apprehension however as Porcia's lace-like features unbound themselves. The wild fervour of her looks then possessed the rest of her delicate figure as she dramatically scrunched up the skirt to her gown in two small fists and ripped the garment open to reveal her right thigh, stained with both dry and fresh blood. With a trembling hand the stoical woman peeled back the scarlet bandage and displayed her glistening, gory wound. Porcia had sliced into a major vein in her leg with a small knife that she used to cut her nails earlier in the evening. She wanted to prove to herself, and her husband, that she was strong - and could conceal a secret. Cherry-red blood still oozed out of the cut.

Brutus - shocked, cherishing - hastily pressed the blood-strewn gauze back onto the unsightly wound and with his other clasped his wife's head to his.

"I'm so sorry. I should have trusted you. I love you so much. I don't deserve you," Brutus half whispered, half moaned, whilst tears streamed from his eyes - tears of sorrow, devotion and rage. His marble heart crumbled. He kissed her on her snow-white cheek, slaked lips and brackish eyelids. Porcia, drained, barely heard what Marcus said. She just felt that a weight had been lifted from her heart and dreamily smiled whilst leaning into her virtuous husband.

He picked her up like a child and carried her into their room. All through the night Brutus attended to his wife. He redressed the wound and sent for a physician. Not once did he let go of her limp, but responsive hand. After the surgeon departed, and Porcia had regained some of her strength, Brutus poured out his dilemma to his wife. As tempted as the young woman was to influence her husband - for although she kept it from Brutus she had never forgiven Caesar for her father's suicide - Porcia for the most part just listened. She knew how much Marcus admired and loved Julius as a friend, or father figure even. Porcia felt more concern for Brutus' torment than vengeance towards Caesar. The morning sun eventually poured through the window like honey. Porcia drew her husband close, tenderly kissed him on the temple and whispered, "I know that you will do what you believe is right, my love."

11

Octavius opened his eyes, squinting in the half-light. His stiff limbs ached and his head felt like an anvil after a day's work at the blacksmiths. Briseis was no longer lying beside him, having crept out before dawn to avoid being caught in the young master's bedroom by a loose-lipped slave or soldier. The room still reeked of wine and body odours, as well as the girl's cheap perfume, but Octavius smirked when recalling the scenes of the night before.

After their encounter outside of the house, Briseis, wordlessly, suggestively, led him by the hand into the bath house of the estate. The love-struck youth followed her. She immediately placed a finger over his lips when Octavius tried to say something, and then kissed him teasingly, with the unspoken promise of more kisses to come. Water sizzled across the red hot stones, producing even more steam. The comely serving girl gently ran the back of her hand down her master's arm, following and stroking in the droplets of perspiration which formed upon his skin. She then sat him down on the large wicker chair which occupied the centre of the room. His eyes only diverted themselves from hers when he glanced and admired the rest of her provocative curves.

Again he tried to speak but Briseis grinned and shook her head as she crouched down and placed her hands into a bowl filled with warm water and a sponge. Her skin and eyes glowed in the mellow light of the torches which adorned the chamber. First she removed his sandals, dusty from the bouts of walking during the day. For a moment the water tickled as it trickled down his foot, but then the sensation grew more sensuous as she freshened his skin. Her eyes slinkily gazed up at his servile aspect as she knelt before him. Once his feet and calves were washed, scraped and dried, Octavius, unable to contain himself, reached out to touch the girl but Briseis deftly moved away, denying and arousing her master with a playful, chiding look. He grinned, lasciviously. She smiled, deliciously, as she knelt before him again and, dipping her hand into a small bowl beneath the chair, rubbed olive oil into his feet. Slowly, deliberately, alluringly, Briseis moved around to the back of her lover. With neither master nor mistress issuing a word she began to loosen his tunic. Octavius drew in the scent of her breath, skin and damp hair as if it were the finest of fragrances. Briseis, hardly able to contain her own self now, leaned over Gaius and, before he had time to fully respond, kissed him hungrily upon the mouth. He tried to turn his head and return her amorous sortie but once more the girl tantalisingly retreated and shook her head, indicating that he was breaking the rules or not playing to her script. The pace again grew slower, sultrier, as Briseis returned to her position close behind Octavius. Her left hand stroked his ear and cheek as her right, soaked in oil, massaged his chest - delving down to his stomach and beyond.

Octavius soaked up the warm sensations - the seduction. Yet he could not totally tame his excitement; his heart pumped blood into a somewhat different but equally ardent organ and he tapped his foot impatiently. Anticipant.

Gaius closed his eyes and cocked his head back, emitting a sound of pleasure - which somehow eased his troubled soul as well. Briseis couldn't help but sigh with gratification, half-lost in the eroticism, too. But then the handmaiden suddenly ceased her caresses. All was silent, apart from the noise of Octavius breathing - and the slight rustling sound of the seductress disrobing. Octavius remained speechless as Briseis appeared before him, naked - her ripened flesh glistening with perspiration and oil. She licked her lips, moistening their splendour even more. The look the lovers shared conveyed a million words - playful, carnal, and intimate. For a brief second or two a shy teenage girl was also to be seen in the sexually powerful woman as Briseis coyly bit her bottom lip and smiled a little nervously - but then her prowess returned as she grasped the two wooden arms of the chair and inserted her slender legs each side of her master, to perch herself upon his lap. Octavius clasped his hands around her waist and brought the girl towards him, her firm yet soft breasts pressing against his chest. Despite the fervour of their passion the maturing lovers kissed each other tenderly. He then kissed her neck as Briseis pulled her head back in response to Octavius stroking his fingertips up and down her back.

They made love.

A cold bath succeeded their exertions in the steam room.

The blazing torch of the sun had also extinguished its orange embers. By the time Octavius returned to his room the moon shone supreme in a cloudless sky. His face buried itself in his pillow. Although exhausted his thoughts were still enlivened by the sensations and memories of his lovemaking. Gaius soon missed her - and desired her again. And Briseis soon duly re-appeared, carrying a jug of wine and bowl of figs, under the cover of nightfall. Waiting until her jealous sorority of servants were asleep she had changed into one of her mother's old dresses - which left little to the imagination (but fired it just the same) - she slipped in and out of the shadows towards the young Caesar's room.

Octavius creased his brow, trying to remember how much wine he had consumed the night before, and how many times they had made love. Dehydrated, Gaius turned to the table beside his bed to see if Briseis had left him a jug of water. She hadn't. It was perhaps the only thing she hadn't thought of yesterday he speculated, grinning.

The groggy youth tried to get back to sleep but his thirst finally conquered his desire to rest and so he arose from his bed. The sundial in the atrium confirmed his internal clock. It was late morning, approaching midday. He would have to miss his afternoon lesson with Cleanthes. The tutor would be disappointed, but forgiving. Octavius would feel guilty later but at present he was too tired to feel anything too keenly. Where Octavius more often than not had been outside the house during this part of the day he was suddenly struck by the sight of the redolent rays of the sun striking one of the mosaic-filled walls decorating the atrium. The mural was a replica to that which adorned Caesar's family home; Venus and Aeneas populated both Caesar's wall and ancestry. Senators struck poses and soldiers won victories within the mosaic, lineage, with the triumphs of Caesar himself dominating the lavish and awe-inspiring picture. His great-uncle had once stood before a statue of Alexander and wept. "I have something worth being sorry about, when I reflect that at my age Alexander was already king over so many peoples, while I have yet to achieve anything remarkable." So too Gaius felt hollow, shame again, in comparing his life to Caesar's. His life did not merit even a solitary tile upon the mural.

*

Spain.

The site of the camp, especially reconnaissanced by an experienced centurion, was set on a vast undulating plain. A sedate and crystal clear river flowed along its left side. The ground was hard, crisped by the Iberian sun, but still workable. It had not taken the legions an undue amount of time to dig the deep trenches and build the ramparts which encircled the camp. A nearby forest had provided the timber which had been used to construct the four watchtowers which stood at each corner of the rectangular encampment. The commander-in-chief's tent, topped with a gloriously bright and rippling vexillion, dominated the skyline as Octavius, still seated behind the decurion, approached the camp.

He was immediately and intensely awe-struck by the scale and order of the sight before him, inspiring in him a feeling that was particular to being Roman he imagined - a martial pride. A couple of large tents flanked Caesar's own. Octavius would later find out that they housed an engineering workshop and quartermaster's store. Two main 'streets' ran down from Caesar's tents - which were marked out by rows of spears - called the Principalis and Via Praetoria.

To prevent attacks from flaming enemy arrows and artillery fire, a gap was set between the palisades and the vast grid of tents which housed the army. The area was then filled with the army's livestock (mules, draft oxen, pack horses), as well as prisoners of war and various plunder.

Broiled beef, sour wine, ordure and the smell of leather assailed Octavius' nostrils as he slowly made his way through the gates of the camp and up the Principalis. Such was the spectacle and sensory influx of the scenes before him that Octavius was even distracted from his thoughts concerning his imminent meeting with Caesar. Men sat around hunched over bowls of steaming hot porridge or glugged down water or something stronger from their skeins. Choruses of laughter, occasionally counter-pointed with the odd curse or scuffle, also coloured the air. Half of the men seemed to bustle with industry and discipline (or just habit) whilst the other half, off duty, relaxed in various ways - yet all remained fit for service should the trumpets sound. Most ignored the ragged party accompanying the returning cavalry patrol. Others couldn't help but stare at the fair-haired and studious-looking youth, hazarding a guess as to who he might be.

Caesar.

His dark brown eyes were warm and lively, but the strains and privations of the constant campaigning over the years had weathered his complexion a little in the time since Octavius had last seen his great-uncle. He was as close shaved as ever and his hair was trim and carefully spread over his receding crown. Caesar wore a leather breastplate with matching greaves - the armour inwrought with a golden eagle on each impressive piece. A gladius hung from his left hip.

Julius looked his nephew up and down. His features softened with relief and pride; a charming smile also enlivened an already engaging countenance as Caesar noticed how a poppy-seed stubble had replaced the down upon his cheeks from when he had last seen Octavius.

"I hear you have bested both Neptune and the Pompeans to reach us. It bodes well, for if they link up through Sextus recruiting an army of pirates then Caesar might have to call on his nephew to defeat them."

The men, those from the shipwrecked party and the general's staff, grinned and laughed a little at their commander's joke. Octavius blushed, partly because he did not know how to accept the comment.

"But I should not let my manners be enveloped by my happiness. You must all be both famished and tired. Decimus, please see to all of the men's needs. Spare no luxury. I thank you all for delivering my nephew to me. This will neither be forgotten nor go unrewarded," Caesar gregariously declared. Decimus, an adjutant upon Caesar's personal staff, immediately carried out his orders, instructing others to lead the shipwrecked party off and provision them. Sprits were lifted. The result of their commander's commending words produced an almost metaphysical alchemy in the souls of the party. They now suddenly looked back at the experience of the last few days with pride rather than bitterness.

"Lucius, Roscius, I would detain you a little longer. Please, join me for some wine. I dare say you must all be thirsty."

Octavius dismounted - with the decurion and his patrol taking their leave - and tentatively approached the dictator. Caesar, who observed and was a little saddened by his nephew's wariness of him, pretended not to notice Octavius' nerves. He first addressed the loyal centurion and legionary who stood to attention before him.

"Relax, my friends. You are not on the parade ground now. How are you Roscius, are you still keeping your officer out of trouble?"

Not for the last time over the next few weeks, Octavius would be struck by his great-uncle's familiarity and affection for various soldiers, from all ranks, under his command.

"I'm trying Caesar," Roscius replied, smiling.

"Nay, it rather seems you are succeeding. And I thank you for your service to him, and me."

Octavius would think to himself that evening that for all of the criticism Caesar received for him acting like a king, or deity even, few senators deigned to ever lower themselves to talk with such courtesy and sympathy to the lowliest soldier or citizen. He admired Caesar's graciousness. Gaius promised himself that he would always try to emulate his great-uncle's virtues - albeit his tiredness and deep slumber that night temporarily relieved him of the ardour of his new vow.

Caesar turned to Oppius. The general heartily clapped his hand upon his officer's shoulder and embraced him. Octavius also observed the brief, solemn nod of gratitude he offered his centurion after their embrace. To Oppius the gesture and expression meant more to him than any flattering speech or token honour.

"Before the battle at Munda Lucius, I wished you by my side. But such is the service you have done me in bringing my nephew to me, I am glad that you were with him rather than me. You have my gratitude once again, my friend. Caesar will not forget this."

There was a history and mutual admiration between the two men that one couldn't help but be conscious of and intrigued by. A day or so later Octavius discovered how Oppius had been the famed anonymous standard bearer of the Tenth Legion, who had inspired the army to capture the beach against the Britons. Octavius had perhaps been no older than ten when he had first read about the deciding moment in the campaign. The attack was faltering. The Britons still held the beach. The water was deep, the currents strong. A torrent of rain - and missiles - lashed down upon the legions; they steadfastly remained in the relative safety of their transports, furrowing their brows and shaking their heads at the prospect of trying to take the beach. Either from a sense of madness, or ambition, a nameless standard bearer acted - and offered up the legionary's prayer.

"Jupiter Greatest and Best, protect this legion, soldiers every one. May my act bring good fortune to us all."

To the amazement and condemnation of his comrades, Oppius leapt over the rail of the vessel and plunged into the murky ocean. The gleaming head of the legion's standard first appeared out of the foaming water. The eagle was the pride of every soldier. When in camp the standard was kept at an altar, surrounded by lamps which burned all through the night; both the eagle and the ground it stood upon were deemed to be sacred. The protection of the standard was every legionary's duty - and its loss would blight every soldier's honour. Roscius followed his aquilifer into the surf out of friendship, yet the rest of the Tenth Legion bravely, absurdly, followed the silver eagle - to protect and fight for it. And the eagle seemed to come to life itself as it soared upwards and into the chest of the first enemy cavalryman who opposed the seemingly suicidal standard bearer. The fizzing spray of the ocean blurred his vision so Oppius did not see the second cavalryman attack his flank, yet he heard the sound of him shriek and fall as Roscius' pilum skewered his stomach. Support was soon mustered around the precious standard though. Witnessing the Tenth's courage - and success - the Seventh Legion also abandoned their transports and advanced towards the shore. Caesar swiftly ordered reinforcements. By the time the sun lowered on the horizon the sea seemed to be weeping blood, but a beachhead was finally secured. "You captured my respect and loyalty today Oppius, as well as that beach. You have earned my gratitude - and a promotion," the enigmatic General remarked to his new officer in a private meeting that evening. Reciprocated respect, loyalty and gratitude would be further earned from that day hence.

Both men had aged since that night, but Oppius had been a young man at the time. Octavius couldn't help but notice however the lines and wrinkles in his great-uncle's visage as Caesar approached and surveyed his nephew. A touching paternity could be seen in Caesar's fond expression, which was all the more marked due to the seriousness which had been carved into his demeanour of late. Tears glistened in his eyes, but fell not. For once he could be Julius again, not "Caesar". He beamed - cherishingly, happily, memorably. Octavius smiled back and his apprehension and aching limbs vanished into the ether. Although he was conscious of wanting to appear manly, Roman, he couldn't help but feel the urge to run to his uncle and bury his head in his chest. As Caesar proposed to speak to Octavius and opened his arms to fulfil this desire, a figure and voice intruded upon their familial reunion.

"I came as soon as I heard. It seems you have a Caesar's determination and luck, Octavius," the voice, alien to Octavius yet over-familiar, expressed. The soldier's warmth and flattery were intended more for his general's ears than the boy's however.

"Octavius, this is Mark Antony," Caesar cordially remarked. Although irked a little by his lieutenant's intrusion upon his private moment with his nephew, Julius was a practiced enough actor to be able not to show his displeasure.

The celebrated soldier's forehead was smooth and broad. The lines of a strong and square jaw were softened by a well-kept beard. A short-sleeved tunic showed off his muscular biceps, seemingly hewn from bronze. Not without some credence Antony claimed descent from Anton, a son of Hercules - and from his build and soldierly virtues few people found cause to argue the point against his supposed bloodline. His chestnut brown eyes sparkled with masculine charm and good humour, or wine. His glossy black hair was artfully brushed upon his head in a perfectly formed centre parting. A large spatha (cavalry sword) hung down from his left side, its gold-plated guard and pommel encrusted with semi-precious stones.

Antony had not fought at Munda. He had been in Rome. After hearing of Caesar's decisive victory though he had sped like winged Mercury to the dictator's side to congratulate him and share in the jubilant mood of the army. The Civil War was finally over. The soldier had been all too pleased to vacate Rome, tired and harassed as he was by the constant petitions and the business of office that Caesar had asked him to attend to in his absence. More so though Antony had attended to his mistresses, cronies and vintner.

"Julius has told me much about you, Gaius," Mark Antony cheerfully expressed whilst placing a hand on Caesar's shoulder, as well as Octavius'. It was Antony's custom to treat Caesar with such familiarity and affection - but on this occasion the lieutenant did so to mark out to the nephew how close he was to his great-uncle. Whether he was conscious of it or not Mark Antony was jealous of the unique bond between Caesar and the youth. His jealousy would grow more pronounced over the next couple of months as the dictator spent more and more time with his nephew.

"And all of it was good, I can assure you," Mark Antony added, clapping the slender built adolescent on the back. Caesar's lieutenant was affable, without ever being as naturally witty or charming as his mentor.

Octavius raised a corner of his mouth in a gesture towards a smile, but he reciprocated not the soldier's familiarity and warmth. Indeed if anything Antony's behaviour reinforced the young stoic's pre-disposed dislike of the renowned soldier and bacchant. Octavius was familiar with some of Antony's history. In his youth the pleasure-loving aristocrat had attached himself to Clodius - a self-serving demagogue who had courted the mob and reduced politics to little more than criminality. Antony's capacity for drinking and womanising was notorious. When he did attend to his duties in the Senate he would often arrive hungover, or debauched. Vomit rather than words would issue from his mouth when he was due to speak, although Octavius fancied that his oratory would be scarce more eloquent than vomit should it ever be given voice. His retinue was filled with low-born prostitutes and actors - and often at least one wife of a fellow senator. Octavius also disparaged his uncle's lieutenant, however because he was partly envious of the popular, powerful soldier.

"And Lucius, it's good to see you again," Antony remarked at seeing the centurion, walking up to his old friend and embracing him. "I've already arranged some wine and women for you, although you might want to take them in the opposite order," the carouser added, laughing at his own joke.

As he looked at him then - and as Octavius thought about Mark Antony now in Apollonia - an expression of suspicion and disdain laced his features. Octavius smiled at recalling Cleanthes' comment about Antony.

"I don't know much about him. But what little I know makes me want to know him even less."

*

Whilst Caesar made preparations to return to Rome - and formulated his tactics to deal with the guerrilla war which would ensue with Sextus Pompey's remaining forces - the general instructed Roscius to introduce his nephew to military life during their remaining weeks in Spain.

Firstly the legionary issued the new recruit with a uniform. He was given a linen military tunic, which was longer than his civilian one and reached down past Gaius' knees. As to the style of the day though Roscius taught the youth how to bunch some of the material up over his military belt - and leave the bottom of the tunic curved as he did so. He was at the same time issued with caligae - the tough, leather hob-nailed boot of the Roman legionary.

Although he seldom wore it over the succeeding weeks (the scorching heat and sheer weight of the garment suppressed the inclination) Octavius was given a mail cuirass formed from hundreds of tiny iron rings. The armour was both strong and flexible and Roscius assured Octavius that the shirt would one day save his life - for it had his own on many occasions, the standard bearer was pleased to confess.

To top off his uniform Octavius was given a standard legionary's helmet. The bronze bowl owned a peak at the back to protect the neck and also large protective cheek pieces, designed to leave the ear uncovered so as one could still hear orders. Such was its size - and the youth's slender head - that, to almost comic effect, Octavius found himself having to continually adjust the helmet, either tilting it backwards to prevent the rim from slanting over his eyes or pushing it forward to stop the bowl from slipping off the back of his head.

A gladius - with a blade around twenty inches long - and scabbard were next handed to the youth in the quartermaster's area. The sword felt heavy and unfamiliar in Octavius' hand, yet the sensation was still prized (and he suitably swished the weapon about that night in his tent, cutting down and slaying invisible foes). Roscius also handed the new recruit a pilum - the lethal javelin of the legions. Octavius felt a tinge of pride as Roscius described how Marius (the legendary consul and general who had also been Caesar's uncle) had re-designed the weapon. Marius changed the manufacture of the pilum so that the metal between the shaft and point was soft and pliable. Once the pilum was thrown - and lodged into a target - the shaft sagged down and the weapon was rendered useless should the enemy wish to throw it back. So too, should the pilum strike an enemy shield, it was awkward to remove.

"This, as much as this, has carved out Rome's progress," Roscius then somewhat sagely announced as he held up a shovel, as well as his own razor sharp gladius. A dolobra (a military pick-axe), saw and bill-hook were also exhibited to Octavius as being the tools of the Roman legionary.

Finally the veteran produced a scutum - decorated with the Bull emblem of Caesar's famed Tenth Legion - and presented it to the youth. The shield stood four feet high and was as thick as a man's palm. Rectangular and semi-cylindrical in shape, the shield was made from plywood and covered with a layer of canvas and calfskin - and was reinforced with a bronze central boss. The scutum was strong and flexible - and such was its weight that it had to be supported by both the hand and forearm through leather straps across the reverse. Within just a minute of holding the legionary's shield Octavius' arm ached and he felt again a wave of doubt that he would be able to live up to Roscius' - and more importantly Caesar's - expectations.

During that first day Roscius took Octavius on a whirlwind tour of the camp and he immediately began to appreciate the scope and specialist nature to the make-up of the army. Caesar's nephew was introduced to engineers, craftsmen, clerks, cooks, surveyors, farriers, artillerymen, surgeons and drill masters alike. Partly as an attempt to echo the virtues and manner of Caesar, Octavius was attentive and friendly towards everyone he met. He made a conscious effort to ask and remember everyone's name - and was genuinely interested in certain facets of various tasks and trades.

That evening Octavius listened avidly as Roscius told him more stories of their general's exploits and achievements. He reported an anecdote of when Caesar was once invited to a meal by a friend, one Valerius Leo - and the asparagus somehow got accidentally dressed with myrrh instead of olive oil. Caesar however ate the dish, courteously ignoring the mistake. Others in his party though complained and composed snide comments. Before long however Caesar reprimanded the ungrateful - and ungracious - group. "If you didn't like it there was no need to have eaten it. But if one reflects on one's host's lack of breeding it merely shows that one is ill-bred oneself," Roscius reported Caesar as saying.

Roscius had also been there in person when the army had been forced to stop marching one storm-filled night. The only real shelter that was available was a farmer's hut. When offered to Caesar however he refused the accommodation, arguing that "honours should go to the strongest, but necessities should go to the weakest.' He subsequently slept in the roofed doorway of the building, allowing the injured to take refuge inside the dwelling.

"Soldiers respect Caesar, because Caesar respects us. Whether it be because of his ability, or his luck, we know that he will do his best by us. We are loyal to Caesar, rather than the Senate, because if and when we ever get discharged we know to look to our general, rather than some politician back in Rome, to look after us - and maybe provide us with a plot of land somewhere that we can call our own. Caesar rewards loyalty. The Senate, filled with over-weaned aristocrats who live off their family name

- and who look down on the soldier class - would happily wash its hands of the legions after their service to the state though. And why do soldiers love Caesar? He doubled our pay to two hundred and twenty-five silver denarii per year," Roscius finally said with a grin on his face, whilst raising a wine-filled cup to his absent commander.

Realising how late the hour must have been though Roscius suddenly brought a close to their evening, for the legionary was all too aware of how long the following day (and following two weeks or so) would prove for the youth. For the remainder of Octavius' stay within the bounds of the camp he received regular rudimentary weapons training and drill instruction. Moreover Roscius was conscious of developing Octavius' physical condition - and although the youth could not justly claim to have attained the standards of fellow new recruits, Octavius brimmed with a sense of achievement in relation to the change in his constitution and abilities.

12

Marcus Vipsanius Agrippa had woken early that morning - yet his father was still up and dressed before him, impatiently waiting to give his son his chores for the day. Summer was coming, if not with them already, and Domitius Agrippa wanted his eldest son to service the series of mini-aqueducts - that Marcus Vipsanius had himself designed - which helped irrigate some of his farmlands. Although the youth had plans for the day, Agrippa duly complied with his father's request. Rather than completing the task by himself however, he quickly trained up half a dozen slaves to clean and service the matrix of stone and oak channels that provided water to a particularly arid corner of his family's estate.

And so by noon Marcus was racing across the olive groves of neighbouring properties in a shortcut to reach the Roman fort, situated just outside of the main town of Apollonia. The camp was a hive of activity and preparation in lieu of Caesar's imminent arrival. The historic campaign could then begin in earnest. The talk was of glory, eastern riches, the retrieval of the standards that Crassus had lost - and the tits and virtues of Parthian women.

Sweat dripped down his plain-looking and honest face and a

smile seemed to brighten Agrippa's features because, and not in spite of, his arduous run. The guards had now grown used to the tough but good natured youth turning up at the camp. His introduction to the fort had first come via Octavius. Yet while he had increasingly devoted less time to his martial education over the months - choosing to spend his time reading and in the company of Cleanthes - Agrippa received the training and conditioning that Octavius could and should have benefited from.

When his schedule allowed him the time Oppius himself took the enthusiastic and fast-learning Agrippa under his wing, teaching him about basic tactics, swordsmanship and survival techniques. The centurion had first noticed the youth through overhearing a bunch of legionaries chattering during their evening meal of fish stew. Agrippa was among the group. They were discussing which god they'd offer up thanks to before entering a sea battle - Mars, Jove or Neptune?

"I wouldn't want to impress Neptune too much with my devotion, in case he took me down into the deep with him," one legionary jokingly piped up.

"And too many legionaries offer up prayers to Mars, so I'd worry if he could hear mine over the rest," his comrade countered. "So who would you give thanks to, young'un?" the man, idly whittling away a piece of wood into nothingness, added.

"I'd offer up thanks to the man who invented the corvus," Agrippa drily posited.

Oppius, hearing the unfamiliar voice and unconventional answer, abruptly turned his head. The centurion was amused and impressed to hear such a thing come from such a young recruit. The next day Oppius asked Casca about the would-be soldier. After hearing the old legionary's report, the centurion invited the youth to train with his own cohort. With an air of confidence, rather than arrogance, Agrippa fought and bested many of his own men during combat practice. Before long Oppius was tutoring the recruit personally, imparting his knowledge and sharing his experiences with the lad. Agrippa's rapid progress even infused in the stern and insular centurion a feeling which was something akin to paternal pride.

*

An open, contented expression could be found on Octavius' face as if his sister were actually in the garden with him, rather than just a name upon the top of a letter.

Dearest Octavia,

I have missed you, and not just because you helped share the burden of mother's dotage.

Thank you for your last letter. I am well. I am sometimes afflicted with the ague of boredom, but thankfully I am keeping myself busy and, although one cannot perhaps totally remedy the mutating disease, prevention is as good as a permanent cure.

Please pass on my thanks also to Athenobus for the copy of Plato's Laws. You may wish to add that I said to you that he is a superior tutor to

Cleanthes - and that I have remained a devotee of his Plato, rather than an adherent of Cleanthes' Aristotle. I can forgive myself the lie, if you can - for the sun will be shining that much brighter for the old librarian when you tell him.

However, I cannot lie to you sister. You asked how I was progressing in my military training. My progress marches on like myself, slowly and out of step. I try, but I often also fail. I am perhaps still more versed in the conquests of Catullus than I am in the campaigns of Scipio. But I do not fear the rigours of military life as I once did, albeit I warrant that I'll be about as useful in a battle to the army as a knife and fork would be to Tantalus.

Marcus is also fine. I can't help but admire him. I often think that I should perhaps envy or resent him, such are his virtues and accomplishments, but he possesses such a noble nature - and I love him so much - that I would rather part with all that I own than lose his friendship. Marcus is twice the soldier I am Octavia, but I would be perhaps half the soldier I am, if it were not for his instruction and encouragement. In return I have helped him with his other studies. Together we could perhaps take on the world. As I often write about him to you - and speak of you to him - I am very much looking forward to a time when I can introduce you. If nothing else it will save me both time and energy in acting as a go-between.

Salvidienus is also doing well. He will make a marvellous advocate. He has perhaps been rehearsing for the role all his life, such are the lies he tells himself and others. I shall miss him when I depart for Parthia though. He has been a good friend. We are at present planning a day together and fishing trip so we can say our farewells properly.

Should you receive this letter in time you might want to request to return with mother. I would dearly love us to spend some time together before I embark upon the campaign. You could also mediate between mother and me when we argue - it'll be just like old times!

Octavius loved his sister - and admired her. Her virtues were as plentiful as the summer harvest. She was patient, generous, loyal, kind and forgiving. He occasionally found himself having to invent flaws for his sister when describing her to people, for fear of his true opinion and portrait appearing too biased or unbelievable. She was perhaps as equally intelligent as him, yet Octavius himself could not be sure, as Octavia had spent half her life concealing the education she had given herself in private. For fear of earning people's prejudice, or envy, she never flaunted her intellect or engaged men on their own level, except when conversing privately with her brother. Yet she was content, or seemed so. Octavia was far from beautiful in a classical sense - she was no Clodia or young Servilia - but yet she was pretty. Her hair was fair, straight and just shy of shoulder length. Her features were round and soft, her light brown eyes gentle and charming.

Octavius had been sincere in his wish to want to see his sister again; if anything he had understated his desire. He hoped however that his brother-in-law, Marcus Marcellus, would be too busy to accompany his wife. Partly Octavius disliked and distrusted the eminent senator because of his initial siding with Pompey during the Civil War, as he had even been the one to hand Pompey the ceremonial sword to defend the Republic against the outlaw Caesar, but perhaps more so Octavius was jealous of his brother-in-law. Octavia - who he had shared so much with and loved more deeply than anyone else in the world - had to be now a wife first and sister second.

For a minute or so Octavius chewed the end of his stylus and pondered whether to tell his sister about Briseis - and how and what he should say - but then he desisted. He did not want to come across as a lovesick poet, worthy of the satires they had both read when younger. So too Octavius was worried that his sister - who appreciated modesty and duty - might think less of him for bedding a servant girl.

Despite his fondness and affection for Octavia though - and his intention to finish the letter quickly in order to dispatch it - the comely figure of the serving girl danced before his mind's eye again and distracted the youth from his correspondence. Did he love her? He would never be allowed to marry her. Yet he would not ask permission. Octavius briefly imagined the scenario of what would happen should he declare his love for the serving girl to his family - and society. He would be ridiculed and shunned. Caesar perhaps might even turn his back on him. Yet the young romantic felt that he would sacrifice the entire world to spend just one more night with the girl, who had touched him in a way like no other. His heart beat faster just thinking of her. Pictures, both carnal and poetic, were painted in his mind's eye. The afternoon sun baptised his face in apricot light and Gaius surrendered to his daydream. His was an affair to rival that of Paris and Helen, Catullus and Lesbia.

Let's live and love, my love,
Ignore the snide talk
Of all these crabbed old men.

The sun sets, and rises:
Once our candle's snuffed
We're out for a long night.

A thousand kisses, then,
A hundred thousand thousand,
Till we will lose count.

Don't keep score, for no
Evil eye can blight us
If our love seems infinite.

The glowing expression across Octavius' face suddenly altered however - and he wryly, or even scornfully, smiled to himself. Cynicism succeeded idealism, love. Cynicism should act as life's strigil, scraping away unwanted and dead or dying material. The selfishness of Paris and Helen doomed Troy. Clodia was unfaithful - Catullus, conceited. Gaius was a victim of lust, not love - yet he would still surrender to it, he indulgently mused. Rather than Catullus, he now recalled Cleanthes. The brief cautionary tale that the tutor told to his hormonal student was originally composed by a satirical Jewish playwright who Cleanthes had once encountered in a brothel in Capua.

"If Man was put on this earth to serve the Gods, then was not Woman created to serve the god in Man? Originally there was only one sex, Adam. Gloriously endowed was he, the personification of the gods. And, in the beginning, the gods were proud of their son. But when Man began to stand on his own two feet, not only did the gods start to envy his mortal magnificence, they also began to fear this spark that Adam burned autonomously of his origin. The gods did not want an heir. Adam was created for their amusement. But nevertheless the subject of Man became no laughing matter, for they feared that one day this zealous son might strike out at his father. So the High Council of the gods called a secret meeting to address what was to be done about this issue. Ere the hammer could crack upon the block to open the meeting the flame-haired Mars barged in and declared that "The gods should lift up the clouds and squash Man like the louse that he is!" But not only did the brash Mars underestimate the resilient pest of Man, more importantly he was not thinking that secret thought of the even prouder gods. If the deities compelled Man by force it would mean that they would be treating him as a worthy opponent, or equal; Cronos battling Neptune is a fair contest, but noble Achilles is in a no win situation if he defeats a lowly helot. Then Venus, lisping like an asp, spoke. She announced that she could concoct a potion to induce Man to fall vainly in love with himself, "he will do nothing but look in the mirror all day". But Zeus objected and ruled that even perfect Apollo would get bored with such a fate after a time. "No", proclaimed that god whose name I dare not mention, "we must subdue Man in such a way so he knows not he is being subdued; and even if he should discover that he is under the spell of such a force then its sweets will compel him anyway.

This force must be weaker than Man, yet stronger. This diversion I shall create and call Eve," He sagely ordered to much approval, obsequious or otherwise. *"But what if Eve falls in love with Adam - and confesses the ruse?"* an impish Pan called out from the back benches. *"I have thought of that comrades. I will make Eve innocent of her attractions; her modesty will prove all the more alluring to Man. He will be possessed in possessing her - and in their contract he will be a slave to being her master."* *"But if Man serves Woman he serves not the gods"* Seth posited, his brow wrinkled in either worry or scepticism. *"Then we cannot make Eve's love as faithful as ours is,"* He stolidly replied, *"We must also drug Man with the tonic of boredom once in a while. He will adore Woman - and he will praise us for creating her for him - but Man cannot make an idol out of just one of the creatures. He cannot live for her solely, else it will lead to bad faith and other blasphemies. We should prick him as such so that as soon as he has eaten of her fruit he'll look to pick another. If he doesn't, then either he is mad or then one of our Angels has escaped again."* Only when the gavel was struck to seal the motion did Tiresias know that there would be sufficient quiet for him to be heard. *"But what if Eve should dare eat from the Tree of Knowledge?"* But by then it was too late - and the rest is History.

Octavius was duly amused by the story but also conscious of the lessons it tried to impart. Rather than a Helen he wanted to find his Penelope. Conscious of how much time and energy he was devoting to the self-serving girl, Octavius shifted the tone of his thoughts towards her, in order to denigrate and dismiss Briseis' significance. His affair would not be, could not be, akin to some plot by Plautus - where obstacles are overcome and love conquers all. Reality always plays chaperone. She would not enchant him like Circe - and have him behave like some mere animal or lovesick slave. He was a Roman, a Caesar. As such Octavius turned again to his sister's letter and read over the news concerning the city and its dictator.

"The Games were as grand a spectacle as ever, with Caesar competing with himself - and winning. An artificial lake was created on the site of the Campus Martius and scaled down fleets of ships acted out battles, as well as gladiators and teams of Roman cavalry defeating British chariots ... Jaws dusted the ground and eyes were rubbed into the back of heads when a creature called a 'giraffe' was exhibited, which Caesar had imported from Africa. As you can see from the sketch I've done for you its neck is as long as Cato's face - and the animal can run faster from danger than mother can to a shoe sale."

13

Rome.

The meandering Tiber, glassy in the moonlight, attracted his attention through its serenity and nocturnal beauty. Caesar stood on the balcony of his Janiculum villa - the 'Mons Aureas' (the golden hill of sand). Situated west of Rome, Caesar had given the extensive and luxurious property to his mistress, Cleopatra.

Cleopatra. He still recalled their first meeting, as if it was burned within his memory. The smell of Egyptian oil of roses still lingered in his nostrils. A similar balcony adjoined a similar reception room, but the eastern sky was ruby red, oozing heat. Various official papers, like now, littered the chamber. Confusion and faction-fighting reigned supreme in Egypt back then. Caesar was close to returning to Rome. He was fatigued, bored perhaps of the east - and he had his own civil war to attend to. His epilepsy had also returned. Balbus, ever loyal and quick-witted, had explained away a fainting fit as heat exhaustion.

An exotic looking slave, Apollodorus, appeared before him. Oil or sweat glistened across his bare, muscular torso. Over his shoulder the Nubian carried a finely decorated carpet, a gift no doubt.

"Yes?" Caesar rudely demanded, unusually curt from tiredness or tedium, after a pregnant pause between the two men.

Without a word said the slave bowed to Caesar, smiling slightly and awkwardly like one unpractised in the art - and then rolled out the carpet.

Cleopatra. Caesar could not remember the last time that he had been so astonished, or aroused - perhaps the one fed off the other. The Conqueror of the World was rendered temporarily speechless.

Her eyes, oriental-like, were rimmed with ash - and would prove both engaging and unreadable, shaped either in perpetual satisfaction or desire. A satin tyrian purple skirt, worn low upon her hips to display a bejeweled navel, clung to her thighs and reached down to her feet - where pretty toes, painted gold, peeped out. A V-shaped split ran down the satin skirt, revealing tantalising glimpses of silken thighs. A low-necked sable cloak adorned her shoulders and breasts, leaving most of her arms bare - and shone as glossily in the candle light as her long jet hair.

"I come to you both as a queen and supplicant," the girl issued, her voice strong yet feminine. She bowed before him, yet her eyes - equal in pride, ambition and charm to the Roman's - met his. An alluring face, more Greek than Egyptian, gazed up at him. Her full, sensual lips, which would prove as amorous as they could be eloquent, were slightly parted. The tawny skin of the nubile girl, barely out of her teens, glowed like the burnished gold decorating her ears and long-nailed, tapering fingers. Her perfume was as intoxicating as her singular beauty. Only mistresses could entice and enthral Caesar so - never wives.

Apollodorus silently excused himself, his task completed.

Cleopatra, Queen and the Goddess Isis incarnate, rose and unclasped the scarab brooch which fastened her cloak. The garment slid from her shoulders and onto the floor, revealing her young, succulent flesh and breasts.

"I am your slave," she issued playfully, ardently.

Caesar was tempted to reply "No, I am yours", but refrained from doing so. He merely drew the beautiful, sensuous girl towards him and kissed her.

"My father was known as Ptolemy the Flute-Player. I too will show you how I can use my mouth and fingers."

The evening was memorable, to say the least, Caesar judged, half-smiling.

Pillow talk was of politics, the grain supply and the strength and tactics of armies. He was impressed by her intellect and ambition. The woman batted not an eyelid when plotting the usurpation of her brother-husband's throne. She was both a goddess and a whore - and as manipulative as both Caesar fancied. Yet she had seduced him. He remembered again making love to the exotic queen on her imperial barge, soaring up and down upon the rhythmic waves - the eastern sun kissing and massaging his skin, along with the woman he was with. She complained not when he took another mistress (which he rarely did for once, satisfied and excited as he was by his semi-divine lover) yet Cleopatra was wise enough to remain faithful to Caesar. The dictator told himself that he had still not been swayed by the woman into doing anything that Caesar didn't want to do - but then Julius smiled, knowing it to be untrue. He had fought and won half a country for her. Mark Antony had joked that, in terms of the young queen, Caesar could also declare, "I came, I saw, I conquered" - but rather could not the Egyptian say that in reference to the Roman?

Was it their advice, or the veiled threat of his legions to abandon him, which convinced Caesar to finally free himself from the seductions of the east and return to Rome - to attend to his own civil war, rather than those of his paramour? Caesar had returned though, bringing his trophy mistress with him and establishing her in his Janiculum villa. And she had given him that which he most craved, a son.

The dictator yawned and rubbed his brow - being careful not to disturb the laurel wreath which rested on his head and half-disguised his balding pate - as he gazed out over the undulating, turquoise river. A voice, doused in wine and amours, breezed out from the bedroom.

"Come back to bed."

Her appetites could rival Mark Antony's, Caesar mused.

"Give me a moment or so," he replied.

After this evening he would return and stay with Calpurnia, his wife, for a while. He missed her uncomplicated devotion and friendship. Her love had become unconditional, like his mother's and Julia's had once been. He still missed his daughter. For a while Cleopatra had filled the void, but not anymore. Caesar recalled the incident, argument, of yester night between him and his mistress.

"But Caesarion is your son!" she had posited, her eyes ablaze with the heat of a passion far removed from love.

"But he is not my heir. Octavius is," Caesar had firmly replied.

The young queen and mother responded with a tantrum. Curses, in a language Caesar was unfamiliar with, emanated from the woman, as well as cat-like hisses and wild protestations. Her arguments seemed scripted though to Caesar - and he had already made his judgement. He intended to adopt Octavius. Eventually he silenced the politic queen, either through his rhetoric or the threats implicit behind his words.

"Julius," she called from inside, now demanding, yearning.

An increasingly familiar mournfulness, or atrophy, overcame the dictator again - darkening his mood and eyes, as if a veil had been placed over him. Even Caesar could not conquer time, old age. He tried to muster his spirits. The Parthian campaign would be his last, but greatest, triumph. He looked forward to seeing Octavius again, imparting his memories and wisdom to him. More than his mistress, his nephew made him feel enthused and purposeful again.

"Julius," she exclaimed once more, her musical voice a little less harmonious - harder and flatter. The queen was not used to being ignored, or defied.

Would he even return from the campaign? He honestly didn't know he conceded - and occasionally of late a world-weary Caesar thought to himself how he didn't care.

*

Spain.

Ribbons of cloud, like deft white brush strokes across a light blue canvas, striped the sky. Lowing cattle could be heard in the background, perhaps moaning about the oppressive heat. Caesar fanned himself with some papers that he had just finished reading and signing. He sat with his nephew in a carriage, cantering along - but still tarrying too much for the dictator. Finally they were on their way home.

Caesar closed his eyes in a vain effort to suppress an oncoming migraine. Finally he had earned a moment or two of peace - and private time with his beloved nephew. Since dawn, since their party had set off, Caesar had been hard at work - replying to urgent matters of state that Antony had ignored and re-writing chapters of his book with Hirtius, which would recount the history of the recent civil war. Julius also caught up with his personal correspondence. Among which Cassius Longinus had composed a servile and long-winded petition to be considered for the Praetorship of Rome. Cleopatra had written to him, stressing how she loved and desired Caesar - and that she had remained chaste in his absence. Aemilius Lepidus was memorably forgettable in a routine, fawning letter. Atticus still wouldn't sell his life-size bronze statue of Aeneas, yet Caesar perhaps admired the art-collector more for prizing beauty over money. Added to a clear and insightful review of the mood in the Senate, Brutus had also written a critical but fair appraisal of *"The Journey"*, a poem that Caesar had recently composed.

Whilst Caesar closed his eyes Octavius, sitting opposite and half-reading a play by Terence, surveyed his uncle. Although the youth had been impressed by his general's infectious energy and dynamism in front of his legions and staff, Octavius had spent many evenings of late with the dictator - and Caesar could not sustain his public face in private. His tanned skin could not quite conceal the small clusters of liver spots dotting his head, which would have been discernible to all if not for the civic crown or bronze helmet which the dictator wore. Wrinkles increasingly carved themselves, as deep as scars, around his neck and brow. Caesar joked to his nephew that they were just 'laughter lines'. He slept more, often dozing off in the middle of reading, or during his evening meal. Octavius would often take the book or plate away from his uncle on such occasions, not wishing for anyone else to see him so vulnerable looking. When he would wake, Julius would smile to himself, appreciating his nephew's consideration. His head seemed to weigh heavier in his hands when deep in thought. His joints ached during cold nights. So too Caesar secretly asked his quartermaster to forge a new, lighter cavalry sword. He could no longer leap up and mount his horse from behind, yet the keen rider derived the utmost pleasure one afternoon from teaching his surrogate son to perform the trick. "Not even Caesar can conquer old age," Julius confessed to Octavius one evening, his wistful smile eventually faltering. He confessed to bouts of falling sickness also to his nephew. Although saddened by his slight demise Octavius felt privileged that his great uncle should allow him to see him at his most human and fallible.

The wheels of the carriage, along with four hundred hooves and numberless hob-nailed infantry boots, spewed up dust along the corrugated track, enveloping the entire army almost in a sandy mist. The curtains were closed over the windows of the regal carriage, but still gusts of dust infiltrated the compartment and made the two passengers cough.

A scroll and a pair of ewers upon a tray, containing the dregs of some watered-down Falernian, fell to the floor as the carriage suddenly jolted, having passed over another large rut in the track. Caesar scrunched his face up in frustration and condemnation. The dictator thought to himself how he could have worked through his correspondence in half the time if they had been travelling along a Roman road. Roman roads were valuable as things in themselves - as arteries for both trade and the military - but equally so they embodied Roman superiority and progressiveness. Their flagstones marked out and extended the Empire.

After a pause - during which Caesar gazed through a crack in the window and up at the sapphire sky as if he were an augur searching for or receiving inspiration - he spoke in confidence to his nephew in an attempt to justify himself to the boy, or perhaps himself.

"People will doubtless scoff and claim that I fought this war for myself. I would be lying Octavius if I said that that was not partly true. But know that I have sacrificed part of myself for this triumph. I have been cruel as well as clement. I have lost many friends and comrades. But I fought for them - and for peace. I freely admit to you that I, in part, acted in pride in defying the Senate. Caesar could not have those self-serving parasites and honourless politicians sit in judgement on him. But didn't Caesar merit such pride? But if I was proud, they were envious. Aye, their envy condemned me. They dusted off ancient laws for convenience - but remember that they served not their own precious laws and traditions when they overturned the rightful petitions of the tribunes and proclaimed me an enemy of the state - a state which I had enriched and served for over a decade.

I honestly believed that my rightful cause would not instigate such a terrible war. I was not the only one to be prompted by pride. I did not force Pompey to abandon Rome. He was flattered and manipulated into challenging me. If we could have only talked face to face, imbued in each other that same spirit of trust and equanimity that we shared when Julia was alive; we could have ruled and bettered Rome together, perhaps.

But the past is dead. Pompey is dead - and I have mourned him enough. More than perhaps his conceited and ambitious sons did.

If they could not see that the old order was dying, how could they have possibly imagined anything different, more enlightened? - A Rome re-born. The Senate is but a cartel run by a few ancient clans, who have become so in-bred as to be retarded. Merchants lobby the Senate and direct Rome. The people are taxed to fund the Empire but their interests are not represented or respected. Only their taxes, not their rights, reach the Senate House.

But I will change things when I return Octavius - that I can promise you. Caesar has to be Caesar," the eloquent and forceful dictator expressed, yet this final statement was conveyed with perhaps a tinge of sadness - as if "Caesar" was its own animal, too powerful and proud for even its own creator to control.

The carriage bumped over another rut in the track, causing Octavius' book to fall to the floor.

"And I promise you also that this Spanish road, or poor excuse for such a thing, will become a Roman one by the end of the year."

*

The surface of the Tiber shimmered, like the jade-coloured silk gown Cleopatra was wearing over her soft tawny skin - if she had not already disrobed by now. The wind soughed through the stone vents of the balcony. The sky grew leaden, dampening out the stars. Caesar continued to glare down upon the hypnotic swirls and currents of the mournful river. *"The Tiber was full of citizens' corpses, the public sewers were choked with them and the blood that streamed from the Forum had to be mopped up with sponges,"* Cicero had written, in response to the violence and civil disorder during the years when Clodius and Milo fought for political supremacy on the streets of Rome. Caesar recalled the lines again, briefly and morbidly imagining a corpse-strewn Tiber - but then the dictator permitted himself a self-satisfied smile, for no longer would his beloved capital suffer such scenes. Caesar had brought peace, reconciliation to Rome. His life - and the sometimes compromising means he had adopted to achieve his ends - proved justified. He had fulfilled his self-appointed destiny.

"Julius," the voice issued again, this time purring - sultrily rather than sulking. Caesar finally ventured back inside.

"I'm tired," the dictator exclaimed, before even entering the chamber. Before seeing her Caesar encountered her scent. The queen's musky perfume reached almost as far as her voice, albeit the Roman turned his nose up at the overly potent fragrance. His villa smelt like a brothel, Caesar disdainfully thought to himself.

"I have enough love for the both of us." The purring was now somewhat slurred. She had been drinking again.

"I haven't any for either of us," Caesar was tempted to reply, but refrained from doing so.

14

Time passes.

The wind seemed to shush itself as the skeletal branches of the willow trees, swaying in the breeze, swiped over the three youths like giant hands. On more than one occasion Octavius nearly had his sun hat knocked off and Agrippa had to nimbly dodge left and right to avoid the top of his bow - which was slung over his shoulder - from being caught up in the trees. The scent of pine and salt mingled in the air.

The three adolescents finally came to the end of the disused woodland trail. They stood on top of a cliff looking out across an ocean glowing purple beneath the embers of dusk. Beneath them was 'Monster Bay', named as such because of the steep jagged cliff walls and semi-circular shape to the bay, as if a titan had reared up from the ocean and taken a bite out of the coastline. Winged clouds scudded the crimson horizon. Agrippa rubbed his face - routinely checking to see if his stubble was duly transforming itself into a beard - and grinned, appreciating the sumptuous view. Salvidienus however, surveying the same seascape, still wore a look of disgruntlement on his haughty countenance. The Roman aristocrat was still cursing the fact, beneath his breath, that he had to carry his own provisions and fishing equipment, having been out-voted by his two friends on the subject of whether they wanted slaves to accompany them on their expedition or not.

The companions had spent the afternoon fishing. Agrippa had won the unspoken competition between the three as to who had caught the most fish. They had then cooked and eaten their catch, washed down by some Arvisium wine which Salvidienus had borrowed from his father's cellar. The friends had laughed, argued, and then slept on the riverbank. Realising that the light was falling they decided to venture to the coast. Their plan was to shoot fire arrows out into the ocean - again in unspoken competition with each other to see who could shoot the furthest.

Octavius took in the memorable seascape, but yet he was still absorbed by the contents of Octavia's most recent letter. Rome was thriving again. Caesar's reforms were working. By enfranchising a number of colonies in Gaul and Spain - and investing in the regions - Caesar had encouraged emigration from Rome. Overcrowding and crime were also down due to the dictator having cut the number of recipients of the free corn dole - thus those who had once over-relied on the state had to emigrate or find employment. Public amenities were again being built and maintained. To pay for these state projects Caesar had confiscated the estates of eminent Pompeians who had refused to surrender after Pharsalus. So too he had levied fines and taxes upon the Spanish and African towns who had opposed him during the Civil War.

Yet, although inwardly proud of Caesar's regeneration of the capital, Octavius still brooded over the contents of his sister's correspondence.

"Whilst in the market yesterday, concealed in my litter, I heard a water vender call our uncle the new Gracchus." Octavius, conscious of his history, briefly and darkly wondered if Caesar would meet the other legendary reformer's fate.

Success breeds as many enemies as failure.

*

The prow of the sleek vessel cut through the water like a freshly-sharpened plough moving through virgin soil. The trireme had been built for speed, its crew bred for violence. The wind fed the sails, giving the ship's oarsmen a well-earned rest. Many of the crew whetted blades, in preparation for the raid. Dice tumbled upon the slick deck. Lucky talismans were kissed - and prayers offered up to Neptune - out of superstitious routine. The spray from the ocean freckled piratical faces.

The breeze hissed. The signet ring on the hand of Sextus Pompey tapped upon the figurehead of a lion, painted gold, which gazed out from the bow of the ship. The commander's gaze was as adamantine as the vessel's totem. Internally he was uncharacteristically anxious for once though, for his crew were a long way from the waters in which they usually operated. Yet the ambitious commander wanted to expand the frontiers of his marine empire and influence. Rome shuddered at his name, or so the young man believed; soon Greece would suffer for Caesar's sins as well.

A sun-polished complexion gifted an already attractive countenance a healthy glow. His build was that of a soldier's but his features, mannerisms and dress were those of an aristocrat. His hair was blond, as golden as his lion's mane, and was styled and fixed into a distinctive quiff at the front, to help pronounce and remind people that he was his father's son. An air of brooding melancholy made the famous, or infamous commander, even more handsome and enigmatic - but the Roman corsair finally permitted himself a slight smile, for the bay seemed perfect. Perhaps the gods were smiling on this new campaign after all.

"Do you want to disembark now, or head further down the coast?" his loyal lieutenant, Menodorus, asked.

"Here will be fine. We will be in danger of being seen if we venture too close to a settlement. We are far from home my friend. Surprise must be our ally."

"I will get the men to ready the anchor and launch the boats. Hmm, it seems we have a small audience," Menodorus then remarked, squinting up at the cliff face, rippling the vicious scar which ran from his temple down his right cheek.

The commander's piercing blue eyes scrutinised the three figures approaching from above - assessing their age, social status and the potential threat they posed.

"Give the nod to Alexander and Pollux, just in case," Sextus Pompeius finally ordered.

"That's neither a merchant nor military vessel," Agrippa said gravely.

"But these waters are supposed to be free of pirates," Salvidienus argued, unconvincingly. "What shall we do? Surely we should run back and warn someone?"

"We have the higher ground. We also have fire arrows, which will not react too kindly to their timbers or sails," Agrippa wryly announced, grinning.

"Are you saying we should fight, rather than flee?" Octavius asked.

"Perhaps we should do both. One of us should run back and sound the alarm. We have warships in port that can set sail immediately and hunt them down," Agrippa replied.

The pirate vessel continued to skim closer towards them, borne upon the incoming tide. There is such a thing as animal cowardice, as well as animal courage. The former - whilst gripping Octavius' heart like a bear trap - dictated that he should run as fast as his legs could carry him. Although Octavius did not want to volunteer to be the one to sound the alarm, hope swam through his veins like adrenaline that Marcus might suggest that he be the one to escape any perilous confrontation. Yet so too a voice sounded within Caesar's nephew, that he could not leave his companions. "Nobility has its responsibilities," Caesar had remarked.

Whilst unhooking his bow from his shoulder and unsheathing the quiver of arrows which were specially coated so as to set them on fire Agrippa spoke, or rather commanded: "Rufus, you're the fastest runner over a long distance, so you must head back to town. Octavius and I will do our best to stop their raid from here."

A short silence ensued, as though the reality and risk of the situation fully dawned upon the three adolescents. They might never ever see each other again. Their laughter and reminiscences beside the riverbank not two hours ago now seemed a world away, unreal. Octavius nodded, as if trying to convince himself, as well as Rufus, that it was a good plan and everything would turn out well. The pirates appeared to be without horses. Should a group of the raiders land and make their way up the steep track, which was located over the other side of the bay, then Octavius and Agrippa could still make their escape without their pursuers even knowing in which direction they had fled.

A nervy Salvidienus nodded back and smiled encouragingly at his two friends. He would repay the relief he felt at being picked to sound the alarm by running as if his life depended on it. As the wiry youth dropped his provisions and bow to the ground, Octavius advised him to:

"Make haste slowly. Pace yourself. We'll be okay, so don't you burn yourself out with the burden of our safety on your shoulders, Rufus. Even Oppius couldn't hit us with an arrow from down there - but even you couldn't miss in terms of us shooting down upon their ship," Octavius reassured his companion.

"I'll be back before you know," Salvidienus replied.

"Aye, and bring a bottle of Falernian with you this time, to toast our victory," Agrippa exclaimed, attempting to lighten the mood.

Salvidienus nodded, filled his lungs twice with the sea air, and sped off.

*

"And now there are just two it seems," Sextus remarked to his second-in-command.

"If they have any sense they'd all be off. We should not suffer the young fools gladly. But rather we should gladly see the young fools suffer," Menodorus drily replied, whilst polishing the decorous ball of amber on his sword.

"Unhoist the sails. Bring us to a stop. Put down the anchor. We are close enough I think," Sextus quietly informed his lieutenant - who then bellowed out his commander's orders - all the while not taking his eyes of the two youths on the cliff top.

"You're not worried about those two cubs are you?" Menodorus asked, observing the slight disquiet in his friend's expression.

"More curious than worried I'd say. Why haven't they all fled? Are they ignorant of our intent? Or just curious themselves?"

"Either way, they'll pay for their ignorance or curiosity - and they'll either be dead, slaves or hostages worth ransoming by sun down," the pirate replied in his raspy, Spanish accent.

Menodorus now removed his gladius and, with a sharpening stone that he wore like a lucky pendant, he began to whet an already well kept edge. The blade gleamed, mirroring the cold glint in the sadist's eye. He licked his lips in anticipation of the youths' imminent deaths, for deaths presaged plunder, good food and women. Indeed Menodorus couldn't remember the last instance when so much time had passed without him having killed someone; such had been the length of their voyage. Sextus had sensed the men's disquiet too - Alexander and Pollux were only too pleased to be let off the leash - which is partly why he had finally decided to launch his first raid. So too he had sailed in these waters many years ago, with his father, and recalled the relative seclusion and affluence of the region.

*

The claret firmament faded to a dull brown. The timbers of the pirate ship turned black, the sea charcoal grey. The first flaming arrow shot across the sky like a comet, roaring and then thudding into the deck of the ship. For a second or two mouths were agape - and hearts stood still - as if the fiery bolt had been sent by the gods. But petrification but lasted a moment before half a dozen men frantically ran to the shaft and stamped out every cinder of the unexpected, abominable missile.

Fire stokes the nightmares of every sailor. Ships seldom sink, but they often burn. People drown in silence, but the death rattles curdle the blood of men being burned alive. Even the imperious air of the self-titled 'Son of Neptune' was shattered. Menodorus bared a set of small, sharp yellow teeth and spat out a curse.

"We have more arrows than you have feet to stamp them out. You would do well to leave these shores," a youthful but purposeful voice issued from above. Sextus could but make out the build of the figure above, as Octavius too failed to pick up the facial features of the person he addressed.

Sextus allowed himself a brief, begrudging smile at the audacity of the youths.

"What's your name, boy?" the commander then bellowed up, in an attempt to buy some time.

"You can call me Teucer," Gaius replied, naming himself after the famed Greek archer in the Illiad. Agrippa had no need to warn Octavius about not using his real name. Either the pirates would not believe him, or they would target him as a hostage worth ransoming.

"Well then young Teucer, how would you like to cut a deal?"

"I would much rather cut your throat," Agrippa replied, his voice echoing through the air and scaring off a brace of gulls who were loitering on the cliff top.

"And who might you be?" an amused, rather than threatened, Sextus Pompey replied.

"Ajax," Marcus Agrippa immediately retorted, taking the name of Teucer's brother. "What's yours?"

"Odysseus," the wily commander answered, smirking. Sextus did not want to reveal his presence in the region quite yet. So too the youths might just have figured that he was lying - trying to scare them - should the Son of Neptune have announced himself. "I'm actually beginning to like these two scoundrels. It's somewhat apt though that they've named themselves after a couple of dead heroes," Pompey remarked to his lieutenant. Menodorus barely registered the comment however, watching as he was the two figures of Alexander and Pollux nimbly scaling the cliff face.

"Your first shot could have but been guided by fortune. Prove to me that you're a threat, rather than just lucky - and we'll be on our way."

Octavius this time allowed Agrippa to nock his arrow, set the tip alight via the uncovered lamp that rested on the ground, and fire the shaft down at the stationary vessel.

An arrow once more thudded into the deck of the trireme - with pirates and buckets of water this time extinguishing the dangerous bolt with less drama. Sextus raised his eyebrow in appreciation of the keen eye and strong arm behind the missile. He grinned to himself however as well, for the adolescents had risen to his bait - and arrows would now be absent from their bows for when Pollux and Alexander surprised them.

Their limbs ached but the two cutthroats gave no indication of their fatigue as they suddenly and terrifyingly emerged from climbing the cliff face. The first, Pollux, had been a gladiator, freed by Spartacus. He had escaped over the Alps years ago and made his way to the Spanish coast, turning pirate there. A harelip gave the muscular Athenian a permanent mocking expression, which now chilled the blood of Octavius. The second assassin, Alexander, was as wiry as his comrade was brawny. His dark eyes glittered with prospective sadism, his villainous grin revealing a brace of dog teeth in his radish coloured gums. Both men removed their swords from the backs of their belts, seemingly in unison. Sextus would reward them well for a job well done - and they would relish the easy kills.

Octavius and Agrippa edged back immediately, out of range of retrieving their arrows. Octavius gulped and was perhaps on the brink of running - and abandoning his friend - or begging for mercy.

First there was the faint sound of the knife scraping against its sheath. Then there came the whisper of the weapon darting through the air. Then there came the abrupt thud, as Agrippa's hunting knife found its target of the pirate's barrel chest. The freshly sharpened blade managed to puncture the former gladiator's heart and lungs. Although his twisted mouth was agape in agony, silence but issued forth from the Athenian.

Agrippa no sooner observed his hunting knife buried up to its hilt in the large cutthroat's chest, than he quickly turned to Octavius and grabbed the fishing knife from his friend's belt. He deftly threw it at the second assassin. Disbelief first lined Alexander's expression after observing his friend Pollux felled by the adolescent, but shock was quickly displaced by rage. Not only was Agrippa's second throw less accurate than his first, but the slender fishing blade lacked the power and potency of his own knife.

The dog-toothed pirate seethed in pain as the knife lodged into his left shoulder. The air was filled with curses and spittle. Rather than wait for the pirate to attack him however Marcus suddenly launched himself at the assassin. As Alexander was half-way through swinging his gladius at his target, his shoulder - and seemingly his entire left side - flared up in fiery pain as Agrippa's bow, carved from yew and horn, smacked into his upper left arm. Steel jagged into bone and sinew. Taking advantage of his enemy's brief disorientation Agrippa proceeded to grab the hilt of the knife, twisting it in unison with the sneer which appeared on his face. With his other hand Marcus grabbed Alexander by the throat. Within half a second he pushed the weakened pirate back, throwing him off the cliff. His scream curdled the air. Sextus and his crew were gripped by the sight of the flailing figure fall to his death in the shallow waters below, yet none could discern in the falling light whether the victim was friend or foe.

Pollux lay upon his back, semi-conscious. Blood trickled out from his mouth, accompanying the shallow breathing of the giant, but vulnerable, man. The large hunting knife was still lodged in his sternum, the ribs acting like teeth, chomping down on the blade. Agrippa's hand slipped off the handle of the weapon at first, such was the amount of slick blood covering it, but once he had wrestled the blade free the remorseless youth immediately cut the assassin's throat, terminating the gurgling noise of his shallow breathing completely.

Despite his exertions Agrippa's demeanour still appeared calmer than Octavius'. Octavius had remained rooted to the spot during the entire fight and now gazed at his friend - who peered over the edge of the cliff for further assailants - as if he was a stranger. There had been both a sense of method and instinct in the actions of Agrippa during the fight. One would have scarcely believed that the youth hadn't killed before. Later that night Marcus would replay the encounter - and he would suffer fearful nightmares based upon how the violence could have unfolded; yet more so he felt a sense of purpose and pride in regards to what had happened. Finally he'd had an opportunity to test his skills and mettle. He had killed an enemy of Rome. And he had protected Octavius, as if it had been his duty to do so.

Agrippa collected his thoughts for a few moments and, briefly, an expression of pensiveness and something else overcame him - borne from the overwhelming experience and emotion which besieged his nerves. But then he reined himself, took two deep breaths and picked up his bow.

The scarlet sun finally sunk over the horizon, darkening further the young lion's glowering countenance.

Sextus Pompey nervously bit his bottom lip and glanced up at the cliff top. He stood at the prow of the ship so his men could not observe the burgeoning worry and frustration in his features. Surely Pollux and Alexander had dispatched the two irksome youths without any trouble? Or had the boys not been alone? Perhaps they had been with their girlfriends - and they'd been trying to impress them by challenging the pirate ship? The two brutish assassins had enjoyed themselves with women before – 'spoils' they had called them. But just as Pompey sensed that something was somehow wrong, he was duly proved right.

The bow creaked, almost wincing in pain, as Agrippa drew the string back more than perhaps he had ever done in his life. Anger fed his strength. The following morning the youth would offer up a prayer of thanks to Mars for inspiring him the night before - but equally his heart pumped oxygen and adrenaline through his body to power his bulging forearms. The bow sang, twanged, and the flaming arrow roared through the raven-black air, akin to the sound of the air whooshing inside a seashell. The bolt rained down like a fist of molten lava from a volcano.

Missile after missile was unleashed, pimpling the deck and rigging in flames. Octavius would hand the arrow to Agrippa. Agrippa would set the bolt into place and draw the bow. Octavius would then hold the lamp up and, as soon as the arrow-head caught alight, Agrippa would fire. Before the shaft even found its target, Octavius would have another shaft ready.

"Back! Back! Retreat you dogs!" Menodorus snarled at his company of oarsman, whilst the rest of the crew scrambled around the vessel, attempting to stamp and douse out the growing epidemic of small fires.

Smoke, instead of the familiar smell of sea air, filled the nostrils of the Son of Neptune. If he wanted to land and raid now - and take his revenge on those sons of fortune above - then he would be in danger of losing his ship and means of escape. Sextus Pompey appreciated the value of living to fight another day however, and had ordered Menodoros to sound a tactical retreat.

The rhythm of the drum, which set the pace of the company of oarsman, skipped a beat as one of the accursed missiles landed at the stroke-master's feet. He further comically lost time by trying to stamp out the potential blaze, whilst simultaneously attempting to keep stroke. An oarsman was even gruesomely struck in the neck by an arrow, his eyes bulging out of his head - but his comrades either side of him principally regarded the dying man as motivation to row quicker.

The pirate ship finally began to crease the sea around it and move away from the shore. Menodorus marshalled the bucket teams and oarsman. Before long Agrippa had to fire up into the air to reach the vessel, instead of just down upon them - and eventfully, despite pulling a muscle in his shoulder, the trireme was out of range. Finally his efforts caught up with him and Agrippa, his arms feeling like jelly, dropped his bow and gasped for air. Octavius put a fraternal hand on his back and retrieved his canteen of water for his fatigued friend.

Sextus Pompey saw the last arrow sizzle into the ocean behind him. Ribbons of foam littered the sea, but for the most part the sea was as black as the pirate commander's mood.

"Perhaps they are worthy of their nicknames. If only those two nobodies realised who they had just encountered Menodoros," the Son of Neptune posed, allowing himself a brief philosophical smile amidst his ire and frustration.

"It's a shame we don't know who they are," his lieutenant replied bitterly, "as I'd cut their throats without you even having to ask."

15

Under a gibbous moon the two friends sat down and toasted their victory. Their drunkenness provided a welcome release for the pair's frayed nerves and erratic hearts. Exhilaration had succeeded terror within the space of ten minutes. Octavius especially was edgy, shifting between nervous laughter and energy - and then sinking into moments of chilling gloom. After one such bout of silence between the two youths, Octavius suddenly retrieved his good humour and asked, "How did you learn to throw a knife like that?"

"The harder I practise, the luckier I get," a grinning Agrippa replied.

Octavius raised a corner of his mouth in a knowing smile, yet later that night when contemplating Oppius' tutelage of Marcus he felt a stabbing sense of jealousy, that his friend had somehow eclipsed him and was favoured by the centurion, who was supposed to be attending to him.

Envy again would hiss in his ear like a snake a few days later. Agrippa revealed how Oppius and Roscius had taken him into town. They had spent the night in the tavern - and then brothel -

as a reward for the youth's first kill. "He has lost his virginity as a soldier, now he has to as a man," Lucius had drunkenly proposed to Roscius. The two men then pooled their funds and paid for a clean whore who specialised in first-timers. Her make-up papered over the cracks of her fading beauty, but she was coaxing and patient with the handsome youth. By the morning Agrippa had lost his shyness without losing his courteousness and the woman said that he should come again, which he did.

Yet more than envy, Octavius experienced an overwhelming sense of gratitude and love in regards to his friend. They shared an uncommon and unspoken sense of trust and respect. They would share in each other's successes - and be a pillar of support for the misfortunes. If they argued, they could forgive as well. Their interests differed, but not their values or sense of humour. "To have a friend is to be one," Cleanthes had once expressed, and Octavius was now fortunate enough to understand what he meant by it.

Oppius headed up the group of cavalry, which arrived a couple of hours after the pirate ship had long since been swallowed into the night. He first questioned the two youths as to the size of the vessel and its crew compliment. The officer then sent orders back for a couple of warships to disembark and patrol the waters in the direction to where the vessel was heading.

16

The Ides were a public holiday, to mark the end of winter. Hydra-headed Rome was rousing itself early this morning, in preparation for the day's festivities. Wine had been uncorked before even the dawn had un-bottled its honey-coloured light. Best tunics had been washed and were drying on the line. Picnics were being packed for those who were visiting the delights and quietude of the countryside. Even the horses and bullocks seemed ebullient, chomping on dewy hay and best, crunchy oats. The paint was still moist and glistening upon gaudy and garish banners, competing for attention in wishing Caesar well for his forthcoming campaign. It was as if the city was a creature coming out of hibernation and he now craved sustenance, society and merriment.

Drovers, dyers, farriers, furriers, tanners, tonsors, waggoners, wharfmen, carpenters, cobblers, blacksmiths, boatmen, surgeons, shipwrights, merchants, mid-wives, perfumers, pastry-chefs, rope makers, ribbon-sellers, quaestors, quacks, actors, aediles, augurs, jewellers, jugglers, vintners, vendors, haberdashers, herbalists, upholsterers, urchins, kitchen-hands and knife-sharpeners all buzzed around the streets, as industrious and content as a colony of bees.

*

Caesar woke and was briefly startled to see, hazing in and out of focus in his sleep-filled eyes, various attendants positioned around his bed, smiling obsequiously or gawping. Fury briefly knitted his brow before the statesman realised that he had instructed many of his staff to be ready to attend him as soon as he arose.

Dimpled serving girls held strigils, oils, soaps and sponges in their hands, ready should Caesar wish to take a bath. An over-worked but ever-ready secretary stood poised with a wax tablet and stylus, should Caesar suddenly decide to write a letter. Two dressers, brothers, held a woollen, circular-shaped piece of material aloft which - after meticulous draping, folding and pleating - would be transformed into Caesar's magisterial toga.

For a telling moment the pontifex maximus, and dictator perpetuus, closed his eyes again after waking, perhaps wishing that the bothersome retinue could vanish and he could continue to bury his head in the swan down of his pillow. But the purple, gold-bordered garment loomed large in the tired fifty-five year old's eyes, reminding the consul of the significance of the day ahead. It was to be the last gathering of the Senate before Caesar departed for Apollonia - and then onto Parthia.

He yawned and stretched simultaneously - the yawn dovetailing into a small roar. Caesar duly put the clicking of his joints down to the frigid morning air, rather than his age. Julius smiled winsomely at his retinue.

"Would you like some breakfast Caesar?" Joseph, one of the dictator's oldest servants, asked. 'Joseph the Jew' as he was called, to mark him out from 'Joseph the Carpenter' (who was also a Jew), had been with the Jullii household for as long as Julius could recall, to the point where the duteous and sometimes over fussy manservant had asked his master's father the same question once as a serving boy.

"A cup of water will suffice Joseph, thank you."

"Is that all Caesar?" Joseph replied, with a hint of disappointment and criticism in his voice. The servant was forever trying to encourage his master to eat more.

"If you're worried it's not enough Joseph, I'll have two cups," Julius replied, his features bright with fondness and charm. The good-humoured smile ebbed from Caesar's expression however as he noticed his wife's absence from the other side of the bed - and the uncommonly ruffled state she had left it in. Was something wrong?

*

The early dawn had been snuffed out by leaden skies. Slowly but surely though the overcast clouds, slate by slate, had been lifted and fine sunshine sprinkled itself over Rome as if nature wished to give the city a climate deserving of its jubilant mood.

Brutus stood, where others leaned, next to a pillar in the large portico before Pompey's Theatre. Cassius had once satirically commented that the praetor's posture was "as upright as his morals". Sometimes his ashen expression seemed watchful, sometimes pre-occupied. He bit his nails again. The rings around his eyes marked out a sleepless night. Brutus had tried to read to take his mind off things but familiar friends - such as Cato the Elder, Carneades and Hesiod - brought little or no consolation for once. The words seemed empty, or loose on the page, as if a gust of wind could blow them all away. And the bookish praetor would have noticed not, or cared little, should they have done so. Books could not help him now. Where once a copy of Plato's Symposium rested in the inside fold of his toga, there now resided a dagger.

Usually the stoical statesman dressed himself in the morning, having been taught by Cato how to don his toga without assistance, but this morning Porcia had helped him. His hands had been shaking too much. She had also calmly placed the ceremonial dagger, used for religious sacrifices, into the large inside pleat of the garment. Again, the conspirator covertly touched his midriff to check if the weapon was still there.

"He who many fear must go in fear of many."

At first the words but sounded as loud as an echo in his ears - and they emanated from a man who appeared and disappeared in front of his person in a blur. But then reality, oppressive reality, took hold. The quote was from a play by Liberius - and Cassius had adopted the phrase as code for the conspirators, to indicate that a member would be in his designated position. Brutus but caught the back of the libertore but he recognised the figure

166

as Servius Galba, a former general of Caesar's in Gaul. Was his cause the Republic? - Or was Galba rather acting out of envy or revenge, for being passed over for promotion in Caesar's new campaign? Brutus sadly already knew the answer to the question.

The ill-at-ease senator seemed strangely out of place in the gay, bustling square. The mood seemed especially fraternal. Citizens had even been considerate enough to avoid dumping their toilet buckets on passers-by beneath their windows this morning, the praetor had noticed. Banter and laughter were freely exchanged, between friends and strangers alike. Gossips twittered like crickets. People were either purposeful in the act of shopping, or setting up shop. Brutus overheard the latest epigram doing the rounds and, for the first time that morning, his dour countenance fleetingly broke out into a smile.

> *"I have heard that Fulvia cries*
> *Ev'rytime her husband returns home late.*
> *Either Mark Antony must change his ways*
> *Or his wife will dehydrate."*

The ardent Republican surveyed the scene however and his expression became pained. Was this really a tyranny? Was Caesar really a tyrant? More than the people and Caesar even, had it not been resentful patricians and the taxed merchant class who had propagated the idea of the consul acting like a king? Brutus even posed that some had perhaps feted and honoured Julius - commissioning statues and awarding him further bombastic titles

- in order to build him up and inspire jealousy, breeding reasons to knock him down.

"He who many fear must go in fear of many."

The words sent a chill down the conspirator's spine. Instead of a sense of duty the call to arms began to stir feelings of doubt, guilt. The line this time had been uttered by Decimus Brutus, a distant relation and a man Marcus had perhaps admired more before the instigation of the conspiracy. Where once he had thought Decimus intelligent, he now thought him politic; ambition whispered in his ear as much as a sense of justice. Cassius had called Decimus "a good man" but he meant it in the treacherous rather than true sense of the term, Brutus despondently judged.

Taking charge somewhat of the libetores' final gathering it had been Brutus himself who had recommended that Decimus be the one to make sure Caesar attended the Senate meeting on the Ides. And so Marcus now watched his fellow conspirator walk off in the direction of Julius' house. His voice and resolution were too weak to call him back.

The die was cast.

*

Caesar was torn. The duty of office, rather than a desire to do so, suggested that he should attend to the Senate. Yet Calpurnia had asked him to remain at home for the day. First she had said that she was unwell, which from her abnormal pallor and strange manner Caesar could well discern himself - and then she had argued that they did not have that much time left before he departed on his new campaign. She wanted to spend some time with him. It was uncharacteristic of her to plead and make a demand on her husband's day in such a way, which is why Caesar wanted to oblige her. Unlike Cleopatra, Calpurnia seldom asked anything of Caesar.

Rather than answer yes or no, then and there, the consummate politician had told his wife that he would think about it - and make his decision after his morning shave. As to their daily routine Caesar took his chair and Joseph stropped the razor. The dictator liked to be clean-shaven to the point of it seeming an obsession. He once joked to his servant that he liked to remain so because it gave the impression of him having more hair upon his head.

"I'm a dog caught between the call of two masters Joseph, the Senate and my wife. What would you do?" Caesar posed, half-jokingly, as he sat down.

"I would pray to my God for direction."

"And what do you think He would say?"

"For an easy life He will say whatever my wife tells him to," Joseph said after a short mock-philosophical pause, the barest flicker of a smile upon his face. Julius smirked, enjoying the dry wit of his old friend. Behind closed doors Caesar gave licence to Joseph to say anything he wished to his master.

"You have a wise God, Joseph."

"Or a frightening wife," the old Jew wryly replied.

*

Brutus nervously fingered the dagger beneath his toga, repositioning the weapon once more. A small volcano of terror suddenly erupted within his stomach, thinking how if Caesar should embrace him he would notice the knife press against him. His breath quivered. The logician reined himself in however by arguing that Caesar only embraced him after an absence of seeing him - and had he not last seen his former mentor only yester night? There had been a dinner party at Lepidus' house. Brutus' stomach had tightened and the blood drained from, and then flooded his face in succession as the topic of conversation turned to "a good death". A pregnant silence filled the room just before their dictator spoke.

"Let it come quickly and unexpectedly," Caesar had expressed. Brutus darted an anxious glance towards Cassius, but his co-conspirator merely popped a grape into his mouth and nodded in agreement with the dictator, briefly raising a corner of his thin cruel mouth in an amused smirk.

"One cannot spend one's life constantly worrying about and trying to prevent one's inevitable demise. The sands of time will always slip through our fingers. Cowards die many times before their deaths; the valiant never taste of death but once."

"Wise words, Caesar," Lepidus ingratiatingly pronounced in reply, raising his cup of second-rate Chianti and toasting his consul. The Master of Horse's most pronounced feature, in Brutus' eyes, was his mediocrity. He was as bald as Caesar, as uneducated as Mark Antony and as self-serving as Cassius. His virtues as a general were that of being a good administrator and following the orders of his superiors. Cassius, who had served with Lepidus in Spain, thought little of him - but Cassius thought little of everybody, Brutus mused.

It was an act of courage, bravado and hubris for Caesar to dismiss his bodyguard like he did. "There is no worse fate than to be continuously protected, for that means you are in constant fear," Julius had remarked to Brutus in private. Cassius had exclaimed that it was fitting that it should be Caesar's pride and arrogance, those traits that had made him First Man of Rome, which should also be the authors of his downfall.

Out of the corner of his eye Brutus saw now his sharp-faced co-conspirator, leading his own personal bodyguard of a dozen gladiators. The plan was for them to be stationed outside of the Senate meeting, just in case Caesar's supporters should come to his aid. Cassius had not informed them of the plot, only that he might call on them to restore order. Trebonius, Pompey's former fleet-commander, also stood in place. His task was to detain Mark Antony, so he would not be present when the deed was done. Everyone was now in their place, like actors waiting for their cues upon the stage, except for the villain. For so long Julius had been Marcus' hero. He owed Caesar gratitude and respect. As well as a gift of a necklace or silks for Servilia, his mother's lover would always bring the budding scholar a copy of the latest translation of Plato or Euripides. So too it had been Julius who had financed the opportunity for Brutus to further his education and visit Athens all those years ago. He was still the greatest man Marcus had ever known, eclipsing even Pompey, Cato and Cicero in his range of virtues and accomplishments.

Punctuality was never one of the dictator's most prevalent virtues, however. Or had the conspiracy been uncovered? It surprised Brutus how much this last thought did not alarm him. Perhaps he just wanted for the day to be over.

"Either this dagger will end Caesar's or my own life by the end of today," he had flatly stated to his wife that morning.

*

"You have not usually suffered from such superstitions before my dear."

"I have not suffered such a dream before," Calpurnia replied. The couple sat ensconced in a small arbour within the villa's garden. Lilies bloomed at their feet. Ivy hung down like the auburn ringlets framing Calpurnia's once elegant, now grief-stricken, features. A tardy lark warbled its dawn chorus. Dark rings still circled her teary aspect - and the image of Caesar, bloody and dying in her arms, still plagued her inward eye. She had at first lied, pleaded and then raged to keep her husband at home for the day. The violent nightmare scarred her waking reality. Caesar had been loving and patient towards his wife all throughout her pained histrionics - all the while rehearsing his arguments as to why he still needed to attend the Senate meeting that morning.

"I dreamed you were murdered."

"Even if death is calling, duty is also calling my love."

"Are you not worried about the auspices? It might be written in the stars."

"Then I shall change the calendar again if need be," Caesar replied, tenderly cupping her distraught face in his strong hand - and smiled that smile which had conquered more hearts than just his wife's. "Let it not be said that Caesar does not know how to compromise. I will be as quick as I can in dealing with the Senate - and then I will return home and we can spend the day together. Indeed I promise to spend so much time with you my love that you'll be veritably sick of me by the time I leave."

Calpurnia let out a laugh cum sob at her husband's sardonic wit. More than anyone, Julius knew how to judge his wife's mood and make her feel good. It had not always been the case. Their marriage had originally been one of political convenience. So too Caesar nearly divorced his high-born wife, offering her to Pompey in order to maintain strong relations with his fellow triumvir. Yet fondness, respect and love eventually fostered themselves into the union. Calpurnia's cold patrician humour melted under the light of Caesar's charm; duty turned into devotion. Caesar appreciated his wife's faithfulness - and forgiving nature; she tolerated his indiscretions, moods and vanity. She nursed him like his mother and Cornelia - and kept it secret when he suffered from his increasing bouts of falling sickness. Julius in return enjoyed lavishing her with gifts of jewellery and clothes (although Calpurnia would rather have had her husband spend time, than money, on her). He even made love to her outside of her cycle, when she was least fertile. It had frustrated and saddened Caesar that Calpurnia had not been able to furnish him with an heir, but after being informed that his wife might be barren Caesar dismissed the idea of re-marrying. Julius had of late appreciated his wife's Roman virtues in light of his mistress' recent behaviour and demands. When Cleopatra had witnessed an attack of his epilepsy Caesar somehow felt ashamed or vulnerable in the politic queen's eyes; when it similarly occurred under the gaze of his wife, he absorbed love and compassion in her maternal aspect. Calpurnia was, as much as Mark Antony and Marcus Brutus, a friend and confidante. He had enjoyed the dinner last night, partly because he could see how much Calpurnia had enjoyed it, basking in the attention and honour of being Caesar's wife. When they had returned home Calpurnia had read to her husband (which, as much of a pleasure as it was, it had of late became a practicality - as Caesar's eyesight seemed to be receding as quickly as his hairline).

Caesar paced up and down in the courtyard of his villa, his sandals clacking over the veined marble floor. He ruminated still upon his wife's unnerved - and unnerving - state of mind. She had said how she had never ever asked anything of Caesar, except to stay at home with her for this one day - and she was right. Guilt prodded at him, like a blunt bodkin into his ribcage.

"Morning Caesar," a bleary-eyed Mark Antony tiredly but amiably announced when entering the courtyard. Caesar smiled, thinking how, even hung over, his lieutenant was strikingly handsome and good humoured.

"Late night?"

"Let's just say I spent half the evening drinking with Lepidus

- and the other half eating with his niece," Mark Antony replied, lazily raising a corner of his mouth in a boyish smirk.

"You seem to be systematically working your way through our Master of Horse's stable. I would ask you to refrain from riding his wife though Mark Antony," Caesar expressed, with the hint of a warning.

"Fear not, she's a nag. So are we off to the Senate today?" the soldier asked - and then yawned. He hoped that Caesar wouldn't have any official business or role for him to perform at the session. Sleep was beckoning him like a mistress to bed.

"No, you are off to the Senate today my old friend, alone. Announce that I have urgent business to attend to. Calpurnia is unwell. I promised to spend the day with her."

"Nothing too serious I hope. Would you like me to summon a physician before I attend to the rabble?" Mark Antony asked with genuine concern in his voice for his friend and his wife. His disdain for the Senate was equally sincere.

"No, I have a feeling it will just be a twenty-four hour fever, but thank you. How is your wife by the way? I didn't get the chance to speak with Fulvia last night."

"Lucky you. Two of her slaves died this week. She says she has nothing to wear. Her brassiere keeps pinching. And she's putting on too much weight. I've never heard her complain so much. In short, Fulvia's as happy as she's ever been and back to her old self. Never mind wedding feasts, the party should come when people divorce."

Caesar laughed, happily and unaffectedly. It would be the last time that he would do so.

"I am going to miss you my friend when I leave for Parthia. I can't quite decide whether you have been a son or brother to me Antony, but Caesar would not be now Caesar without you."

A sense of gratitude and love permeated the heart of the sybarite and wastrel. Caesar was the only man who Antony could, or would, serve as a lieutenant to. The two men shared a brief, wordless moment. Mark Antony approached his surrogate father and older brother - and hugged him as such. Tears glistened in soldierly aspects.

*

Mark Antony formally nodded to Decimus Brutus as he exited the courtyard. The two men tolerated rather than liked each other. Mark Antony couldn't help but notice the disdain and disapproval which Decimus cultivated in regard to the dissolute soldier. In return Mark Antony was suspicious of the patrician's sobriety and ambition.

Decimus Brutus had served under Caesar in Gaul and, although from a prominent optimate family, he had sided with Julius in the civil war. His military successes had been many - and many of them had been key. Yet his victories had always been under Caesar's banner. Decimus believed that he deserved to share some of the pages of history that had been written by Caesar, Pompey and Lucullus - rather than just serve as a footnote to their triumphs. Like so many of his fellow libertores he trumpeted the cause of the Republic, but more so it rankled with the patrician that scoundrels like Mark Antony had been promoted to consul ahead of him. He seethed with resentment as well, believing that Caesar intended to announce his nephew as a successor. Caesar wanted to establish a dynasty, as well as a monarchy. His dagger would plunge deep into such transgressions Decimus had promised himself and the others, baring his teeth as he did so. "Let us see how immortal the self-proclaimed son of Venus is," he had sardonically added in a private chamber of Servilia's house, where the conspirators had hatched their plan. Trebonius had called it a coup, yet Decimus argued that, rather than a coup or revolution, they were merely re-establishing the rightful government of Rome.

The middle-aged senator straightened out a pleat in his toga and smoothed his oiled hair. Baring his teeth, this time in the form of an oleaginous smile, Decimus approached Caesar.

"To what do I owe this unexpected pleasure, Decimus?" Caesar exclaimed upon seeing his former General, clasping and scrunching his shoulder in fraternal affection.

"I was just passing, Julius, and I thought you might like some company in walking to the Senate meeting."

"I'm afraid you've had a wasted journey, Decimus. I will not be attending the session today. Mark Antony has just left to send word of the fact. Would you like some refreshment?" Caesar said, distracted somewhat as he took in the new pastoral landscape which Calpurnia had purchased to decorate a wall of the atrium. As such the dictator did not notice his friend blanch, or almost choke on his words before he replied.

"May I ask why?"

"Calpurnia is unwell, or rather she had a bad dream last night and she remains unsettled." Julius pursed his lips, pouting almost, and gently nodded his approval at the picture. The landscape was a little too symmetrical, artificial, but the colours and style of the painting were striking. The deep blue sky briefly reminded Julius of the woad-dyed faces of the barbaric Britons. Caesar smiled, remembering his triumph over the distant isle, but then his smile faltered as he remembered the cost of his victory.

"Permission to speak freely Caesar?" Decimus asked, as if he were back upon the battlefields of Gaul.

"Granted," Caesar replied, curious and concerned by his friend's tone.

"It might be interpreted that you are somehow dishonouring the Senate, should you listen to your wife's dreams rather than the dictates of your duty."

"The Senate has been dishonouring itself for years Decimus. Another day will not make much difference I warrant."

"But more than criticise you Julius, they will laugh at you. The Senate can abide the judgement of Caesar directing the governance of Rome, but I fear they will not be able to stomach the dreams of your wife dictating policy and state business. The paint of the graffiti artists will have dried upon the cartoons before the close of day."

Creases found their way into his brow at Decimus' frank words. Caesar pursed his lips, in deliberation. Calpurnia was asleep.

He would be home before she woke, he argued. Caesar did not wish to leave for Parthia with a chorus of laughter or satirical comments echoing up from the city. More than his love for his wife Caesar ultimately cared for his own pride and auctoritas - and Decimus knew the dictator well enough to play upon Caesar's weakness, and strength.

"You're a persuasive fellow Decimus - and a good friend. I feel that not even Massilia was besieged as much by you as I am now. To Pompey's theatre then. 'Tis time for a final performance before I leave this stage for good," Julius exclaimed, clapping his lieutenant affectionately on the back and leading him out.

*

Marcus Brutus heard the procession before he saw it. The praetor was standing outside Pompey's Theatre.

Caesar's litter was unmistakable and unrivalled. Disgust, despondency and envy fought for pre-eminence in the Republican's heart as he witnessed various people, from the Sabura and Palatine districts alike, throng around their consul, behaving like beggars more than citizens.

The procession and adoration was akin to that of an official Triumph, at which a Roman general would celebrate a historic victory over the city's enemies. Rather than a chariot however Caesar rode in an ornate litter - the polished gold of which radiated in the sunlight, giving its occupant a further divine aura. Yet, unlike a Triumph, Brutus judged, no voice would be now whispering in Julius' ear, "Remember you are mortal, remember you are mortal". Would Julius even hear such sage advice though at present, over the chants of "Caesar? Caesar!" which rose up like puffs of smoke and choked out all other sounds?

People continued to flock towards Caesar, like iron filings to a magnet. A young couple finished kissing, people gave up their places in the queues for various food stalls and augurs lost their audiences. And the litter continued to make its way through the undulating sea of people. Heads bobbed upon necks, as if they were pigeons about to be fed, as the adoring crowd attempted to sneak a peek at the dictator. Maybe Cleopatra was with him? "She can turn more heads than a garrotte" a cartoon had once commented on a wall next to the Forum.

Faces beamed with religious adulation. A few children were crushed in the chaos. Drunken cheers were thrown up for no apparent reason. Rome had forgotten its sober spirit, Brutus lamented.

Even through the frenetic and knotted forest of limbs Brutus could still discern the calf-length red leather boots of Julius as he stepped out from his carriage. The roar from the various supplicants eclipsed even that of what had come before, as if the people were attempting to send man-made thunder from earth up into the heavens. Brutus was not the only one to close his eyes and shake his head in derision at the raucous din.

Across the portico Cassius sneered at the ignoble exhibition. His eyes became two slits as he tried to focus on the swirling and slavish congregation and pick out Caesar; the sight of Julius' self-satisfied and pompous air would feed his blood-lust. The senator's knuckles turned white as he viciously clasped the hilt of his dagger beneath his toga.

The brawny litter bearers formed a protective cordon around their master, albeit even they found themselves buffeted by the force of the eddying mob. Caesar, in the eye of the hurricane, was a picture of imperious calm however. He gratefully collected scrolls and petitions which were thrust over and through the arms of his entourage. He smiled and waved, sparking a sense of devotion and satisfaction in every soul he interacted with.

Brutus was suddenly checked in his derision by the sight of a friend of his, Artemidoros, a Greek teacher of public speaking, fighting his way through the tightly-knit horde in order to contact Caesar. Brutus squinted in an attempt to better observe the exchange. Artemidoros seemed to be trying to articulate something to the Consul - and hand him a scroll. Caesar cupped a hand to his ear yet still couldn't understand the strange petitioner above the applause of the crowd. Brutus wasn't aware that Artemidoros was on familiar terms with Julius. The Greek orator had even stayed over at his house a week ago - Brutus gave his friend permission to use his library and study - and he hadn't mentioned having any business in regards to Caesar.

The scroll contained details of the conspiracy. Julius was momentarily tempted to peruse the document then and there such was the singular manner of the fellow who had made such an effort to give it to him, as if his life depended on it. But he merely passed the document over to his clerk and continued to make his way towards the surrogate Forum for the day.

Pompey's Theatre. It was rare, if far from unprecedented, that the Senate would gather here. The grand building, constructed to celebrate Pompey's equally grand victories, was the first stone theatre to be permanently housed in the capital. The stone seating, preferably softened by a cushion, could accommodate close to ten thousand people. The monument was a testament to the great man's achievements as well as his (then) unparalleled wealth and unrivalled status. The semi-circular theatre was situated on the edge of the Campus Martius, next to - and towering over - various other temples and buildings dedicated to Rome's triumphs and heroes over the centuries.

A boisterous sun reflected off the luna marble as Caesar gazed up at the row of elaborate statues built into the monument. Venus Victrix (Venus the Victorious) was the most prominent and beautiful sculpture. Julius allowed himself a brief smile, thinking how he had stolen her as his mistress from Pompey, as well as the title of First Man of Rome.

At seeing Brutus, Caesar waved off his entourage and walked towards his old friend. The dictator nodded his head backwards at the commotion behind him and rolled his eyes to express how he felt suitably divorced from the scenes in the square, and a little embarrassed by them.

"Morning Brutus."

"Morning Julius."

"You look a little pale my friend."

"It's nothing. I think I was just close to being bored to death by

Lepidus last night, that's all. I spent all this morning remembering to forget his insights into the merits of satin compared to silk - and how his augur is exceptional at reading the entrails of seagulls and quails, but not blackbirds."

"In other words, he was talking shit. I tell Aemilius that the reason why I keep him busy so much is that I trust and value him as an administrator, which I confess I do - but more so I am just trying to save other people from suffering his company for too long."

Brutus smiled. Julius was one of the few people who could make him laugh.

A group of senators walked past the two men. Out of sight of Caesar, a couple eyed Brutus anxiously. Sweaty palms clutched their stylus cases. Rather than writing implements though, the cases carried their daggers.

"Right, let's get this over with. Are you coming in now?"

"I will be with you in a moment," Brutus replied. Whether Brutus knew it or not, the cancer of guilt had already lodged itself into his soul.

"If I don't see you afterwards, please try and call on me before I leave. Calpurnia and I would dearly love to have yourself and Porcia over for dinner. Just the four of us. Have a good day, my friend."

Marcus could not quite look his friend in the eye as Caesar said this, and clasped his forearm in a Roman handshake. He quickly turned away, sheepish, pained - and observed that, as to plan, Trebonius was detaining Mark Antony in the portico outside the theatre. As instructed the libertore was advising the consul on how he could consolidate his debts and decrease his interest payments.

*

Julius strode into the meeting and sat down on the gilded throne, which resided next to, but above, Antony's curule chair. The murmuring gathering quietened. Sleepers were nudged and woken up. Some still gazed down at the speeches they had prepared. Caesar apologised for his lateness and then immediately asked if there were any urgent petitions which needed to be addressed.

A few statesmen duly approached the dictator, some clutching scrolls or pieces of papyrus. Julius was far from impressed at seeing Tillius Cimber step forward however. This was now the third time that he would try and persuade Caesar to permit his brother to return from exile.

"You are wasting your time. Hannibal has more chance of returning to Rome than your brother. And my patience is now growing short with you," Caesar exclaimed, responding to Tillius' petition - shaping his features so as to leave Cimber in no doubt as to his displeasure at having to address the issue again.

Pretending to be desperate and unhinged the libertore suddenly rushed up to Caesar and grabbed him by the arms, pulling the dictator's toga tight. "Once Cimber has grabbed his toga, we strike, all of us," Cassius had coldly ordered at the final gathering of the conspirators. Caesar was at first shocked and disgusted at the supplicant's unbecoming display, but then Julius saw the glint of the first blade.

Servilius Casca was the first assassin to strike. He aimed for the dictator's bare neck but, with reflexes and strength hewn from years of campaigning, Caesar managed to free himself from Cimber and avoid the intended blow. Instead of stabbing his neck Casca merely sliced his chest.

"This is violence!" the dictator roared, calling out to his friends. But only his enemies sped towards him. Caesar wounded Casca in the arm with his stylus, but as he did so Julius felt the point of a dagger skewer into his side. The pain brought Caesar down onto one knee, but he gritted his teeth and rose again, punching one assassin in the throat and throwing another off. Such was the confusion and unwieldy strategy with which the attackers each attempted to get their blow in that many ended up stabbing or cutting each other. Blood flowed and stained like wine. Already a number of senators ran for the door, believing themselves to be fleeing for their lives.

Such was Cassius' determination to deliver the fatal blow that he actually pulled off one of his fellow conspirators to get to Caesar, who was still fending off many of his attackers. The blade arced over the shoulder of a blood strewn libertore. Cassius screwed up his face in bitterness and fury, exorcising all his jealousy and hatred in a paroxysm of violence. The dagger was just about to stab at Caesar's once imperious - but now crimson and contorted - countenance when it suddenly failed to reach its target. To Cassius' astonishment he witnessed Caesar standing there, his forearm bulging, his hand dripping blood from where he had hold of the blade up to its hilt. For a second, not even that, the two men glowered at each other - Caesar with contempt, Cassius with venom - before the dictator finally floored the wiry assassin by knocking him to the floor.

Julius fought on, leonine. A knife cut into the back of his right leg, slicing his hamstring. Again he fell to one knee. The old soldier found a dagger on the floor and returned to his feet. A wounded, cornered animal. Yet blood increasingly seeped out of him, sapping his strength.

For a time Brutus had but watched on, mournfully transfixed. He had believed that by the time he delivered his obligatory blow Julius would have already perished - and he would not have to look his friend, the man who had spared his life, in the eye. Marcus finally got to his feet and approached his enemy.

Julius stumbled once more, his right leg giving way, but he rose again, his visage still showing signs of life and fight. It was not just his blood now which splattered the marble floor. Such was their wariness of Caesar that, to re-group and check the extent of their wounds and losses, there was a lull in the attack as they circled their victim.

The groans of injured assassins and the sight and sounds of panicking senators fell into the background as Brutus entered the cordon of assassins, which surrounded their prey. For a second or so Caesar believed that Brutus had come to save him, but then the praetor plunged his dagger into the dictator's stomach.

"You too, my son?"

"I'm sorry," his killer immediately whispered, unsure as to

whether his victim had heard.

Caesar slumped to the floor for the third and final time. His mind was becoming, like his sight, a blur. Tears cut streaks into his bloodied face. Twenty-three stab wounds punctured his body, which lay beneath the cold gaze of Pompey's statue. He would not allow them to hear or see him suffer though. Caesar would die as he lived - with dignitas. Julius' final act was to cover his toga over his head.

Terror and confusion reigned in the Senate, rather than a sense of justice and liberty. Brutus finally woke from his trance-like stupor and realised the ensuing state of anarchy.

"Cicero, Cicero. Rome needs you again," the praetor suddenly shouted, noticing his former mentor fleeing the scene as well.

But the elder statesman, after hearing his name being called out, merely turned around to the assassin and shook his head - either in condemnation of the deed, or to convey his inability to bring order to the pandemonium the conspirators had unleashed.

Dapple-grey clouds flocked together over the city and cast Rome in darkness.

17

Dear Atticus,

You will forgive me if this letter lacks niceties and pleasantries, but know that your friendship is one of the few things which I still have faith in.

The thunder-clap has no doubt reached you by now. I will recount however what transpired after the deed. I'll attempt to be brief - to save both your time and mine - and so too you may already have received news of the assassination and aftermath from other sources, albeit that news might contain more garnish that Gaulish stew.

Where rumour is married to truth is that, immediately after the killing, my name was called out, either as a cry for help or to lend my authority to the bloody act. Suffice to say the 'libertores' should have applied for my help and to lend authority to the deed earlier. We would not now be in the state we're in, so to speak, if they had. So the tyranny survives, though the tyrant is dead.

The theatre emptied, faster than if a troupe of lepers should have taken to the stage. Fear and panic were legion. Mark Antony was perhaps as frightened and confused as anyone - and it was only after when he realised that everyone was terrified that he emerged from his hiding-place.

Three loyal servants returned for the body and took it back to Caesar's house.

Come late afternoon I ventured out and appealed for peace. I also appealed for Brutus to take a lead as praetor, who along with others had taken refuge in the Capitol. But instead Antony took the lead, as consul. We overestimated our authority, but more so we underestimated him. During the dead of night he seized control of the treasury and also Caesar's papers and will. He also secured the support of Lepidus - and therefore the soldiers under his command which are posted just outside of Rome. Where were we? Sleeping, or biting our nails.

The morning appeared to bring a certain amount of hope and conciliation. A Senate meeting was called, albeit, claiming to fear for his life, Antony was notable by his absence. Neither the optimates nor Caesarians wanted to inflame the situation too much, partly because neither knew the strength of the other I suspect. The sole exception to this was Cornelius Cinna, who denounced Caesar as a tyrant and that not only should his legislation be decreed null and void, but his murderers should be declared heroes and rewarded.

Brutus and Cassius appeared before us. The murder, Brutus argued, had been an act in the name of peace, not war. He would refuse any money or honour offered to him for deposing Caesar. Rome had been their cause, not personal ambition (I think we are both raising our eyebrows to that one my friend). Cassius then moved centre-stage and was fulsome of his praise of his fellow libertore. Brutus, he exclaimed, had "fulfilled his destiny". As his noble ancestor had delivered Rome from the tyranny of Tarquin the Proud, "our Brutus" had once again saved Rome from despotism. Once again "Rome would be a republic, not a monarchy".

A bout of cheering here issued forth from their supporters, but although they won over many they did not win over a majority.

Deputations from Antony then addressed the Senate. It was and would be the consul's duty to maintain order. "Peace and order" would be sovereign. Despite the danger to his own personal safety his representatives announced that the consul would address the Senate the following day.

That afternoon Brutus appeared before the people. He was eloquent and persuasive, although far from inspirational. He listed Caesar's crimes or 'illegalities' as he pedantically called them and argued that the dictator was in fact a tyrant. Corruption was rife (but, unlike the beard Marcus has taken to growing, hasn't it always been in fashion?). Caesar had employed the law arbitrarily. I sensed that people left the Capitol feeling partly satisfied with Brutus' arguments, though more so they were still just in shock and worried that civil war could again break out.

The following day saw Antony appear before the Senate - with Brutus and Cassius now absent, fearing for their lives. Although he had sworn an oath to protect Caesar and avenge his death - Rome, public order, peace, took precedence over one man's honour. I must confess I even begrudgingly admired his performance in certain respects. Yet it was "because of the dictates of peace and order that we should not regard Caesar as a tyrant and ratify his legislation" he exclaimed. For stability's sake Dolabella should succeed Caesar as consul. Moreover the various positions and promotions that Caesar had planned should be honoured. As you can well imagine a large number of senators nodded sagely in agreement with this proposition, being beneficiaries of the policy. "Peace is what we are all trying for," Antony reiterated, before positing that "If we nullify one act of Caesar's, must we not do so for all? And who will tell Caesar's veterans, entitled to their land settlements, that they now own nothing?" Fear swept over many of the neutrals now, if indeed one could have still considered them neutrals.

Can you imagine how shocked and suspicious I was to then not only hear Antony amiably call my name, but also agree with me in that we should establish an amnesty for the assassins? "We should pardon both Caesar and his murderers," he generously proclaimed, to the approval of the majority. The motion was speedily passed. To cement a bond of trust and good faith Antony then motioned to abolish the office of Dictator, a motion which was also duly ratified. The dramatic session ended with the announcement that Caesar's will would be opened and read the next day.

The will was read by Piso, as self-important and insignificant a fellow as one could hope to avoid, at Antony's house. I attended, despite the tasteless decor. In a predictably self-glorifying gesture Caesar bequeathed his gardens upon the Tiber to the people to enjoy at their leisure, for free. Added to which he bequeathed to each citizen 300 sesterces, a sum so generous as to be ridiculous, and they'll surely never even receive three sesterces of the entitlement.

The most dramatic revelation however, which was unbeknown even to Calpurnia, involved the news that Caesar had apportioned three-quarters of his estate to his great-nephew, Octavius. Yet can we now not rightly call the boy his son? For Caesar also stated in the will that he had legally adopted the child. Even Antony's solemn countenance displayed flickers of distress and amazement.

The news filtered through to the great unwashed and people perhaps now loved Caesar more in death than they did in life. Their love and sympathy increased for Caesar as markedly as their shame and disdain for Decimus Brutus, who was named in the will as a legatee. Even in death Julius is still out-manoeuvring us all.

A few days passed without major incident. Cleopatra thankfully left Rome, taking her child of dubious parentage with her. Decimus made a tactical retreat back to his province in Gaul. Antony, Brutus and Cassius met for dinner. I was absent but I was informed that the mood was conciliatory. I dared to hope.

I have dared not commit to such folly since the funeral however. For once, I believe that Mark Antony was sober. We should perhaps be thankful that he is usually drunk, for in his oratory and stratagems that day he reminded me of his esteemed grand-father. I sensed that it was not just his hand behind the speech and spectacle which followed though. Suffice to say I spotted phrases and techniques borrowed from Hortensius, Caesar and even myself. Antony has a new lieutenant, one Enobarbus, who has come to my attention. My sources tell me he is both an accomplished soldier and orator. Unfortunately my agents also tell me that he is unswervingly loyal to Antony. Or maybe Fulvia is sticking her oar in and stirring up trouble. She was not one to rule a household when she could rule a consul instead.

The pyre was a work of art in itself my friend, indeed such was its impossible height that you might have even witnessed its peak from Greece. The duteous consul and mournful friend took up his position in the forum next to Caesar's bier, facing an already captivated and emotional audience.

The colourful panegyric came first, listing Caesar's titles and achievements. After praising Caesar's accomplishments as a general and statesman he then artfully listed his virtues as a friend and mentor. The men nodded in fraternal appreciation, the women batted their eyelids at the handsome - but sensitive - consul to such extent as to create a draught. Antony recounted the oath that he had taken to protect his general and avenge his death. The collective gasp here sucked in the draught before Antony assured everyone again that peace meant more to him than his own oath. Cue applause.

Tears came next, from Antony. I was somewhat underwhelmed in regards to Antony being overwhelmed. But the pliable crowd drunk down his lies like a bottle of cheap Massic. Such was his seeming loss of self-control that eventually Antony began to speak as if he were Caesar himself, trying to make sense of the heinous crime, apologising for being misunderstood - and them damning his murderers. "Did I save these men that they might murder me?" he finally, dramatically, expressed as a wax figure of Caesar, replete with painted wounds, was brought into view. Women - and men - wailed. The pyre was lit - and the flames of people's passions fanned. Mourners fuelled the flames as all manner of junk (jewels, wreaths, and robes) was tossed onto the pyre. Stools, benches and curtains followed. Antony created the spark, but the conflagration of hate and lawlessness fed itself. Rioting ensued. The Senate House was set alight. Enraged mobs marched through the streets, torches and weapons in hand, seeking vengeance upon the assassins who had felled the "people's champion".

For more than a few days Brutus and Cassius became prisoners in their own homes, such was the appetite for destruction and revenge from the mob. Order was eventually restored, although one suspects Antony could have restored it sooner. Concerned for their safety - and to get rid of his rivals - Antony proposed that Brutus and Cassius take over the governance of the corn supply in Asia and Crete respectively. Without either accepting or refusing the offer, both conspirators abandoned Rome. I too followed them, fearing that Mark Antony might get around to considering me an enemy or, worse still, a potential ally.

And so a number of the noble but daft libertores - and myself - met at

Antium yesterday. I advised Brutus that he should accept Antony's way out and re-group in Asia. Antony has not been as clever as he thinks I argued, for rather than raise taxes and crops, Brutus will hopefully raise an army. My intention is for Cassius to do the same in Crete. I also have faith in Decimus Brutus to defy Mark Antony when it comes to him handing over his province in Gaul, later on in the year. This triumvirate will cut Mark Antony down to size. Brutus is the key however in unlocking the gates of the Republic again. We must protect, laud and fund him. Both the patricians and the people trust him. Once I cited how he should not only venture to Asia for his own safety, but for Porcia's, he saw reason. I fear I will have to rely on Brutus to persuade Cassius though. Looking most valorous I assure you, the picture of a warrior, Cassius announced that he had no intention of going to Crete, "Should I take an insult as though it were given as a favour," he protested. His fate is linked to Brutus' though. And he's astute enough to know that the capital is controlled now by Antony. He has the support of enough of the people and enough of the soldiers who are camped just north of the city - like the Sword of Damocles hanging over our head.

I should just mention that Servilia was present at the meeting also and got on her high horse about my involvement, especially when I lectured the group on failing to deal with Mark Antony originally, "A pity you didn't invite me to dinner on the Ides of March. Let me tell you, there would have been no leftovers," I remarked. Suffice to say that Servilia has grown too old and dry for anyone to look up her skirt whenever she gets on her high horse, though. I warrant that old age is making me cantankerous my friend. Everything irritates me.

Gaius Matius lamented, before I left for Antium, that "If Caesar, for all of his genius, could not find a way out, who is going to find one now?" Perhaps I agree with him. War seems inevitable. Sullans, Marians, Populares, Optimates, Caesarians, Republicans - Rome is perhaps fated to be divided. I used to ask "Who will bring harmony to the classes?" Now I think to myself, 'Who can?'

I have just received news from Salvidienus in Apollonia that Octavius intends to come to Rome in order to claim his inheritance. Salvidienus also insists that he is at my and the Republic's disposal. Not two months ago he was making similar ingratiating noises to Caesar.

I understand that the boy has a tutor, which you recommended the family to. Are you still in contact with this tutor? Can we trust him? Does he have any influence over the boy? - And can we influence him?

If I can get to the boy - before some assassin's knife - then we might be able to use him. Antony will never freely hand over his inheritance. With his new name - and the fact that he can afford, unlike Antony, to win over the ardent Caesarians by promising to avenge his great-uncle's murder - Octavius may be able to create a schism in the Caesarian camp.

Balbus has no doubt been informed of the news or it might even be the case that he influenced the boy's decision. The old Spaniard has been suspiciously quiet. I have received but one letter from him, in which he expresses a desire to maintain the peace at all costs and, for the moment, make friends with Antony. In short, as much as I enjoy his company I don't trust him a yard. One letter is perhaps as stingy as Crassus also, for such is the proximity of our estates that the secretary could deliver it himself.

Take care my friend. My apologies for this abrupt ending.

Cicero

18

Octavius gazed back at the Apollonian coastline, conscious of the fact that he might never see its shores again. The ocean appeared as black as Styx. Aye, was he now sailing to his death? Had Caesar taken charge in Hades by now? The lights from the harbour blinked but they were soon enveloped by the kohl-black night.

Oppius, once he had dried his own tears, had given the boy the news. Octavius betrayed a flicker of resentment and additional shock after hearing that Marcus Brutus had been part of the treacherous act, but otherwise he remained stone-faced. Only when alone did he break down and weep for his great-uncle. A pit, or grave, opened up inside of him – grief was like a vacuum, consuming all. All the sadness in the world could not fill the black hole. Only hate and revenge could help clot the void, he darkly surmised. Octavius asked Oppius for the names of all the murderers, he refused to call them libertores. He etched them into his mind; only their deaths could erase them from the list, branded upon his thoughts as the names were.

His step-father had entreated Octavius to remain in the care of Oppius and the loyal legion at Apollonia. Cleanthes too had warned his student about acting rashly. "Let the light of reason guide you", the philosopher had advised. But the light of a funeral pyre, made up of the bodies of his enemies, held a more powerful sway in his mind's eye.

Octavius still wore the inky cloak of his black funeral toga. He felt frustrated that he was so far from Rome – and his enemies. The youth had composed an oration for his great-uncle - or rather now father - which no one would ever hear.

"Caesar was not just a father to me but rather he was a father to Rome – a protector and provider ... Caesar was loyal to his friends, compassionate towards his enemies ... He believed that Rome should provide prosperity for the many, not the few ... the self-interested Senate judged Caesar a tyrant, but rather, upon opening his will did we not discover that he was Rome's benefactor? Will Brutus bequeath his library to Rome, as Caesar opened up his gardens? How many sesterces will Cassius give to each citizen in his will? Hopefully enough for us to purchase a dagger and plant it in his grave before any floral wreath ... And how can we trust Decimus Brutus to honour the land agreement for the legionaries when he dishonourably murdered the man who made that promise? ... It is not just I who has lost a father. We have all lost a father."

Agrippa slept peacefully in the corner of their cabin. Tiro Casca, Roscius, Cleanthes and Oppius sat around the table, a half-eaten meal of salted squid and olives before them.

"Can we trust Antony?" Casca asked.

"No," Cleanthes replied.

"Yes," Oppius argued, defending his friend and Caesarian comrade. "Antony will want to avenge Julius as much as any man – more so even, as he has the means to do so."

"The means coming from Octavius' inheritance," Cleanthes drily stated.

"Antony is not our enemy. We should trust him, partly for fear of earning his distrust."

Roscius kept his own counsel but sensed that Oppius was trying to convince himself of Antony's loyalty as much as he was the group.

"Antony holds the reins of power within Rome as consul – and through Lepidus and his own relations with those legions loyal to Caesar he controls enough of the army," Oppius went on to say. "In some ways Antony is Caesar's heir."

"Are you suggesting that we get into bed with Antony?" Casca asked, believing that it would not be such a bad move to ally themselves with the consul. With Caesar gone Antony could lay claim to being Rome's greatest general, too.

"Antony has enough bodies in his bed already I warrant," Cleanthes remarked. "Gaius should be his own man."

"But he's just a boy," Oppius replied, shaking his head. "I appreciate your loyalty and affection for the lad, Cleanthes, but I must ask why you think we should share your faith in him?"

"I'm not asking you to share my faith in him, I'm asking you to share the faith that Caesar had in him."

A short pause ensued. "So the plan is still the plan? We are to venture to Puteoli, to Marcus Phillipis, Atia and Balbus," Casca determined.

"And Cicero," Cleanthes added.

"It looks like Gaius may have found another pro-consul who wants to adopt him," Oppius wryly asserted.

*

Agrippa slept on in the corner. Tiro Casca could be heard snoring and – due to his missing teeth – hissing in the adjacent cabin. Oppius had decided to take some air. Roscius and Cleanthes worked their way through the remaining wine.

"It seems that you can hold your drink Cleanthes, but can you hold your own in a fight too?"

"I can unsheathe my wit, if you think that'll help."

"Just stay close to me if we get into a scrape, or run."

"To live to run away another day. I can drink to that."

The two men grinned and clinked cups.

"You know Oppius as well as any man it seems, Roscius. One can see how much he was devoted to Caesar. To what extent is he devoted to Octavius though? How deep is his loyalty to Antony? I fear sooner or later that Caesar's heirs will have to fight for their inheritance. Upon whose side do you think Oppius will stand?"

"Lucius gave his word to Caesar that he would protect Octavius."

"But Caesar's death may have relinquished Oppius of that duty."

"Not in his eyes. Lucius is a soldier Cleanthes, not a politician.

He will keep his word. I will confess to you that Lucius was far from enamoured with his task of protecting Gaius. Should Caesar had lived Oppius may well have asked his General to free him from his duty. But rest assured both Lucius and I will stand between Antony and Octavius should it come to it. I dare say we will be but his second line of defence, though."

"And his first?" Cleanthes asked, whilst pouring the dregs of the wine.

"He's sleeping over there in the corner."

*

Octavius stood at the bow of the ship, his aspect as foreboding as the mushrooming clouds upon the horizon. The sea was still relatively calm though, unfurling itself before the vessel like a blank scroll. His future was similarly blank, or black, Gaius reflected.

"This is a bad decision," Cleanthes judged after hearing of his student's intention to travel to Rome to claim his inheritance.

"Nothing is good or bad but thinking makes it so," Gaius replied, quoting from a text that the tutor had recently instructed him to read.

"Rome is like an un-weeded garden at present."

"It's why I'll need a gardener to accompany me."

"And how are you going to pay me?"

"In compliments."

"Ah, the currency of Cicero."

Although Cleanthes had disagreed with Octavius he nevertheless supported his student and chose to join his party. Oppius had asked Casca if he could commit to one last campaign for Julius. He said no, but he could commit to his first campaign under the banner of Octavius. "Roscius, I've spoken for you," Lucius had told his comrade. "Just so long as you don't drink or whore for me on the way," the legionary replied.

Agrippa had been the first to offer his unconditional support for his friend however. The two youths sat in the garden under a night sky more lustrous than their hearts. Six months previous the adolescents, working their way through one of Marcus Phillipus' vintages, would have told each other lewd jokes or discussed Herodotus.

"You have my sword, Gaius."

"I'd rather you kept it, I'm useless with the thing. You are the brother I never had and the friend I always wished for Marcus. Caesar's work in Rome is but half finished. I cannot do what I mean to do alone, but together we can be greater than the sum of our parts and complete Caesar's vision. We will find a Rome built with brick, but found one clothed in marble."

"There's a storm on the horizon," Oppius remarked, raising his voice above the swirling wind.

"Do you mean here, or in Rome?" Octavius replied, staring out into the churning ocean.

"Both."

"Tell me about Balbus."

"First Pompey - and then Caesar - found Balbus indispensible as a secretary. He will whisper in your ear but that does not mean that you have to listen to him. Be aware that there will be self-interest as well as wisdom in some of the things that he counsels – not that those two things are mutually exclusive. But for the most part he can be trusted. Partly through envying his wealth, partly through looking down on him as a foreigner, the Senate has little love for Balbus. He has no great personal loyalty to Antony but Balbus was devoted to Julius. He will support your cause. Rumour has it that he instructed Lepidus to use the troops outside of Rome to avenge Caesar's death immediately after the Ides. But as much as Balbus loved Caesar know that Cornelius is a politician – he loves himself more."

Oppius gazed at the steely-eyed youth. Thunder rumbled ahead.

"No more will I wear this funeral toga. This son should avenge his father, not mourn him," Octavius expressed, as much to himself as the centurion.

"I will not lie to you Gaius, this could well be a suicide mission that we're on," Oppius issued whilst placing a hand on the youth's shoulder.

Octavius appreciated the centurion's candour and, with a wry smile lining his features, replied, "Julius would've liked those odds."

19

Late morning. Although approaching midday a violet gloom still entombed Rome, dulling its lustre and stone walls. Grey showers gushed down, fuelling rather than washing away the filth and funereal air of the city.

Mark Antony, his toga awry, slouched across Caesar's old throne in Pompey's old villa. Bleary-eyed carousers made their way out of the opulent chamber, either trying to remember - or forget - the depraved events of the night before. A few of the revellers - be they senators, soldiers, actresses, usurers - were still draped over sofas or slumped over cold tiles. The bouquet of yester night's wine had grown as stale as the atmosphere. Insects and rodents devoured half-eaten delicacies - sugared cucumbers in cream, spiced asparagus, lamprey in cranberry sauce, duck stuffed with truffles, Damascus plums and oysters, which either raised one's sex drive or turned one's stomach. Stolas, togas, goblets, olives, figs and the like also littered the room. A young, exotic Jewish prostitute retched in the corner, next to one of the Numidian marble statues of Hercules which populated the hall. For a brief moment one could have imagined the Nemean lion coming to life and attacking the whore, for spoiling his mane so. Wine - and a less seemly fluid - ran down her leg.

Upon the floor, by the Consul's feet, rested his cavalry sword and heavy red cloak, which the former lieutenant wore in imitation of his former general. His cloak however had been sequestered as a blanket by his new mistress, Tertia, an actress and former lover of Cassius. Her uncovered breasts were still stained red from the wine that Antony had poured over them and drunk off during the bacchanalian festivities.

The evening had not just proved a success because Antony had secured a new mistress; as well as feeling that he had won over a number of moderate Caesarians and the more pragmatic (corrupt) Republicans, Antony had also secured the loyalty of his co-consul, Dolabella, through paying off his considerable debts. Dolabella would now support any of his legislation; he would be Antony's subordinate, as much as Bibulus had been a consul in name only during Caesar's first tenure in the office. It was known as the consulship of 'Julius and Caesar'. Antony here drowsily smiled to himself, thinking that he might inspire similar comments and be compared to Julius. His smile faltered however at recalling just how much money it had cost him to clear his co-consul's debts. In a small way Antony even admired his profligacy. But it would be worth it. Dolabella was now indebted to him. And who was Antony indebted to? The boy - seeing as it had been part of his inheritance that Antony had used to buy Dolabella's loyalty. But Caesar's bastard had more chance of fencing with lightning than receiving a single coin out of his war chest, Antony vowed.

The sound of the giant oak doors closing juddered through the room and Antony, or rather his headache, cringed at the noise. He was just about to berate and dismiss the unwelcome attendant when he noticed that it was his capable lieutenant.

Domitius Enobarbus stood at six feet tall. His build was trim, his features pleasing. He briskly, efficiently walked towards Antony. The lieutenant raised his eyebrows in wry amusement at the scene of the party's debris around him. His eyebrows were raised in a questioning fashion, as well as in amusement, as he reached his friend and glanced down at the girl sleeping at the consul's feet.

"Her name's Tertia," Antony said, answering his lieutenant's unspoken question, whilst rubbing his brow in a vain attempt to massage away his throbbing headache.

"I take it then that Chrythis has left for Greece?" Domitius replied, asking after Antony's actress mistress. One of her patrons had requested that her company perform in Athens. Antony, looking upon her prospective absence as an opportunity to taste more forbidden fruit, magnanimously allowed his mistress to further her career.

"She sailed yesterday evening."

"So did Octavius Caesar, if the intelligence reports are true. I fear his destination is Rome, rather than Athens, though. In anticipation of this move I posted a couple of men to Brundisium a week ago," Enobarbus conveyed, lowering his voice.

"Assassins?"

"No, just a couple of my agents. I've ordered them to just shadow the boy."

"I received a letter from Salvidienus Rufus, the father of one of the boy's friends in Apollonia, confirming your report. Rufus pledges his support to our cause. I'd rather he put his money where his mouth was and pledged sesterces. So do you think the whelp will come to Rome?" Antony asked, sadly confident that he already knew the answer to his question.

"If he's smart, or even if he isn't, he will at some point seek the advice of Cicero or Balbus, or both - if they haven't already contacted the boy themselves. I can imagine that both will counsel the heir to come to Rome, if only to stir up trouble and undermine your support with the army and ardent Caesarians. Yet there is a chance that Octavius might listen to his step-father also. I believe that Phillipus will advise the boy to refrain from coming to Rome and claiming his inheritance. But you've met the boy. What are your thoughts?"

"He'd be nothing without his uncle's name," Antony remarked with a sneer, remembering the slight youth with the studious manner who had somehow wormed his way into the affections of Caesar and supplanted him as his designated successor.

"But with his name, what is he capable of?"

Antony paused before answering, as if during that pause he was deciding the youth's fate, rather than thinking about the question.

"His own downfall. We can't let him get to Rome or obtain the support of any of Caesar's legions. I already have enough to contend with here, juggling more balls than a Cretan acrobat. Are Gravius and his cohort still encamped on the Campus Martius?"

Enobarbus nodded, both to confirm that they were and also to convey that he understood Antony's unspoken order.

"The road to Rome is rife with bandits is it not?" Antony remarked with a murderous twinkle in his eye.

"If it's not, it soon will be."

The consul smiled. Caesar would have approved of the swiftness and expediency of the decision - if not the victim of it – Antony mused.

*

His belt used to hang below his waist in the name of style, but now it had become fixed there due to his burgeoning pot-belly, Antony thought to himself. He was beginning to cultivate the figure and lifestyle of a politician rather than a soldier. Sulla, Lucullus, Pompey - all had grown to seed to an extent when they had swapped their general's cloak for the toga of office. Only Caesar had worn both well.

Antony's self-castigation was perhaps prompted due to comparing his physique with that of his lieutenant's, as he invited Enobarbus into his study. Unopened scrolls and unanswered correspondence littered the desk, along with goblets filled with the dregs of various beverages.

"Any other news to report?"

"Cicero is ensconced in his villa in Puteoli. All important correspondence is being handled through Tiro - and the man is as slippery as he is incorruptible," Domitius expressed, privately admiring the former slave who Cicero had freed, educated and employed as his personal secretary.

"The old man can cause us little trouble now. As much as Brutus might still heed his out-dated ideals Cassius is far too proud to be led by our former self-titled saviour of Rome. Soldiers matter now, not scribblers," Antony judged, disdainful of the elder statesman.

"I can devote fewer agents to him if you wish," Domitius replied, secretly believing that Antony might be letting his contempt for Cicero blind him from his influence and potential threat.

"Feel free to do so. What else?"

"I believe that Balbus is starting to court the favour - and whisper into the ears - of Hirtius and Pansa."

Antony here stopped cutting himself a slice of venison from the joint of meat which rested on the table. Having served with Caesar for so long Antony had experienced first-hand the cunning and sway of the Spaniard. As Antony had been Julius' lieutenant on the battlefield, Balbus had been Caesar's principle agent and strategist in his political campaigns. It was even rumoured that Balbus had been the author and facilitator of the triumvirate between Caesar, Pompey and Crassus.

"Do you think it's possible to court and whisper into the ear of Balbus? He was sympathetic to us after the assassination."

"That was when he believed that you would avenge Caesar's death."

"I still might. Can he not be persuaded, or bought off?"

"The wily old Spaniard has riches enough - and Balbus has devoted his life to the art of persuasion, rather than being persuaded."

Antony compressed his lips in either deliberation, or frustration, but then his rugged countenance regained its natural amiability and confidence.

"Well, my friend, we fought on two fronts at Alesia and triumphed. History will just have to repeat itself again," Antony posed, with an assurance which convinced its author more than audience.

*

The Campus Martius began to crackle with the numerous camp fires which sprouted up in the gelid darkness. A crescent moon shone but half-heartedly over the city, as if sympathising with the mournful mood of the soldiers who had so recently lost their general. Talk and rumour were rife - and varied. Some whispered that they would not serve their Master of Horse. Some would serve under Antony, but only if he avenged Caesar's death. Yet most soldiers ironically craved peace over all else, having experienced the bloodshed and privations of the previous civil war.

Domitius Enobarbus made his way through the rows of tents. Ribald jokes (one involving an Egyptian eunuch and a boar's tusk), drinking songs and hushed discussions swirled about in the air like the smoke around his ears, but he appeared oblivious to it all.

Enobarbus was from patrician stock, but his father - through bad investments and living beyond his means - had squandered away most of the family's estate. Refusing to allow his son to become a soldier - both because of his wife's protestations and the shame that would befall the family name to have a son toil in such a profession - Enobarbus joined the staff of a legate and commenced to go on campaign that way. The educated and diligent Enobarbus was proficient in his duties as secretary to the legate, to the point where he performed most of the legate's responsibilities himself. But he always aspired to be a soldier, rather than administer to them. After his father's death the young man proceeded to gain a commission to realise his ambition.

Enobarbus originally encountered Antony during his posting as a junior officer in Syria. He admired the courageous and charismatic Roman from afar however, as he observed Antony being the first man to scale the fortifications of an enemy town. Though outnumbered, he outfought the defenders upon the ramparts and led the army to victory.

He continued to idolise the famous son of Rome, desiring to join Antony's feted company of cavalry and emulate his gallantry. Enobarbus admired Antony for being a great tactician and popular leader, as well as esteeming him for his personal bravery. A young and idealistic Enobarbus would write back home positing how Antony was a "man of honour", humane to the soldiers under his command and gracious in victory. After defeating Archelaus, an Egyptian Prince, Antony sought out his body and arranged a funeral with full royal honours.

People often criticised Caesar's lieutenant for his vices and profligacy but his debts were due to his generosity, Enobarbus could argue. He smiled, relieving the tension in his habitually serious-looking countenance, as he recalled the incident with the steward. Antony had ordered that a sum of two hundred and fifty thousand drachmas, or a decies, be presented to a centurion to accompany his promotion. His steward was astonished at his master's liberality, believing that Antony was underestimating the size of the gift. In order to subtly inform his master of the extent of the sum the steward decided to place the amount upon the table before him. Aware of the steward's ploy, Antony decided to further shock his servant and reward his centurion. "I thought a decies amounted to more than that. This is just a trifle: you had better double it!"

Antony was generous with his time and energy though, as well as with his money. He often exercised with his men or sat with them at the mess table, happily sharing a joke or amphora of wine with them. So too the arch-seducer would often play Cupid, rather than Dionysus, and devote himself to the affairs of his friends. Enobarbus had lost his own virginity thanks to the advice and encouragement of his commanding officer.

Yet more than the delights of love Enobarbus was conscious of being indebted to Antony for his very life. Alesia. Enobarbus and his cohort were fighting on the outer rim of the ramparts, repelling the relief force which had arrived to support Vercingetorix's besieged army. The fighting was as ferocious as it was unrelenting. An arrow pierced Enobarbus' left shoulder, knocking him to the ground. Before he could recover a giant, flame-haired Gaul stood over him, his axe strewn with Roman gore. His blood-curdling scream, emitted as he raised the terrifying weapon above his head in preparation to bury it into the Roman, was suddenly drowned out by the tamp of a cavalry horse. At full gallop Antony propelled himself off his grey gelding and floored Enobarbus' assailant. With little use or desire to emit a similar barbaric howl, Antony first plunged his cavalry sword into his enemy's stomach - and then, with swiftness matching ruthlessness, chopped off his head with a single blow. The timely arrival of Antony proved not to just save Enobarbus' life but it inspired the legionaries fighting around him as well as diminishing the ardour of any Gaul who witnessed the fall of their formerly head-strong champion.

With the arrowhead still lodged in his shoulder Enobarbus fought on that day. Antony noted the young man's bravery and transferred him onto his staff. Such was the industry of his new officer, in military and clerical matters alike, that Antony suppressed the urge to praise the youth in Caesar's presence, for fear that his general might poach him for his own staff. Enobarbus eventually became aware of this situation and was content to remain in Antony's employment and subdue any ambitious urge he might have in relation to being promoted to Caesar's inner circle. He owed a debt of gratitude and loyalty towards Antony. Moreover Enobarbus rightly reasoned that both he and Caesar's lieutenant had time on their side and would be well placed when someone would succeed their general.

As much as Enobarbus admired Antony - and as deep as the bonds of friendship reached - Enobarbus wasn't so partisan as to be blind to the consul's faults. Pleasure too often took precedent over duty, he was too easily swayed by women and he could be at the very least lazy - and at worst inept - when it came to the details and demands of political office.

Yet in the same way that the loyal lieutenant could forgive Antony's faults in light of his virtues, so too he now buried his feelings of unease in the name of duty - in regards to Caesar's nephew. Enobarbus had not known Caesar personally, but he had admired his courage and progressive reforms in relation to Rome and its army. Enobarbus had served Caesar well, serving under Antony, towards the end of his campaign in Gaul and throughout the civil war. It seemed now strange at best - at worst dishonourable - that he should be ordering the murder of Caesar's innocent nephew and lawful heir.

Four legs of salted pork glowed and turned above the campfire. Gravius - and his chosen men - always ate well. Enshrouded in semi-darkness Enobarbus intruded upon half a dozen or so legionaries who sat with their famous, or infamous, centurion. With a brief and subtle nod of his head he instructed Gravius to dismiss his men.

"Leave us," the officer, who was awarded his rank despite not being able to read, barked. Although their stomachs grumbled at the order the legionaries protested not and vacated the campfire.

Gravius would boast that he was the first man into battle, the first man over the wall and the first man into bed. He joked that he had raped more women than Zeus and Apollo combined. Both his boasts and jokes though were often true. Enobarbus had encountered soldiers before who enjoyed fighting (partly because it was the only thing that they felt that they were any good at in life) but Gravius seemed to take things one step further - he seemed to enjoy killing, to the point of it being an addiction. Gravius and his cohort of chosen men were often frowned upon by other soldiers in the camp, yet at heart they recognised their value. They were the first to volunteer to stand in the shield wall, they fought with a savagery that had even made the barbarian Britons turn and run - and Gravius and his cohort never needed to be ordered twice in regards to executing prisoners or hostages, women and children included. War breeds necessary evils.

Gravius, ignoring the formalities of address and rank, remained seated upon his makeshift throne as Enobarbus stood before him. His visage had won more fights than fair hearts Enobarbus judged, albeit he kept the judgement to himself. His powerful arms and torso were tattooed with various scars, collected from all four corners of Rome's dominions. Enobarbus liked to think that he was afeared of no man, but could Gravius be described as human? Those that did not regard him as a wild animal superstitiously believed him to be the son of Mars, sent by the gods to wreak vengeance on Rome's enemies. The only thing that could kill Gravius was Gravius, the legion judged.

"I hope your purse is fuller than this moon, should you want something," the Sicilian centurion expressed, his voice as rough as gravel, smugly grinning to himself at Antony having to lower himself and employ his cohort for more mercenary work. Yet Gravius had no qualms about getting his hands dirty in order for the consul to keep his clean.

"You'll be well paid, double the going rate."

Gravius grunted with satisfaction, or indifference. In truth one man's life, or death rather, was worth as much as another's, he had long since considered.

"Why so much?" the centurion replied, curious rather than suspicious.

"There will be twice the number of people to kill."

Gravius smirked, salivating as much at the prospect of the fight as he was at the fatty joints of pork spitting and roasting before his psychotic aspect.

Enobarbus went on to list some of the requirements of the mission. The centurion would need to enlist at least thirty of his most trusted and capable men for the job. They would also need to be ready to march in the next day or so - and equip themselves with non-military issue weapons and clothing.

"Where are we heading?" Gravius finally asked, after emptying his throat of phlegm - his eyes, one jaundiced, one bloodshot, unnaturally glinting in the camp fire.

"Puteoli," Enobarbus replied, repulsed by the nefarious soldier - but at the same time reassured that he had the right man for the job. As mixed as his feelings might be towards the fact, Enobarbus knew that Caesar's nephew was now as good as dead.

20

The night sky appeared encrusted with diamonds and the ruby red lights of Brundisium's harbour pulsed in the distance. After spying the port on the horizon Oppius instructed the captain of the vessel to alter course. So as not to advertise their arrival on the mainland they would make their landing along the coast, at a quiet beach that he knew of near Lupiae. Money - and the implied threat of repercussions should they speak of their passengers - purchased the silence of the captain and crew.

The crossing had passed without incident, save for the minor storm as evening descended. In a rare fit of superstition, recalling the nightmarish squall during his voyage to Spain, Octavius retreated below deck. He locked himself in his cabin and prayed to Neptune and Venus to spare the ship.

With the merchant vessel unable to venture any closer, for fear of encountering shallow waters, the party clambered into the ship's two lifeboats and rowed to shore. The foaming water slurped as the crafts kissed the shingled beach. Roscius was the first to leap out of one of the boats, relieved to regain the familiarity of land. The sturdy legionary even stamped his feet, in reassurance or even happiness, at the sensation.

Octavius pulled his cloak around him in the blustering wind. His eyes shone in the moonlight and scanned the cliff-top for witnesses to the suspicious party coming ashore.

Oppius, Agrippa, Casca and Cleanthes immediately commenced unloading their baggage and provisions. Weapons were distributed and worn, but concealed. Oppius reminded the group that they should now consider themselves wine merchants - and act accordingly. Suspecting that Brundisium would be populated by various agents - and perhaps even assassins - Oppius would call upon an ex-legionary comrade, who had once served in his cohort, to provide shelter for the evening.

Come the morning, Roscius and Cleanthes would journey into town and purchase a couple of horses and a wagon, as well as a few casks of wine, to authenticate their disguise. By tomorrow afternoon they would safely and anonymously be on their way to Puteoli, where they would call on Balbus and plan their next move.

21

Puteoli.

The buttery rays of the sun spread themselves over the villa and well attended gardens. Mayflowers speckled and scented the air. Wood-finches hopped from branch to branch on the various birch and fruit trees which seemed to be unfolding their limbs in the increasingly vernal climate.

Yet, rather than mining pleasure from the scene outside his window, Marcus Tullius Cicero sat with his head in his hands at his rosewood desk. His fingers stained with ink, his skin sallow with age, he read over his latest letter to his life-long confidante.

Dear Atticus,

What we want is a leader, someone to lend moral weight. Some of the people might well suggest me, but I am too old. I can mentor, but not lead. My agents have reported on potential support for Sextus Pompey. He is starting to make a name for himself, aside from the one he inherited. But we need an army of men, rather than ships, to reinstate the Republic. And

I'd rather not swap a tyrant for a pirate.

No, our energies and capital must be directed towards Brutus. He will venture to Greece, raising both funds and an army (Cassius will do the same elsewhere). I fear that Antony's pockets are deeper and his forces greater however. Again, we have too easily surrendered Rome to the enemy. History teaches us that history repeats itself.

Civil war is certain, as sure as the changing season. I suspect that the first blood will be spilled in Gaul. Decimus will not hand over his troops or governance to Antony, out of pride as much as principle. I am confident that I can persuade Hirtius and Pansa, once they have obtained office, to side with the Senate over Antony. The consuls-elect have little love for Antony. But will our combined forces be strong enough? I'm hoping that Gaul will prove to be the beginning and the end of the bloodshed. But I fear that the impending conflict will touch Puteoli, Greece and edge of the map soon enough. When Rome sneezes, the world gets a cold.

If things stay the way they seem to be now, I find no joy in the Ides of March...

Marcus Phillipus visited yesterday, bringing news that I should expect a second visitor in the near future. The boy has requested to see me. I have of course assented to his request (as tempting as it was to take revenge on Julius through his heir, for how many times did Caesar refuse an audience with Cicero, or childishly keep me waiting?).

Phillipus speaks well of the boy - and not just because, apparently, the boy speaks well of me.

I am still undecided as to how I should play things in relation to Octavius. At present I have more questions than answers. What are his intentions? Will he join, or oppose, Antony? How much can we direct him? How much has Balbus dug his claws into the fresh meat?

... But all this talk of impending civil war has brought on a headache, as well as heartache. Tell me more of the personal, rather than political. How is Caecilia? Please pass on my gratitude for the recipes. You should be justly proud of her. Should she become as admirable a wife as she is a daughter then I envy her prospective husband. She reminds me a little of Tullia, which is both a curse and a blessing. But I weep for Rome now, rather than my daughter.

*

Cicero averted his attention from the correspondence to the door as it creaked open. His secretary entered, carrying a bowl of porridge, sweetened by a mixture of honey and berries. His complexion was dark, but his expression was bright with intelligence and warmth. Tiro had first entered into service for the famed advocate in his late teens. Cicero, recognising and rewarding the youth's virtues, decided to educate - and then free - his slave. Upon gaining his freedom though Tiro devoted himself even more to his former master, acting as his secretary and political agent. Indeed, next to Cicero himself, no one loved or admired the statesman more that the perpetually boyish-looking secretary.

"Is that a grey hair, Tiro?" Cicero exclaimed in mock horror as Tiro placed the bowl of steaming porridge upon his desk.

"I keep telling myself that it's a trick of the light, even at night, but I believe it is." The philosophical secretary had adopted his master's dry sense of humour, as well as his politics, over the years.

"I'm tempted to add your grey hair to the list of crimes I'm compiling, to be read out in the Senate when the time is right, that Mark Antony is responsible for."

As well as some light lunch for the dyspeptic statesman, prepared according to Caecilia Atticus' recipe, Tiro placed a pile of letters on the desk for the senator's attention.

"Thank you, Tiro. What have our informants got to say for themselves, aside from that of wanting more money for their information?"

"Antony has bought off his co-consul. Although we may not strictly define Dolabella as Antony's ally, he will not now provide any source of opposition towards Antony's legislation and ambitions."

"It's now mathematically impossible for me to think any less of that man," Cicero flatly exclaimed, his face uniquely screwed up in derision. Tiro knew that the mere mention of Dolabella, Tullia's dissipated husband, would stir up unhappiness in his master's heart - but the secretary felt duty bound to report the situation.

"Balbus has been composing various proclamations, written in Octavius' name, and posting them up for the legions to see. I believe however that the boy has also been writing his own propaganda. Either he is conceited, or talented. The young Caesar is vowing vengeance for his father's murder - and rewards for loyalty. From all accounts he has the sympathy and support of Caesar's legions in Apollonia."

"But will they follow him into battle?" Cicero asked, absorbing the information whilst blowing upon his porridge.

"That depends on how much he will, or can, pay them. We should not forget though that every legionary who serves Octavius serves not Antony."

"We will then allow the boy to have his toy soldiers. Meddle not in his recruitment drive. Indeed I might even encourage the youth to recruit an army, especially if we can in turn recruit him to our cause."

"I'll be curious to know what you think of him after his visit. I wonder what Caesar saw in the youth, to name him as his heir?"

"Hopefully it wasn't himself," the statesman replied, wincing slightly at the thought rather than at the taste of his lunch.

22

A bedraggled line of wagons, traders, immigrants and would-be labourers snaked into the sea-port town of Tarentum. Oppius gave a small bribe to the official at the gate of the walled city and the wine merchants were duly allowed in without any fuss. From Lupiae they had first travelled to Rudiae - and then onto Uria. The Appian Way now brought them to the bustling port of Tarentum. The air reeked of garum, the ubiquitous food stuff of Rome and her dominions. Made from sardines, spiced in all manner of ways, the fish paste lubricated trade in the Mediterranean as much as wine and olive oil. Octavius turned his nose up at the pungent stench, his eyes almost watering, whilst Roscius and Casca breathed in the moreish aroma as if it were a fine bouquet.

The unassuming party of merchants made their way to the nearest tavern, heavy-legged and empty-stomached. Their journey had been incident free, until now. Whilst Oppius and Roscius ventured inside to inquire about lodgings for the night, the rest of the group were suddenly approached by a dozen men, as dubious in character as they were in appearance. The stale smell of wine on their breath even overpowered that of the garum. The self-appointed leader of the band of men addressed Cleanthes.

"You're new to Tarentum my friend, no?"

"Yes, although such is the hospitable atmosphere I'll definitely be visiting again," the tutor answered. Casca rolled his eyes in exasperation at the tutor's ability to misjudge his audience with his sarcasm.

"So you don't know about the toll charge?"

"I am sure that I don't own the monopoly on ignorance in this place, but no."

The rest of the men, out of work dockers, formed a circle around the outnumbered wine merchants. Casca snorted, either in derision or resignation at the prospective brawl. Agrippa's left leg began to switch, either in nervousness or excitement. Octavius edged behind the wagon, forming the intention to race inside of the tavern and hide should a fight break out.

"Are you trying to be funny?"

"Judging from the lack of laughter, I fear I'm failing rather than trying," Cleanthes replied, giving off the appearance of being amused, rather than intimidated, by the careerist thug.

"You'll be laughing on the other side of your face in a minute." Spittle accompanied the reply. Just as much as the money, or amphora of wine, that he intended to extort out of the merchant, the swarthy ringleader wanted now to teach the wiseacre a lesson in respect.

"No, we'll rather be laughing behind your back. Now fuck off before I, rather than the wine, give you a sore head," Oppius commanded upon coming out of the tavern. He had assessed the situation, as well as the odds, immediately. The centurion also subtly and briefly made a fist to indicate to Roscius and Casca that they should refrain from using their swords. Oppius knew that the authorities could turn their backs on a brawl, but they would not turn a blind eye to murder.

Just as the swarthy docker grimaced and his fingers began to move for the chisel tucked into the back of his belt Oppius' fist slammed into his face, crunching upon the cartilage of his nose. Once floored the centurion methodically stamped on his groin and then his head, rendering his opponent unconscious.

Roscius roared as he quickly grabbed an amphora of wine from the wagon and launched it at two oncoming assailants. The roar transformed itself into more of a laugh as the large porcelain missile found its target. "Two birds with one stone," he would go on to boast later that evening to Casca.

A pock-marked youth cut off Octavius' escape route into the tavern and, for a second or so, time stood still as the two adolescents sized each other up. Fear rather than confidence egressed from Octavius however - and the wiry docker sneered at the wine merchant, anticipating victory. He would have done better to anticipate the punch from Agrippa which quite literally wiped the smile off his face. Marcus followed up the blow with two shots to the body, winding his opponent, before an uppercut left the teenage thug slumped upon the ground at the entrance to the inn.

A girlish scream sliced the air - and was abruptly silenced - as Casca violently grabbed a docker by the hair. He then yanked his head back and - at full-speed - punched the whimpering bully in the throat.

The more cowardly, or wiser, of the would-be extortionists here decided that they would like to live to fight another day - abandoning their drinking companions and scampering off down the street. Some dragged themselves away, whilst others groaned on the cobble stones around them.

Agrippa flexed his sore hand. Cleanthes gently shook his head, either in amusement or disapproval. Roscius and Casca grinned to each other, having visibly enjoyed the brawl. Octavius masked his feelings of shame and inadequacy. Oppius scowled, thinking that they had drawn attention to themselves. He would not now get the chance to taste Tarentum's wine - or women. If he smelled fish tonight, it would be because of the garum he sourly joked.

The sun blazed down over the wagon containing the party and several casks of wine - or vinegar as Casca called, or rather condemned, it. Tarentum was behind then, the outskirts of Puteoli before them. The languid heat inspired torpor in the group but Casca finally spoke up and addressed his comrades.

"This silence is deafening. Cleanthes, Gaius tells me that you used to be a poet. Want to keep us awake, or send us to sleep? Do you remember any of your verses?"

"Poems are like old lovers Tiro, some you remember – those with good lines and that were attractive enough to make your friends jealous. But most one remembers to forget," the tutor replied, smiling and squinting in the afternoon sun.

"Why don't you let one of your old lovers come back to haunt you, or us even, now? As long as you don't bore the horses to sleep you can't do any harm," Agrippa asserted whilst using a sharpening stone upon the edge of his gladius.

"There is a poet in all of us so I'd be happy to let others have the floor, but as I've read enough philosophy to know never to argue with someone who is holding a sword, I'll oblige you. Apologies if my memory proves as rusty as my performance but this humble offering is called *Ode to Indifference*.

> *"Our summer fruit, massaging ray;*
> *Warmth can Indifference display,*
> *For Carefree's platitudes*
> *A Platonic attitude.*
> *He shrugs outside Revenge's fray.*
>
> *Too frothy is the blood at birth,*
> *Age its own carelessness unearths.*
> *Shine your light upon me*
> *Passionate Apathy*
> *In youth's hollows; now show your worth.*
>
> *Oh that I may drink from your cup*
> *When down desired pick me up.*
> *Of Sisyphus they laugh*
> *And Tantalus they starve*
> *But let us from thy harvest sup,*

Those who the gods have played jokes on,
Those fathers who their sons poison
But do not lend the cure.
Let me this night procure
The punch line, antidote; un-con

Life by not falling for its bait
Like an animal that can't wait
To fall into the pit.
Oh Indifference fit
Into my soul, despair placate."

The party clapped and Cleanthes performed a mock bow.

"How was the work received?" Agrippa enquired.

"Ironically, indifferently," was the reply.

"There was a time when poetry would flow out of Caesar," Oppius pensively exclaimed, "a conceit or line would come to him and Balbus would find himself having to transcribe odes and epigrams beneath official legislation. Meetings would be topped or tailed with Caesar and Marcus Brutus trading quotes from Homer. But I look forward now to trading blows with Brutus - and skewering the bastard."

Octavius barely heard Cleanthes or Oppius though as he wistfully surveyed the fertile lines of the landscape and remembered Briseis - and his own attempts at poetry in her honour. He pictured lying next to her in bed, their sweat-glazed limbs entwined. He nuzzled her, their fingers laced together. He whispered the words, like kisses, in her ears,

> *"I want to wake up*
> *To the dream of you.*
> *Your head upon my chest*
> *As the sun pours through*
>
> *Our room, warm with love –*
> *Sweet from words expressed.*
> *Your eyes alight with fun*
> *And the thrill of my caress."*

But even before the news of Caesar's death had annulled Octavius of his desire and any commitment he felt he might own towards the serving girl, Octavius had become philosophical, or cynical, in regards to the relationship. Cleanthes was right; it was lust rather than love. He would now be married to his duty, cause. Women would be but a welcome distraction, to be enjoyed like a fine wine or good play. Romantic love was chimerical. Agrippa and Cleanthes were worth a thousand serving girls.

> *"It was worth getting up in the morning*
> *If the day held her mien -*
> *I would wake to a dream.*
> *Now, when I am not asleep, I'm yawning.*
>
> *She aroused me and gave my life a point.*

The clouds would blow away
Each time her hips would sway.
We belonged, like a ball and socket joint.

But what when her peaks have been mounted, pray
What when the zenith's seen?
We wake up to the dream;
'Tis better to chase than to seize the day."

"How far till we get to the villa?" Agrippa asked, snapping Octavius out of his reverie.

"You'll probably routinely ask that question another two times before we arrive, if that's any indicator. We'll get there when we get there," Oppius replied.

"I just hope that Balbus has been visited by some genuine wine merchants of late. The piss we're drinking is as sour as an aged drab's —"

"Thank you Tiro, for proving my point," Cleanthes chipped in, cutting off the sentence.

"Uh?" the veteran responded, scrunching up his face in slight bewilderment.

"There is indeed a poet in every one of us."

The six friends lazily smirked - and one of the horses whinnied - in the glistering light as the wagon crossed into the verdant pasture of Puteoli, the first step of their long journey almost over.

23

The varnish of his tan concealed the grain of his years. Various papers littered a large cedar wood desk, inlaid with tortoiseshell. Four ornate bronze lions at the feet of the desk surveyed all. Cornelius Balbus composed letter after letter to loyal and wavering Caesarians (clients, centurions, senators, merchants). At present Balbus was drafting a letter to a particularly god-fearing and superstitious client.

"...*Nature abhorred the unnatural act. After the Ides lightening struck the dockyards. Winds moaned through the capital for days, uprooting trees and houses alike. Dogs could be heard howling throughout the night outside the house of the Pontifex Maximus ... There is still a Caesarian cause. There is still a Caesar...*"

Balbus carried on writing, propaganda oozing from his pen like honey from a hive, but his thoughts also turned to this new Caesar again. The secretary recalled Julius' comments about the boy.

"He is intelligent without being conceited, confident without being arrogant. He's aware that the gods gave him two ears and one mouth - and knows to use the former twice as much as the latter ... he sees how things are and how they should be - and I warrant he'll learn how to bridge the distances between those two peaks ... his tutors speak well of him. It's clear he is more of a Cicero than Scipio but ultimately he should become a statesman, not general. I do not want Octavius to spend his life in the saddle on campaign, replicating the glory-hunting of his great-uncle ... he has but asked one favour of Caesar - and that was to intercede on his friend's behalf to release this Marcus Agrippa's brother ... Should anything happen to me Cornelius, I want you to act as Octavius' secretary - and serve him as loyally and adroitly as you have me old friend."

"You are going to announce him as your heir?"

"Not publicly. But I have altered my will accordingly."

"And your son by Cleopatra?"

"He will be provided for, but his mother is too much like his father to be wholly trusted. She can be Queen of Egypt for as long as her immortality lasts, but she'll not get her claws into Rome."

"And what of Brutus? You once imagined that he would take your place as the First Man of Rome."

"I love Marcus as if he were my own. But he longs for a past that never existed in the first place. I want the future to eclipse the past, not be hampered by it. Octavius is the future."

"Should dame fortune cheat on her favourite paramour - and something happens to Caesar - I promise to serve him faithfully, Julius."

"Thank you, Cornelius. And I will make good on my promise

to make you Rome's first foreign-born consul old friend. It'll be worth it just to see the look upon the faces of the old men when the new man is announced."

An attendant knocked and then entered the secretary's study.

"Master, Caesar is here."

For a sublime moment or two Cornelius believed that his old master had returned - after all, hadn't Balbus propagated the idea of Julius' divinity himself in various proclamations? But reason duly took hold.

"Time to embrace the future," the politic secretary remarked to himself, and went out to greet his guests.

*

"Caesar."

Octavius had grown attuned to flattery over the years but still his new name did not chime quite right. The secretary descended the steps of his villa with outstretched arms. Octavius removed his sun hat and courteously bowed to his host.

"Oppius, Roscius. I wish the circumstances were different but it is good to see you both again, nevertheless. Tiro, I have arranged to have you quartered near the wine cellar. You must be Cleanthes? Atticus speaks highly of you. My library is open to you."

"I hope that doesn't preclude me from sharing the wine cellar with Casca, though."

"No, indeed. Well said. And you must be Marcus Agrippa?

Oppius tells me you handle both your drink and a bow well."

"But not at the same time, unfortunately."

Balbus remarked how his house was open to all his guests as an army of servants appeared from nowhere and attended to the party's belongings. Cleanthes would later remark to Agrippa whether the secretary employed a servant whose sole task it was to keep his tongue oiled, such were the compliments that dripped from it.

"We have much to discuss my friends, but such things will wait till morning. Tonight you should rest, unless you would like the wine cellar opened up to you this evening, Tiro? The serving girls may well open up to you too, if you ask nicely, Roscius. Caesar, both your mother and step-father are staying with me. Would you like me to send for them?"

"Thank you Cornelius, for everything," Octavius replied, expressing gratitude not just for the hospitality.

*

The two loyal Caesarians reclined over couches around the fire in Balbus' triclinium. Trophies and curiosities from the four corners of the known world decorated the walls. A sculpture of Odysseus, which for once Atticus was the under bidder on, stood imperiously in the centre of the chamber. A statue of Caesar (which Atticus would have happily been the under bidder on) next to the mantle also naturally attracted one's attention.

"So, Lucius, what do you think of the boy?"

"He growing up and growing on me. But that still may not be enough for what lies ahead."

"I understand that you encouraged him to lead the Apollonian legions to Rome after Julius' murder. Nothing good could have come from that," Balbus remarked, reprovingly.

"I know. I was angry. I just wanted vengeance," Oppius replied, feeling added guilt in that he had also persuaded Agrippa to encourage Octavius to lead the legions to Rome.

"The boy felt the same I warrant, but he did not allow his passions to cloud his judgement. Also, I have spoken to Marcus Phillipus. He implored Gaius not to take the name of Caesar and claim his inheritance. Yet the boy has proved brave and ambitious. So we have intelligence, courage and ambition. If Gaius has inherited some of Julius' blind luck then we may well win back Rome."

*

"We defy augury," Octavius replied after hearing how his mother had consulted a soothsayer as to her son's future. He predicted dark times.

"Would you not be counselled by your mother, or your step-father, instead of a soothsayer then?" Marcus Phillipus asked.

Balbus had provided the family with the guest property on his estate. Gaius, Atia and Marcus Phillipus greeted each other with warmth and tears. They sat down to eat as if it were dinner time back in Apollonia. But once the meal was finished and Balbus' attendants had disappeared, Marcus Phillipus addressed Octavius' fate.

"Your counsel is always welcome, as long as you are aware that I will keep my own counsel too. I love you both dearly but the times call for your son to become a man. I am aware that Antony will view me as a threat for claiming my inheritance. I am aware that the libertores will view me with suspicion, at best. The Republicans in the Senate will look upon the new Caesar with contempt, or be dismissive of me. The Caesarians may be harder to win over than anyone else. Yet I am spurred on by Caesar's faith in me. You did not question his judgement when he was alive, not once. Yet you question his judgement now?" Octavius exclaimed, staring at his parents with a certain amount of disappointment and chastisement.

"We cannot protect you when you go to Rome," Marcus Phillipus warned.

"When I go to Rome, it should be others who should look to be protected," Octavius calmly replied, the long shadow caused by Caesar's statue darkened the youth's already brooding looks.

"Mark Antony will not give up your inheritance easily."

"I know, but in defying my wishes he will also be defying the wishes of Caesar, which will lose him support with the Caesarians."

Marcus Phillipus smiled, admiring Octavius' politic philosophy. Like Julius, he had considered everything. Like Julius, he would not alter his course once his mind was set.

"At least promise me that you will meet with Cicero before you venture to Rome."

"I give you my word," Octavius solemnly replied.

"Then I will give you my support."

Atia was now as resigned as her husband from dissuading Octavius from his course. Tears welled in her eyes again.

"You will always be my sweet-natured boy with his head in a book, who sometimes needs his mother to nurse him in my eyes."

"I just hope that I can still sometimes see me as such," Octavius uttered as he got up, clasped his mother by the hand and sweetly kissed her on the forehead.

"I love you so much."

"I'm pleased to see that you have as great taste in sons as you do dresses, mother," Octavius replied, eyes glistening too.

Atia let out a laugh-cum-sob and the family continued to enjoy their evening together.

24

A couple of braziers flanked Marcus Brutus, flames tasting the salty air. He had asked for his desk to be brought out onto the balcony of his coastal villa. The poetic vista consoled him not, though. He dismissed his attendants, desiring solitude. Porcia was asleep. The russet of dusk had bled into the sable evening. Brutus tilted his head back to drain the last of the undiluted wine and as he did so he caught sight of the Northern Star. Julius had once described himself as being as constant as the Northern Star. Perhaps the boast was closer to the truth than a conceit the praetor mused, for without Caesar to guide it Rome was a rudderless ship - in a storm. The Senate steered it not, fractured and scared as it was. The people were divided, too. Some were distrustful of the Senate. Some recognised the growing tyranny of Antony. The legions marched not under one standard. Was the choice a civil war or Antony ruling by the sword? Or how long would it be before the smell of fear and the tremors of division were felt in Gaul - and an heir to Vercingetorix attacked? Have I, in murdering Caesar, brought about that which I strove to prevent? - Tyranny and the downfall of Rome. Did I spare the wrong consul?

Brutus buried his head in his hands, masking a pained expression. He finally picked up his stylus, which seemed to weigh as heavy as a dagger, and commenced to draft a letter to his ally and mentor.

Dear Cicero,

You wisely set down in On the Nature of the Gods that, "If anyone ever tried to improve anything in the natural world, he would either make it worse or else attempt the impossible." Perhaps the same is true for the political world. We either underestimated Julius' auctoritas or overestimated our own. The ghost of Caesar still haunts Rome, whilst I am in exile. How long before Antony usurps enough power to decree me an outlaw? I should now be presiding over legislation in the capital - instead I am bound for Macedonia, to preside over grain storage …

… What option do I have but to exit the stage for now? But I am yours to direct. This race is but half run - and as Julius once argued it is where one is positioned at the end of the course that matters. Both Cassius and I will glean support and funds to build an army. Antony is not Caesar. He neither possesses Julius' abilities, or fortune. The "feckless boy", as Pompey rightly judged him, will fail - fall. Despite my protestations above know my friend that I am still Brutus and my commitment to rid Rome of tyranny remains as stolid. I am as constant as the Northern Star.

Your friend and student,
Marcus Brutus.

Brutus put down his stylus and pinched the bridge of his nose. He was unsure whether the wine was causing his headache, or if by partaking of some more he would remedy it. He read over the letter again, ruminating upon whether to tell Cicero how the ghost of Caesar was also haunting his dreams.

*

The encampment was just outside Atina, buried in the woods. A thick canopy of trees blocked out a majestic night sky. Lentil soup and a side of honey-glazed venison sat over a crackling fire. Gravius - and a select band of men from his cohort - were now devoid of any possessions marking them out as legionaries. The centurion downed another measure of sour acetum - thinking that he would be able to afford a fine vintage after this job was complete. Most of his men were now sleeping off their own measures of wine, but Gravius was still awake, holding court around the fire with his lieutenants.

"It was shortly after Alesia. We were on patrol and discovered this Gaulish deserter in a cave. After spending ten minutes with Scylla and Charybdis (Gravius here proudly held up his two scarred fists) I proposed some sport with the surrender monkey. We found a length of rope and a dice. He was told that if he threw a one, two, three, four or a five we would hang him. His eyes near popped out of his head as if he had already been hung upon hearing this. But there was also this one shred of hope lighting his expression as he asked, 'What about if I throw a six?', 'Well, if that happens' I said, whilst putting a reassuring arm around his shoulder, 'you get to throw again.'"

The men cackled in unison with the fire.

"But to business. The plan will be to march to Venatrum. Our quarry is currently cooped up in Puteoli. I will send a scouting party along the Appian Way. Our contractor has also placed some agents close to the estate where the boy is staying. Either way we shall be provided with intelligence of the party's position in advance. I know of a perfect spot for an ambush between Venatrum and Allifae. There are to be no survivors."

"The poor bastard won't know what's hit him," one of the lieutenants remarked, shaking his head in sadness but grinning nevertheless.

"I'll know what has hit him. My axe. But let the gods bless the poor bastard all the same - as he's about to make us all rich bastards," Gravius declared.

Again the band of brothers laughed as Gravius sniffed and spat out the phlegm caught in his throat. No one complained as the green missile landed limpet-like upon the venison, missing its intended target of the fire.

*

Marcus Agrippa yawned and gazed at his bed with a look of desire as if the serving girl from earlier was lying across it - but he continued with the letter to his friend.

Dear Rufus,

The night has been long so you will forgive me if this letter is short. We have arrived safely at Balbus' estate. You'd like it here. There are more staff than dishes on the menu, just about - and the staff are dishes in themselves. I caught the eye of a serving girl tonight. I just hope that's all I caught off her.

You ask what Gaius' plans are? I'm not sure if he even knows them. We are like an army marching to battle, not knowing the strength of our enemy. Or enemies. It is a shame that your father would not allow you to join our party. Employ all your arts as a young advocate to change his mind...

... I was talking to Oppius and one could almost reduce it down to mathematics - which side will have the most money to purchase the most legions. At present no one contingent - whether it be ours, Antony's or the Senate's - has the necessary force to defeat the other two... Lucius remarked that our greatest strength at present could be our perceived weakness, for the Senate and Antony are unlikely to collude to see off the threat of an eighteen year old ...

Your tired friend,
Marcus.

25

Citrus sunlight poured down over the emerald garden. The felt lawn was bordered by all manner of ornate flowers. Bowls of grapes, olives, cured meats and sweet pastries were placed on a table, which was housed underneath a tent. Balbus stood to attention and invited his guest to sit.

"Please, let me know if there's anything I can get you."

"This water will suffice, thank you," Octavius replied.

Balbus raised a corner of his mouth in a fleeting smile, recalling how Julius would have the same meagre breakfast. With a nod of his head Balbus instructed his attendants to depart.

"Your great-uncle, or father as we should grow accustomed to calling him, was the most accomplished man I have ever known. If you do right by his name then I will do right by you Gaius."

"I have no intention of seeing his name, or accomplishments, dishonoured Cornelius."

"Now, to business. And the business of Rome is business. One of our tasks is to convince people - the merchant and political classes, the mob, and legions - that by investing in Caesar their futures will be more prosperous. We have retained the support of the majority of Caesar's clients - senators who owe their position to Julius, merchants who have profited from his legislation and favours, soldiers who served under his standard. We must persuade these constituencies that they are, by betting on you, betting on the eventual winner."

Octavius listened intently but refrained from comment.

"As soon as you enter the capital as Caesar you will be crossing your own Rubicon. Are you prepared for the consequences? Power can change a man Gaius; turn him into a monster - a serpent feeding upon its own tail. The course of honours is a race that never ends. Even if one becomes the First Man of Rome you'll still be fated to look over your shoulder, worried about who stands behind you - and as such you may take your eyes off where you're going. Knowing such, do you still want to cross the Rubicon?"

"Aut Caesar aur nihil," Octavius calmly replied, gazing out onto the well tended garden.

"What are you prepared to do? What kind of person are you willing to become? Would you slit the throat of your best friend?"

Octavius thought of Agrippa.

"No, but I would slit the throat of the man that asked me to do such a thing," Caesar responded, with a look as steely as a blade.

*

Oppius' arrow thudded into the centre of the target, adding to the tightly grouped bunch. He proceeded to instruct Agrippa.

"Never ask your men to do something you haven't done, or wouldn't do. Fail to prepare, prepare to fail. Do not break a promise over pay. Train hard, so you can fight easy. Promote discipline, but never be cruel for cruelty's sake."

Agrippa nodded his head and then fired his own arrow into the target next to the centurion's. Again the bolt landed outside the inner circle, where but one shot resided. Oppius raised an eyebrow, hoping that Marcus was just having an off session. They all had things on their minds.

"For as long as I can remember I wanted to be a soldier. Yet I have of late thought that I do not want to solely be a soldier for the rest of my life."

"What do you want to be then, Marcus?"

"A general can build an army - but it is usually for the purpose to destroy something."

"Or protect. But your point is taken."

"We, Gaius and I, want to build something else. Something better."

Marcus pulled back his bow and fired off another shot, which again landed outside the inner target.

"And what is it you wish to build?"

"An empire."

"You're certainly aiming high, Marcus. Nearly as high as that last arrow."

"Really? There I was thinking that I was just getting my eye in," Agrippa replied, nodding towards the target and the make-shift face upon it: a lop-sided grin, nose and two eyes, marked out by his arrows.

*

The breeze wafted through the tent. Wood pigeons darted across the pastel blue sky. Balbus was impressed by the speed at which the young Caesar took things in. The clarity and insight with which Octavius expressed himself also reminded the secretary of his former employer.

"Hirtius, our consul-elect and one time secretary to Julius when he was writing his books, passed this way recently. Suffice to say he can replicate Julius' prose style better than his military or political genius."

"Julius once joked to me that he used his stomach more than his head," Octavius replied, recalling the scene of his uncle whispering the comment in his ear.

"Aye, our Hirtius is quite the gourmet, or glutton. One of the arms of the curule chair may have to be removed, just so he can fit on it. It is doubtful whether Hirtius or Pansa will side with Antony, as my agents report that Antony is reluctant to allow them to inherit the consulship. He wishes to remain as dictator, or serve as pro-consul in Gaul - yet Decimus Brutus has a grip on the office there and would rather give up his mother than his legions. Mark Antony has a number of legions loyal to him in Macedonia. But ultimately he is relying upon winning over our Caesarian legions. Partly because he too wishes to win over the Caesarians - and to undermine Antony - Hirtius will not oppose you or your bid to claim your inheritance. And where Hirtius goes

Pansa will follow. And he has recently followed him to Cicero's villa."

"We must divide to conquer," Octavius remarked, surveying the map on the table and political situation.

"Exactly. We must play a long game - and you have time on your side to do so. There are other positives, too. Our campaign is well funded. We have at our disposal the war chest that Julius was intending to take to Parthia. Marcus Phillipus pledged his support this morning too. Our clients are not without means and the will to finance you, for their present support, will buy future favours."

"And what future favour will purchase your present support, Cornelius?" Octavius remarked, in a spirit of candour rather than offence.

"I want you to honour a promise that your uncle made to me before he died."

*

Whilst Oppius, Casca and Roscius went off to drill the men whom Balbus was providing to escort Octavius to Rome, Cleanthes and Agrippa, finished off their lunch.

"I have to confess Cleanthes, I've been impressed by the amount of drink you can handle," Agrippa exclaimed, as the tutor drained another cup.

"The harder I practise, the luckier I get," Cleanthes replied, winking at his companion.

"Why do you drink so much, if you do not mind me asking?"

"I drink to forget, Marcus."

"To forget what?"

"I can't remember. But no more on that. I was speaking to Roscius last night. He seems to think that you could make a great general one day."

"Wine truth I warrant," Agrippa self-effacingly replied, inwardly cheered by the comment however.

"Perhaps. But to be successful in this life Marcus you should, even more than a great general, be a good husband and father. Your devotion to Gaius and Rome are admirable but make sure that they do not become the sum of your existence. Tullia brought Cicero greater consolation to his life than his study of philosophy or becoming consul. And would not Caesar have traded all his victories to have his daughter Julia back? Remember Marcus, to win on the battlefield you have to dominate, but to succeed in your personal life sometimes you have to submit, sacrifice ground."

"And how successful have you been in your personal life?"

"I forget," the tutor replied, burying a wistful smile in his wine cup.

*

Octavius and Balbus continued to plot. The secretary advised that Octavius should cut his hair; he should address the legions with a short martial style, not that of a floppy-haired teenager. He suggested the date, time and even gate that Ocatvius should use as to when to enter Rome. In order to sow the seeds of the new

Caesar's dignitas and authoritas the secretary would employ his agents and clients to arrange rallies, both for civilians and military constituencies, in towns along the way to Rome. The two men worked on the import and wording of various correspondence and pamphlets. There would be a distinct difference between Caesar's public and private mandate towards avenging Caesar's death. As well as schooling his new master in the sport and stratagems of Roman politics, Balbus shared some stories about Caesar.

"Whilst Crassus used to hide himself away in his treasury counting his money, Julius would be in Crassus' bedroom, counting the times he made love to his wife ... Julius once remarked that though Pompey had more hair, he had more brains ... Sometimes Caesar's clemency was sincere, sometimes cynical ... I remember him quoting Thucydides the evening after returning from Spain and the civil war: *The right way to deal with free people is this - not to inflict tremendous punishments on them after they have revolted, but to take tremendous care of them before this point is reached, to prevent them even contemplating the idea of revolt, and, if we have to use force with them, to hold as few of them as possible responsible.* For all of his charm and brilliance Julius, for me, towards the end, was enmeshed in remorse. He was trying to atone for his past by creating a better future."

Twilight's mellow glow suffused the air. The lines across the map were becoming blurred, Cornelius' hand ached from having written so much. The secretary decided to call time on their day's work. As Balbus did so however one of his attendants strode up and handed him a scroll. He opened and surveyed it immediately.

"It seems that Antony has dispatched Lepidus to Spain in order to recruit to his cause the legions posted there. I warrant his mission is to also sound out Sextus Pompey about his support," the politic adviser remarked, his eyebrow arched in intrigue.

"Should we be worried by this news?"

"The news certainly shows that Antony is worried, if he needs to ask his former enemy for help. We can use such desperation and treachery to our advantage. This news also reminds us how we must get you to Rome sooner rather than later. The stage is set for the young Caesar to enter Rome."

"I have one other stop to make beforehand."

"Cicero? You should keep to our timetable," Balbus warned, partly fearful of Octavius being detained too long, but more so he was worried about the seductive influence the former consul could have upon the studious youth.

"I mean to keep to our schedule, but I also must keep my promise to Marcus Phillipus."

"I count Cicero as a friend - but also a political opponent. Julius admired him greatly. He once remarked that the only things which would endure as much as his deeds would be Cicero's words. Critics of Cicero have called him inconsistent and hypocritical over the years but one could argue that he has always remained constant in his stance - to have a foot in more than one camp. I sense that this new crisis has re-invigorated the old man as well. For many a month he just pined away, mourning for his daughter. For that I can forgive him. Tullia was an accomplished young woman, wise in everything aside from her choice of husband and her blind devotion to the wastrel. I dare say Cicero was also in mourning for past glories and influence. Although Julius admired the former consul - he also often ignored him. Be wary of the wily old man though, Gaius. Marcus Tullius spoke in my defence at a trial in Rome many years ago. Such was his eloquence that even I started to believe that I was innocent," Balbus issued with a twinkle in his deep-set eyes. "If he offers to champion you in Rome, remember that his ultimate champion is Brutus."

"I'll duly trust him as much as he trusts us," Octavius remarked and smiled, concealing however how much he was genuinely looking forward to meeting the revered statesman and writer.

*

The wind rustled the leaves of the cypress trees. Crickets murmured in the background, along with chimes of laughter from the serving girls who attended to Roscius and Casca inside the house. Octavius and Agrippa sat on the porch. The air was still stodgy from the smell of the Trojan Pig, pine nuts and marinated vegetables that had been served at dinner. Stars studded the satin cloth of a clear evening sky.

"How was your day?" Agrippa asked.

"Long, but rewarding. Cornelius can be trusted I think," Octavius replied, going on to recount the latest news and strategy that they had mapped out. "And how was your day?"

"Shorter than yours, it seems. It mostly consisted of a long lunch with Cleanthes. But I intend to have a long night. You must join us. I'll let the First Man of Rome have first choice with the staff."

"I'm not sure. It's late."

"You're Caesar, you can alter the calendar if needs be to make time. Besides, if you're to become a politician you need as much practice as possible at screwing people."

Octavius laughed out loud, the first time he had done so since hearing of Caesar's death.

"What would I do without you, Marcus?" Octavius then expressed, fraternally patting his companion on the back and getting up to join the revelry.

"Not as much is the answer," Agrippa replied, good-humouredly.

26

Antony woke but remained in bed. Despite it being mid-afternoon the consul instructed his attendants to keep the curtains closed. The light hurt his eyes. A couple of candelabras, on either side of his king-size bed, illuminated the chamber. The scent of wine and perfume stained the air. His mistress Tertia - a mime and actress - had long since departed to attend rehearsals. Antony glanced at Caesar's red leather boots, which sat beside Caesar's throne in the far corner of the room. He stared forlornly at them, remembering his former general and how his feet were the wrong size for the boots, as he attempted to wear them yester night.

An attendant announced Domitius Enobarbus, a little too loudly for the hung over consul's liking, and showed his lieutenant in.

"Morning Domitius," Antony warmly said, "excuse me if I don't get up. How was your evening?"

"So good that I can barely remember it," Enorbarbus replied, looking not a little hung-over himself, having attended the lavish and late party.

"That's the spirit. You deserved a night off – and a night on Lucillia. I take it that's who you left with?"

"Yes."

"Did she?-"

"Yes.

"With the?-"

"Yes."

"Whilst she?-"

"Yes."

"Say no more. The smile on your face was as wide as her legs I warrant. May the gods bless the daughters of fishmongers. But there was no need for you to be up as early as a fisherman, my friend. Or is there anything urgent to report?"

"Nothing of urgency but I thought you might like to know that Hirtius and Pansa are now on the road to Rome, after staying with Cicero."

"I hope the fat bastard ate the sanctimonious prude out of house and home. Hirtius and Pansa are even more determined to take up their Consulship after talking to the old man I suspect. They can have their consulships so long as I can have their legions. Can they be bought off?" Mark Antony asked, seemingly as equally concerned with removing bits of spiced mutton from between his teeth as he was with politics.

"Even if they could I fear that that Cicero, using Atticus' money, could outbid us. They are pro-Senate, partly because they are consuls-elect and will head the Senate. They have little love for Brutus and Cassius, though. If they side with the Senate too much it will only drive the Caesarians towards us I warrant."

"What's the latest on securing the Caesarian legions? They

served their General well. Is it not natural that they should want to serve under his lieutenant?"

"I'm afraid that their silence is deafening. Balbus and Octavius have been writing to them, too. Some are zealously loyal to Caesar's name - and Octavius has been self-styling himself as Caesar's avenger, as well as heir. Others are swallowing his promises of increased pay and fulfilling Caesar's land grants."

Mark Antony waved his hand dismissively and replied, "Once the boy has been silenced the legions won't be so deaf to our advances. Have you heard from Gravius?"

"I have kept him apprised of Octavius' movements. He has selected his spot where to unleash his ambush. They will make it look like bandits. Lucius Oppius is accompanying the boy, though," Enobarbus answered, with a hint of caution creeping into his tone.

"Lucius is a good man. Perhaps we should have tried to recruit him from the start. As good a soldier as Oppius is he cannot take on Gravius and his cohort alone, though. Even in a one to one fight with Gravius I'd back our man. Gravius never fails in his missions. His mission is to eliminate the boy. Therefore Gravius will not fail in his mission to eliminate the boy. There, is that not one of your beloved syllogisms? Logic dictates that Octavius is as good as dead. Isn't that right?" Mark Antony pronounced – and then yawned.

"Not quite," his friend whispered in reply, unheard.

27

Dear Atticus,

Octavius is here with me. Gaius Julius Caesar Octavian. He has more names than pubic hairs. His hair is cut short, centurion style, but one thankfully senses he is not cut out for military life. His build is slight. He smiles, but not too broadly or toothily. His eyes often narrow in reflection, or steeliness, but his reserve never manifests itself into rudeness — although I'm not sure if his calmness is not ultimately borne from coldness.

His party, including your friend Cleanthes, arrived this afternoon. Balbus has furnished him with an armed escort — large enough to mark him out as a figure of importance but not so extensive as to provoke the idea that the boy means trouble. Marcus Phillipus introduced us. His followers call him Caesar, but Phillipus does not, so neither do I. I greeted Gaius affably enough but then remarked how I couldn't attend to him immediately as I had some work to complete. I didn't wish to instil in the youth that the world revolves around him (a delusion that his great-uncle suffered from). He showed no offence, which I'm not sure if I was pleased with or not.

Lucius Oppius, Marcus Phillipus, Octavius and I had a late supper. Oppius was silent for most of the evening, which speaks volumes. He ate his stuffed quail with satisfaction but he wants to taste blood even more I dare say. Marcus Phillipus sung the praises of both Octavius and yours truly – music for both of our ears. Octavius is respectful and friendly. The youth is engaging in conversation but loves not the sound of his voice over others. We all seemed to be in unspoken agreement not to speak about Caesar or politics. We spoke of literature, history – indeed everything that is of little importance to us of late. Octavius was witty, articulate, charming. He reminds me of a talented actor who has the skill to attune his performance to each individual audience. He reminds me of my younger self – again, I was unsure whether to be pleased about this or not. This conceit resonated all the more when the actor started to deliver my lines – and quote me! Phillipus asked the boy which lesson he most took with him from his reading of philosophy. His reply was thus, "to get on as best we can, with the aid of our own dull wits". Imitation is the sincerest form of flattery – and flattery will get him everywhere.

In short the boy has a sense of style and a sense of humour. I only hope that he has a sense of decency too. He doesn't wholly trust me – and why should he? – but I will attempt to gain his trust. The last Caesar all but destroyed the Senate. Perhaps, through my influence, this new one may help to restore its authority.

We shall have the day together tomorrow. So I will take leave of you now before sleep blunts my thoughts. Sorry for the brevity of this letter my friend. Let me just say though thank you for the recent loan to finance the restoration of the apartment block I rent out. The structure had become so dangerous that even the rats had abandoned it. Your loans to restore the House of the Senate – and in turn banish any rats there – are similarly appreciated. Finally, but not least of all, thank you for the gift of sending

Caecilia to visit. Her company – and culinary skills – have been of great consolation. She was out most of today sketching and did not have the chance to meet our other guests. She has her father's acumen in judging character though and I'll be most interested in what she thinks of Octavius, should there be a chance for them to meet. Is he the heir apparent or heir abhorrent?

I shall write again anon dear friend.
Cicero.

*

Dearest Octavia,

Thank you for your letters - and apologies for my tardy reply. Taking on the world is more time consuming than you might expect. We arrived at Cicero's estate this afternoon. There is a simple elegance to the estate, reflecting the character of our host. He is in his sixties but still handsome enough to turn the heads of fifty year old widows. Probing, humorous eyes gleam beneath a pronounced brow. His complexion is a little sallow but when he is animated in conversation, or smiling at a witticism (often his own), his expression enlivens to shave ten years off his age. In this respect Cicero reminds me of Caesar. His dress and diet are austere - yet, unlike Cato, Cicero doesn't make a song and dance of his simple tastes and stoicism.

I have just come from dinner. The conversation flowed as easily as the wine. Thankfully we spoke not of politics, although Cicero did drop in one or two barbed comments concerning some of his enemies in Rome. As you yourself explained it has become the fashion in Rome for householders to plant mosaics before their front doors, with a simple welcoming message. Cicero joked how the message outside Fulvia's house should be, "Beware of the dog!" He also described how our "Master of the Horse cannot even control his frisky wife".

We also spoke about literature. I complimented him upon his library, to which Cicero sagely replied that: "A home without books is a body without a soul". I helped to make his evening when the discussion turned to philosophy and I quoted our host. He smiled with such a sense of pleasant surprise - and unaffected gratitude - that the moment made my evening too, I warrant.

Although Cicero is clearly conducting a long term love affair with himself he is healthily self-deprecating and eager to listen as well as speak. I tried to be neither cloying nor distant. Although I wished to impress him I didn't wish to try too hard. As the evening closed he took me aside and expressed the following: "I am in my old age Gaius — the crown of life, the play's last act. I have of late mused that what I do from here on in will decide whether my life can be judged a comedy or a tragedy. Yet I now see that it is what we might do from here on in which will decide my fate - and that of Rome."

Only you - and Cleanthes - can know what his words meant to me, Octavia. I have not taken this path from a sense of destiny, but rather from a sense of duty. To do my duty - to bring harmony to the classes - I must become a synthesis of Caesar and Cicero.

My only sorrow was that Julius - and yourself - were not present this evening. I still miss him. The world seems emptier, lesser, without him. I feel like I am conducting a long term and clandestine love affair with my *grief - and the feeling of revenge to which my grief is married.*

I miss your company and consolation, too. But I shall be in Rome by the end of the month. You asked in your letter if I am ready to come to Rome. Should we not rather ask, is Rome ready for me?

Gaius.

28

Octavius reclined on a chair in Cicero's verdant garden and gazed out over a sumptuous, summery vista. Olive groves, vineyards, and homely stone cottages with wisps of smoke swirling into the air populated the landscape. The smell of freshly-baked bread emanated from the villa. Octavius sat beneath a lime tree. A vermillion sun poured through the branches, sprinkling light across the ground all around him.

"This is one of my favourite views. I come here often. Most people sit here and look back at the villa and admire the architecture. But I prefer to take in nature," Cicero remarked, similarly looking out upon the lush contours of the view. "It's as if the landscape has been sculpted by a god for our enjoyment and admiration. There is an intelligence and order to nature which far eclipses the talent of any mortal architect. I believe that we are in possession of a divine spark, Gaius – and when we witness such a scene as this our spark is inspired to burn brighter."

"All the parts of the world are so made that they could not be better adapted to their use or more beautiful to see," Octavius replied, quoting his host's treatise.

"I should thank Cleanthes for extra book sales. You can quote me better than I can."

"You should rather thank Caesar. Julius furnished me with your works and encouraged me to read them above all others."

"If only Julius would have listened to me, as well as read my books, perhaps we would not be in the state we are in now. I would you listen to me now, though, Gaius. Your uncle, Pompey and I have all made compromises with ourselves and behaved dishonourably. Our divine sparks have burned darkly upon occasions. When most topics were discussed Socrates liked to argue first on one side and then on the other. But on one subject he maintained a consistent point of view: he declared that the human soul is divine. When it leaves the body, it has the power to take the road back up to heaven; and the better and more decently it has behaved in life, the easier this road will be. You still have the chance to save yourself, Octavius. One cannot save one's soul - and Rome."

"You tried."

"I know, but I failed," the elder statesman replied, his face etched with sorrow.

Cicero surprised himself by the candour of his confession - and the affection he was developing for the youth. As much as his counsel had been politically motivated he genuinely did not want Octavius to share Caesar's fate. For once the confident and witty statesman looked sheepish.

"I see so much of myself in you, Octavius. I was far from a robust youth, too. But I thank the gods for my less than perfect constitution, for it encouraged me to remain indoors and exercise my mental faculties. For it is not by muscle, force of speed or dexterity that great things are achieved, but by reflection, force of character and judgement. Despite your adopted name you too, like me, will be considered a new man, as well as a young man, when embarking upon the course of honours. But one does not need to possess a noble name to possess a noble character. Your father, Gaius Octavius, proved that. Gaius was a true servant of the Republic. Even more than Cicero or Caesar you should endeavour to become the man he was becoming, before fate curtailed his destiny. He would have made consul. I would have championed him, as I can you. You do not have to command legions to command respect, Octavius."

Octavius felt an uncommon affection for Cicero for praising his father so. His reposeful expression dissolved into a fond smile. Later that evening he fancied that history may record that, in the same way that Alexander the Great was tutored by Aristotle, Octavius Caesar was tutored by Marcus Tullius Cicero.

The moment between the two figures was broken as an attendant brought Cicero some bread and olive oil. He placed the plate on the small bronze table which sat between Cicero and his guest.

"A meagre lunch I know - and it is not just because Hirtius has visited and my stores have depleted. Did you ever meet Hirtius, when in the company of Caesar? One should eat to live, not live to eat. But your uncle's former secretary is a good man. He will make a good consul. He was devoutly loyal to Caesar, too - and you can trust him with your life, Gaius." Cicero was here tempted to add that Octavius could trust him with his legions also, but that would come in time, the elder statesman hoped. For now, he would just plant certain seeds. In reply Octavius merely gave a nod of his head.

"Certainly you should trust Hirtius above our present consul. Antony looks to the state of his affairs more than the affairs of state. I hear that he's just taken a female mime for a new mistress. She may keep her mouth shut, but the same can't be said for her legs I warrant," Cicero joked.

Octavius smiled, yet again remained enigmatically silent. Cicero would write to Atticus that evening how *"the boy is sphinx-like in his responses. He has perhaps read every word and speech I have composed, yet I cannot even read his intentions for tomorrow."*

"But underestimate Antony at your peril. You will not be able to best him alone, Gaius. You will need the help of the Senate."

Octavius here recalled how Balbus said that the Senate would need his help to subdue Antony, but mentioned it not to his host.

"Even when - and that 'when' is currently an 'if' - Antony's consulship ends he will be in a strong position."

"Nothing is so strongly fortified that it cannot be taken by money," Octavius calmly replied, again quoting from an essay by his companion, "I will win at the odds."

Cicero was astounded by the youth's knowledge – and also hubris. *Perhaps he is the son of Caesar, rather than Octavius,* the republican worried.

*

The bucolic scene strewn before Agrippa on the other side of the estate was equally agreeable. A few woollen clouds ambled across a duck-egg blue sky. The farmland was awash with greens and browns. A goat bleated in the background, in contentment rather than complaint. The sweet scent of dried dates wafted up from the bowl which sat beside him on the bench. But Agrippa noticed not the above as he surveyed the valley beneath him, sketching the scene.

The young woman arched an eyebrow in curiosity, rather than disappointment, at seeing a stranger sitting on the bench she resided upon yesterday as she painted. The girl was dressed in a silk stola, dyed tyrian purple. The colour offset a pair of vivacious blue eyes which could sparkle with both intelligence and humour (a humour which could gently mock others - and herself - but which was never cruel). Her pink full lips were often raised in a smile, which could inspire a similar smile in others. Two blonde curls hung down to frame a sun-kissed face that would be deemed attractive in any age. The rest of her blonde hair was stylishly pinned up on her head. A pair of polished silver earrings, given to her by her father, hung down from her ears but otherwise the girl was unadorned with jewellery or make-up, which was rare considering the fashion of the age. The shimmering dress, which flattered an already enviable figure, reached down to her feet where small, pretty high in-stepped feet wore pretty white silk slippers. She carried her work and utensils herself, having dismissed her over-fussy attendants for the day.

"I am not disturbing you I hope," the girl sweetly remarked. She smiled amiably - yet also in part humorously, as though knowing already that she would be amused by the stranger. She fancied he was a guest of Cicero's, a scion of some patrician family. She knew the type. Haughty perhaps; a trait she was not altogether immune to. Privilege would have bred a vulgar arrogance and sense of entitlement. His education would have been expensive but knowledge would have slipped through his fingers like sand.

Agrippa turned around and smiled when seeing the young woman before him.

"My hope is that you do disturb me," he charmingly replied, friendliness and good humour infused in his tone.

Although retaining her poise she thought him handsome - and unlike most young aristocrats she had encountered. His build was muscular, soldierly. His nose was broad - a fine Roman nose. His hair was short, his tunic plain. Perhaps he wasn't a patrician, she thought. Although he was still a man she judged, interested in one thing in a woman - or two, once he discovered how wealthy her father was.

Caecilia Attica walked over to the bench. Agrippa first politely bowed and then considerately brushed the bench, before the young lady sat down upon it next to him.

"My name is Marcus Vipsanius Agrippa." He continued to grin, almost like a fool, as he spoke. "What's yours?"

"A strange gentleman who asks for a lady's name and gets what he wants may soon ask more from the lady, so I will leave you ignorant for now if I may?" Attica satirically replied.

"You may. I'm no stranger to being ignorant. It's fine."

Attica was amused at the refreshingly self-deprecating reply. The two strangers momentarily gazed at each other with wonderment and something else.

"Now, may I ask something else of you? It's a woman's prerogative to be selfish and demanding, no?"

"I thought such a prerogative belonged to a wife rather than just a woman, but you may."

Her accent and burnished complexion bespoke of a certain foreignness Agrippa thought to himself. Perhaps she was part Greek. Her dress both captured and reflected the saffron light, like her eyes.

"May I see what you are working on?"

"Certainly. Though try not to be as critical as a wife."

His manner seemed uncommonly warm and honest, albeit his wit belied a nobleman's education. She could not recall ever having heard the name Agrippa before – and her father knew everyone who was worth knowing she believed.

Attica raised her eyebrow at seeing the half-finished work. Again this Agrippa confounded any pre-conceptions she had about him. The picture was indeed of the view, although his talent was akin to that of an architect rather than artist. He had captured the form of the landscape, if not its beauty. Yet she was intrigued to see that Agrippa had added to the landscape by inserting an aqueduct and irrigation system onto the plains.

"As informed as your drawing of the aqueduct is, I fear it has ruined the rest of the picture – and will ruin the view before us if constructed."

"The aqueduct is intended to save rather than ruin the valley. The greens will be greener, the browns will be browner. The soil will also be richer, as well as the colours, if irrigated properly. Fresh water will improve the quality of life of the workers, as well as the crops. It should not just be the province of the augurs to look to the future. Aqueducts, sewers and roads should be looked at - as well as the entrails of pigeons and gulls."

Attica scrutinised the stranger, as if he were the work of art that she was unsure of how much to admire or not - both for its accomplishments and originality. She could not quite work him out, both in terms of where he had come from and where he was going.

"So are you a guest of Cicero's, or an architect with a bad sense of direction?"

"I'm a guest in a manner of speaking. I am a companion of Caesar's. And are you too a guest of Cicero's, or a lost wife looking for her husband to nag?"

"I'm the former. If I were a wife I dare say that my husband would be searching for me, not I him. For if I needed to nag him I'd as soon as lose him. But tell me, how close are you to the new Caesar?"

"Close enough to ask you to join us both for dinner this evening. Would you like to?" Agrippa asked, not without a little pride - desiring to impress the sophisticated and beautiful woman with his connection to Octavius. He smiled, with hope gleaming from his aspect. He had only admired such aristocratic women from afar before but here he was, close enough to smell her perfume and hear the rustle of her silk dress.

"No, I would not like to have dinner with Gaius Julius Caesar this evening," the woman exclaimed, shaking her head. Agrippa's smile immediately faltered. He lowered his gaze. "But I would like to have dinner with you, Marcus Vipsanius Agrippa". Immediately the smile returned and he looked the remarkable girl in the eye, his expression as bright as his heart.

*

After dinner Octavius returned to the garden and sat upon the same chair that he had occupied that afternoon. He was accompanied by Cleanthes rather than Cicero now, though. The sky was mauve, the clouds purple, as night settled in. The air was still balmy and sweet with the fragrance of the lime tree that the companions rested under.

"Cicero said that he bought the estate for the views, rather than the house. I can see why," Octavius idly exclaimed.

"If you have a garden and a library, you have everything you need," Cleanthes replied, quoting their host's remark at dinner. "It would be nice to throw in Balbus' vintner and staff too, however. Are you not tempted to purchase a similar villa, with a library and garden? Lucullus retired to his estate and was content to let Rome be Rome. What is stopping you from leading the good life?"

"My duty, to Caesar," Octavius replied, his brow furrowed, his tone as adamantine as his heart. Had grief now wholly manifested itself into revenge? - Cleanthes worryingly thought.

"And when you have fulfilled your duty, what will you do then? Will you, as when Cincinnatus defeated the Aequi, give up your command and live a quiet life? There are still fields of knowledge for you to plough, Gaius. Or have you set yourself upon this course for your own honour rather than Julius? You may be considered a great man if you achieve your ambition and avenge your father, but perhaps the greater man still is he who can relinquish, rather than retain, power."

Octavius listened to his friend in silence, the shadows concealing his brooding expression. He judged his tutor sententious, patronising. He was going to argue that if *his* father had been murdered – and he was in a position to exact his revenge – would he not do so? So too he was tempted to choke the fine blooms of his tutor's moral philosophy with the weeds of political philosophy – and quote Caesar. *"Sulla was a fool for resigning as dictator when he did."*

Yet Octavius bested any ire he felt towards his friend and desisted from responding harshly. He knew Cleanthes meant well, but the Gaius of Apollonia was a fond memory. Octavius Caesar was the reality now. Yet it was with the former's vulnerability and admiration that he turned to his tutor, clasped him on the arm, and expressed: "What will be, will be Cleanthes. Know that I treasure your friendship and wisdom. Please stay with me when we get to Rome. Now more than ever I need someone to remind me that my conscience is more valuable than my fortune. If you wish to retire to your garden again however, I'll understand."

"We used to study history together Octavius. Now we're in a

position to help write it - and someone needs to be here to correct your grammar. As to my garden, I'm far more worried about you getting out of control rather than my weeds," Cleanthes cordially replied whilst squeezing his pupil affectionately on the shoulder. "Now where is your other companion, who will also hopefully keep you on the straight and narrow? Agrippa is a fine young man and equally fine friend. Don't think that I don't know how you often talk together in the evening, going over the day's events and planning for the future."

"He said he had something to do, which could rather well mean he has someone to do," Octavius remarked, arching his eyebrow and the corner of his mouth in a knowing smile.

"Such is his proclivity to catch the eye of servant girls that this philosopher will consider it wise to always sit next to him at dinner so as to be served well."

The two companions here added a chorus of laughter to the nightingale's evening song.

*

Agrippa and Attica had conversed on their bench long into the afternoon - about nothing and everything. Attica felt immediately and uncommonly comfortable and content in his company. Agrippa was neither intimidated by her intelligence or sense of humour. Laughter bloomed from her lips as he matched her witticisms with his own. Attica resisted from telling him her name. So many vacuous would-be suitors viewed her as a trophy to be won or conduit to being a client of Atticus' once they discovered who she was. As charming and gregarious as the girl could be she often felt lonely, isolated. With her father and Cicero alone could she discuss art and politics and be part of a serious or satirical conversation. Her friends were her books. Towards the end of their afternoon together she made Agrippa promise that he would not go back to the house and ask who she was. As tempted as he was to discover more about his captivating companion, Agrippa honoured his promise.

"Now I must keep my promise and venture back to prepare dinner. Thank you for today, Marcus."

"What are you thanking me for?" he replied.

"Just for you being you - and for letting me be myself, that self who I like to be."

She then sweetly walked up to Agrippa, squeezed his hand and stood upon tip-toe to kiss him on the cheek. The stunned and smitten Roman cherished the lingering sensation as the beautiful girl - or was she truly a goddess? - darted back onto the track leading through the woods, her heart skipping, akin to her pretty feet.

*

The moon shone with a mellow, erbium-tinged radiance. Stars glistened with pride, like peacocks showing off their plumage. The night air was still warm. The shutters were left open and Agrippa watched sparrows hop from branch to branch on a birch tree outside. Cicero had given Attica use of a guest villa at the southern edge of his estate. Although possessing all manner of staff Attica had cooked and served the meal herself - freshly picked mushrooms in her special sauce followed by spiced lamb. She dismissed all of her attendants for the evening. Not only did she not wish to intimidate Agrippa with her status, but also she didn't wish to be disturbed (or have one of the staff report back to her father about her guest).

Attica had changed her stola, yet the dress was equally elegant and the pale blue dye brought out the brilliance of her eyes in a different way. Contrary to fashion she also removed the ivory pins from her hair and long blonde tresses flowed freely over her shoulders and down her back. The conversation similarly flowed freely. More than once Agrippa gave thanks to Octavius for having encouraged him in his study of literature and philosophy. He was familiar with the authors his mystery woman spoke so admiringly of - and when she mentioned Herodotus he duly quoted him, *"Of all possessions a friend is the most precious."* Her eyes gleamed with pleasant surprise and the girl shook her head a little, as though the man before her was too good to be true. Agrippa proceeded to talk about his friend a little, recounting a story from their time together in Apollonia.

"For the most part we just went to visit the famed astrologer Theogenes for a joke. Neither of us is superstitious, thank the gods. His study gave off an air of wisdom, with all manner of scientific apparatus and ancient parchments decorating the chamber. The air of the room - or rather the stench of his garb - also suggested that, although devoting his life to foretelling the future, Theogenes was not the best judge of predicting his bowel movements."

Laughter cascaded out of his dinner companion. And her laughter was music to his ears - silvery, sweet, unaffected. Agrippa noticed how her eyes would narrow, yet beam, when he made her laugh or grin - and she would gaze fondly at him as if no one else in the world made her feel like he did or mattered to him like he did (which was indeed the case).

"His voice was as rough as the wine he gave us. First he interviewed me and I gave him the time, date of my birth and so forth. Theogenes then retreated to another room, where he seemed to work his way through a bottle of wine as well as my horoscope. On his return - and I dare say this may have been the drink talking - he professed to have never seen such a favourable fate before. I was destined for greatness, despite my inability to pay him as handsomely as his more affluent clients. Although I had faith in my scepticism, still I couldn't help but be happy with my reading. As happy as Gaius was for me though a gloom came over him when the astrologer turned to commence his reading. Although Gaius jested and appeared indifferent he was worried I think that somehow my fate would eclipse his, or similarly that our paths would diverge. Through a combination of teasing and bullying him he finally agreed to the horoscope. Gaius rarely loses his composure but he did that afternoon as he paced up and down with a fixed look of apprehension across his face."

"And what was the outcome?" Attica asked, leaning towards him over the table.

"Theogenes finally came back. The door seemed to take an age to creak open for Octavius. If the wizened astrologer had been intoxicated whilst conducting my reading his sobriety had returned. He stared at Gaius, his mouth agape. He then fell to his knees and pronounced that Gaius would be "the master of the world". We laughed at the incident afterwards. But then and there, as the old man clasped the hem of Gaius' tunic and made his pronouncement in all sincerity, we somehow felt the hand of fate upon us."

"And will you be a great man, Marcus Vipsanius Agrippa?"

"I'll try."

"In which case you'll succeed. But, tell me, do you have a philosophy by which you will live this great life?"

Agrippa paused before answering, enchanted by the way in which the light of the brazier glowed upon her honey coloured skin.

"Fail to prepare. Prepare to fail," he smiled and exclaimed, remembering Oppius' advice. "And do you have a philosophy by which you live your life?"

Attica gazed at her guest, partly staring into his soul and partly wishing to infuse it.

"Be kind, for everyone you meet is facing a hard battle," she replied, embodying loveliness and wisdom - quoting Plato. She was like no other girl he had met. And Agrippa realised that evening - indeed perhaps at the very moment that she uttered those words - that he loved her like no other girl he had ever met, or would meet.

"Will you be kind now and finally tell me your name?"

She hesitated, but finally spoke.

"Caecilia Attica."

Agrippa's eyes briefly widened in surprise but then everything fell into place - her wealth, knowledge of art, her staying with Cicero. Attica looked down, in fear of witnessing the greed and sense of opportunity in Marcus' eyes that she had observed in others. But as she looked up she bathed in the genuine warmth, good humour, and something else in his aspect. Agrippa had fallen in love with Atticus' daughter, not dowry. And she knew it.

"Will I ever see you again?"

"I'll make sure that the first aqueduct that I construct runs past your house."

Attica but half smiled at the comment, dwelling still on how she might never see him again. He would become a memory, or a dream. Her father had always respected her decision when she did not like the prospective husband who auditioned for her. But would he now respect her choice of someone who he might not consider suitable, both because of Agrippa's class and political affiliations?

"You are to venture to Rome, I back to Athens, shortly," she expressed forlornly. While just before the girl could not take her eyes off her would-be suitor, Attica now averted her glance, for when she looked at him now she saw something, somebody, that might be lost to her. And already it brought her pain.

"Before this evening Caecilia I often dreamed that I would win fame and fortune for myself, or to help Gaius. But now I wish to do so to be good enough in the eyes of your father - and win you."

The girl smiled, but tears began to stream down her cheeks. She sobbed as she spoke and shook her head.

"No, you don't understand. I think I love you. You've already won me. I don't want you to now lose me."

Agrippa tenderly laced his fingers into hers and stood up. Attica too arose and then buried her head into his chest, crying as she did so.

"Fight for me Marcus. Don't give up on me, us."

"I'll wait for you. Should I fall behind, wait for me," he replied, his strong arms cradling her.

"I'll try."

"In which case you'll succeed."

A sob turned itself into a bouquet of laughter. Her face was wet with tears. First Agrippa brushed his thumb over her cheeks. Her slender arms pulled him closer. Their lips met in a sweet, then passionate, then loving kiss.

29

A persistent greasy drizzle had followed the party throughout the morning, but fortunately the skies cleared by the afternoon. The young Caesar stood upon a rostrum in the market town of Casilinum and addressed the crowd - having come straight from the town's temple, where the young man had displayed sufficient piety. Balbus had pre-arranged some supporters but curiosity and the promise of some Caesar-esque largesse had brought people from their homes to the square. Equites, farmers, soldiers, guild members and civil servants rubbed shoulders alike - along with their wives and children - to see the adopted heir of Julius Caesar. There were already plenty of smiles all round as Balbus had organised for a merchant to lubricate the proceedings with free wine, bread and fresh fruit. Heads bobbed up and down amidst the sea of people to get a better view of the Caesar.

A welcome breeze cooled Octavius' flushed features. The sound of the breeze mingled with the whispers which wended their way through the throng. As a soldier's drills will aid him in the battlefield, Octavius had repeatedly rehearsed his speech to suppress his nerves and narrow any scope for errors. He took a deep breath, like an actor preparing to go on stage, and commenced his address.

"I come not to bury Caesar, but to praise him. I come not to bury Caesar's reforms, but to save them. And I come not to bury Caesar's promises, but to keep them."

Octavius' voice was audible and calm. His lungs and temperament would not allow him to bellow. His tunic was plain, but fresh and white, gleaming in the afternoon sun. Balbus had given Octavius one of Julius' old belts as a talisman.

"My father once told me that Rome and its riches should not be the preserve of just Romans and the rich. Before my father we had but two classes, the taxed and the taxing. But the peace he won and the reforms he promoted purchased prosperity for all. He knew, through living in the Subura all those years and campaigning alongside good legionaries from all across Italy that, as the builders say, the larger stones do not lie well without the lesser."

Balbus' supporters, planted throughout the crowd, began to nudge their neighbours and nod their heads - but they were not the only ones to do so.

"How unfair the fate which ordains that those who have the least should add to the treasury of the rich. But that seems to be the fate that the present authorities have in store for us. Taxes are now due to be raised as high as the colonnades on the villas that they are constructing. The only taxes which are due to be rescinded are those imposed by Caesar upon certain luxury goods I have heard. One should be a friend to business, but not to corruption ...We must cleanse the augean stables."

Heads that formerly nodded in agreement now shook their heads in disappointment after hearing such scandalous proposals.

"And certain self-interested factions of the Senate justify their actions by claiming that Caesar acted unlawfully in enacting his reforms, so we must now make them null and void. They are wielding their styluses, as they did their daggers against my father, to attack your freedoms and wealth. They hide behind ancient or brand new laws to defend their actions. But should these self-styled optimates, best men, be standing before me now I would not flinch in telling them that the good of the people is the greatest law."

Clapping and cheers filled the pause that Octavius here artfully allowed. Cleanthes, watching from the performance from the side of the rostrum, smirked - thinking about the irony of Octavius quoting Cicero to endorse his Caesarian mandate. The tutor also recognised lines from Terence and Plato. Indeed, Cleanthes mused, the only person who he wasn't quoting was his teacher.

"Now I can only but hope that I have inherited my father's political acumen and fortune in war. And I desperately hope that I have inherited his abilities in regards to his conquests over women."

The crowd erupted with laughter. Octavius smiled and enjoyed the moment too, yet then raised his hand to silence them. Oppius looked on, impressed, as Octavius started to orchestrate the crowd as Julius had once done so commandingly. Balbus had offered to compose the speech but Octavius merely asked him to read over his own composition - which he edited not. Although youthful in appearance Octavius was projecting confidence and maturity. Cleanthes had coached him a little in regards to his delivery - he sawed not the air with his hands, nor strained his voice - but it seemed he was a natural.

"But I have inherited my father's name and the promises he made - both of which I intend to honour. I have inherited my father's debt, as well as his fortune. His debt to the people of Rome - and I shall see to it that his gardens are bequeathed to the public. And I shall see to it that the gift of three hundred sesterces is paid to every good citizen in Rome, too. And I shall see to it that his promises of land grants to his loyal legions are not revoked." Octavius turned his head to address a section of the crowd consisting of legionaries and centurions and nodded to them in gratitude and respect. "My father craved not a revolution. Nor do I. He believed in the Republic. As do I. He believed in the providence of the gods. As do I. He believed in tradition and the family. As do I. I stand before you now, not just a servant to my father - but consequently a servant to all of you. For who was it who took from the rich to give to the deserving? Caesar! Who was it who gave thanks and worship to the gods, rather than to the senatorial cartel of the Metelli, Claudii and Brutii? Caesar! And who shed his own blood to win our peace and prosperity? Caesar! And who was it they perniciously accused of being a tyrant, but died being our benefactor?"

"Caesar! Caesar! Caesar!" was the reply from the crowd. Fists punched the air. One could not be sure if the throng were cheering for the Caesar past or the one who stood before them. Perhaps the lines had become blurred and it was both.

Though a feeling of anger simmered at the rally for the opponents of Caesar (who if present were wisely quiet), such a mood was eclipsed by a fraternal and celebratory atmosphere. Wine and food continued to be freely distributed. Octavius spent a number of hours listening to the grievances and petitions of a number of his supporters. He took time out to speak to a group of soldiers who had served under Caesar. Cleanthes noted down names and addresses to forward on to Balbus and his clerks - who would write follow-up messages. A widow, not a little charmed by the attractive and well-mannered youth, thanked the young Caesar for his visit to the town. She could not remember the last time that anyone of note had deigned to truly speak and listen to the people. The audience to the scene would later quote Caesar's response, as he warmly clasped the earnest woman by the hands, "my father once told me that the higher we are placed, the more humbly we should walk." Balbus had also arranged for Caesar's heir to have a number of private meetings with key supporters and donors to the Caesarian campaign. For the moderates Octavius trumpeted his new found friendship with Cicero, implying that he would work with the Senate to champion their cause. For the more devout Caesarians however, Octavius expressed himself in more bellicose terms towards the libertores and other enemies.

Oppius and Roscius spent the afternoon in the company of their fellow soldiers, assuring them of Octavius' desire for revenge. Akin to his father, Octavius would reward loyalty, too.

Neither Antony nor the Senate would match the wages that the young Caesar could and would pay. Most of the centurions ended the afternoon swearing loyalty to Octavius Caesar, in the name of Julius Caesar, and promised to extract similar oaths from their comrades.

Agrippa and Casca had the far from onerous task of touring the local taverns, both garnering and measuring support for the Caesar. They sometimes just listened to the gossip and wine truth. At other instances they engaged their drinking companions. The responses to the address were favourable. The affluent did not feel that the young Caesar was a populist demagogue, in the vein of a Clodius. He had no intention of stirring the mob to violence, or championing the poor above all other interests. The Senate were living in the past if they thought they could undo all of Caesar's beneficial reforms and re-establish an oligarchy. Like them, Octavius was a progressive conservative at heart. Yet in the less seemly establishments – which Agrippa and Casca were happily thorough enough to visit as well – the people were equally enthusiastic about the young Caesar. Like his father he had the common touch. He possessed a sense of humour and spoke to them rather than down to them. Although educated his air was that of a tribune rather than a haughty patrician.

*

An old friend of Balbus' and an ardent Caesarian, Valerius Macrinus, accommodated Caesar and his retinue that evening at his estate just outside of town. Gaius, Agrippa, Oppius, Casca and Roscius relaxed in the opulent triclinium over several jugs of Macrinus' finest vintage. The day - and drinking session - had been long.

"Today was a great success. To today - and tomorrow!" Agrippa announced, raising his cup and a smile to his friend. He was, like Casca, far more inebriated than his companions, what with them having embraced their duties earlier.

"Julius would have been proud of you today Gaius," Oppius then earnestly expressed, using up his ration of compliments for the year, and looking at Octavius with not a little affection and approval. They fleetingly shared a private moment.

"Thank you."

"But don't let the praise go to your head quicker than the wine," Oppius added, reverting to his disgruntled self - but warmly winking at the boy.

"To Octavius!" Roscius exclaimed, but before he raised his arm to complete the toast, Oppius stopped him.

"No, old friend - to Caesar!"

"To Caesar!" the companions echoed, clinking their cups.

For once Octavius felt a little uncomfortable in his skin. He smiled and was choked with emotion; he blushed too. He was saved from further discomfort however by Cleanthes re-appearing.

"Valerius has informed me that the entertainment has arrived."

"Please don't tell me that they're musicians," Roscius replied, rolling his eyes.

"I wouldn't call them musicians, although you may approve of how they'll play with your instrument."

Valerius Macrinus here entered the room and ushered in a dozen well dressed women of ill-repute.

"For your entertainment, gentlemen. They're as fine as Caesar's speech - and cleaner than your jokes, Roscius," their host jovially exclaimed.

All manner of lissom figures - some wearing little more than a smile - sauntered into the triclinium. The glow of the fire shone upon tanned, roseate and black perfumed skin alike. Some giggled, some simpered or appeared sultry as they draped themselves over sofas or encircled their prey.

Roscius licked his lips at the banquet of flesh sumptuously laid out before him, not knowing which dish to try first. His eyes bulged, as did something else - beneath his tunic - as he thought to himself how much he preferred life on a political campaign as opposed to a military one.

Tiro Casca gulped as twin sisters sat either side of him and ran their hands up and down his legs. Not knowing how to combat such an assault he decided to surrender to it.

A sweet-faced girl with startling turquoise eyes and a similarly arresting figure perched herself upon the arm of Octavius' chair. She wore an elaborate wrap-around silk stola that he quickly figured out was solely held in place by an ivory brooch in between her breasts. The courtesan smiled alluringly as she ran her hand through his short fair hair and stroked his cheek.

Nearby a strikingly tall Nubian woman sided up to a partly

aroused, partly intimidated Cleanthes.

"And who are you?" she asked, or perhaps demanded, in a husky foreign accent.

"That's a good question. And one which I can happily debate with you in the bedroom."

The woman at first appeared a little confused by the reply but then shrugged her shoulders and led the stranger off to an adjoining room, nearly pulling Cleanthes' arm out of its socket as she did so.

A lithe Egyptian woman caught Oppius' eye, or vice versa. She reminded him of his long-term lover during Caesar's Alexandrian campaign. He smiled as he recalled how her legs would wrap around him so tight than not even Hercules himself could have escaped her clutches - not that he would want to, Oppius mused. The fond smile and glint of dark desire upon his face was invitation enough for this new dusky-skinned figure to straddle the handsome Roman on the sofa and sensuously kiss him.

Agrippa alone resisted the entreaties. He yawned and excused himself from further revelries by citing tiredness, which was indeed the case - albeit not the reason as to why he absented himself. A part of him perhaps wanted to remain and enjoy his host's hospitality - but yet he was content to retire to his room. Lying upon his bed Agrippa dreamily composed a letter and love poem to Attica, his smile as wide as any of his companions.

30

Grey clouds, like slats, were tiled across the sky. The rally in Allifae had been, akin to Casilinum, a success. Indeed the number of supporters had been greater as news of Caesar's arrival preceded him and people from the countryside as well as the town came out to see the heir. Word was spreading. Seeds were being sown - and taking root. The Appian Way was again unfurled before them, its flagstones spotted with rain. Dense woodland flanked the road on either side.

Oppius and Roscius set the pace at the head of the party, along with a quartet of soldiers. The rest of Balbus' men, thirty strong in total, marched either side of the road and brought up the rear. Inside the rectangle were the baggage carts. Octavius rode on one of the carts, attempting to catch up on some correspondence. Casca marched by the cart's side, his expression as dour as the weather.

Behind them were Agrippa and Cleanthes. The grey mare pulling one of the wagons spotted the road with something other than rain, and the tutor had to pull his companion out of the way to save him from stepping in the steaming excrement.

"I'm sure, Marcus, that Attica would not want you day-dreaming about her to such an extent where you did not know where you were walking."

"What? How do you know?" Agrippa replied, astounded that Cleanthes could know about Attica and himself. He hadn't even told Octavius - or he hadn't told him especially.

"I may not be Gordianus the Finder but I'm not blind. You've been walking around with a love-struck look on your face ever since the morning we departed from Cicero's estate. And only a blind man, or a man devoted to someone, would have left the party the other night when those sirens turned up. The wax in your ears was the name of Attica, no? And don't think that I haven't noticed you clandestinely reading Catullus."

Agrippa blushed, but smiled also.

"Of course, I also discovered your secret through having visited Attica on the morning we left. I met her through her father some years ago."

Agrippa laughed and shook his head.

"I could live a thousand lifetimes, Cleanthes, and you doubtless would still own the ability to surprise and confound me. But I must ask that my secret becomes your secret, too. I must ask you to keep this from Gaius."

"Hmm, keeping secrets from each other now are we? You two really are indeed as close as a married couple," Cleanthes joked. "But I give you my word that my lips will remain as tightly shut as Crassus' wallet."

"It's just that I do not want Gaius to be tempted to use my

friendship with Attica for political means, to get closer to Atticus. Similarly Caecilia does not want to tell her father yet for fear of Atticus or Cicero using her to use me to reveal Gaius' intentions. Or indeed they could just forbid our relationship altogether after discovering my loyalty to Caesar. I adore her Cleanthes. She's smart, funny and beautiful. We are each of us angels with only one wing, and we can only fly by embracing each other," Agrippa exclaimed, as much to himself as his companion, quoting Lucretius.

At the touch of love everyone becomes a poet, Cleanthes thought to himself, and smiled fondly. He then remembered *her*, *his* angel.

"For what it's worth you have my blessing, Marcus. Attica is indeed a remarkable and accomplished young woman. As much as I try to forget – and drink aids me in this quest as you know – she reminds me of my first love. My sole love."

Again Agrippa turned to his companion, astounded.

"Can a philosopher fall in love?"

"Oh, I was much happier and wiser than a philosopher then."

"What happened, if you do not mind me asking?"

"We were due to be married. But she passed away," the tutor replied, his wistful expression falling into mournfulness. "Plato once said that one word frees us from all the weight and pain in life. And that word is love. But what he failed to mention was that if one loses that love, then the weight and pain return." Cleanthes was now speaking to himself as much as his companion. Agrippa's countenance couldn't help but mirror his friend's pained one and crease in sympathy.

"When was this?"

"It was a long time ago, although it sometimes feels like yesterday. But I do not wish to speak about it further. I already still think about it too much. Ultimately I'm a bad stoic, Marcus. Or a sad one," the mercurial tutor quietly uttered, rain or tears spotting his cheeks.

Octavius finished composing a letter to Octavia. He smiled to himself on recalling Cicero's words, "And how is your sister? I met her once. She was half her husband's age but twice as clever." Octavius then glanced at the granite-faced Tiro. He had grown fond of the gruff veteran over the past weeks. He was a walking argument as to why Rome bested its enemies.

"Tell me, Tiro. You've fought on all corners of the map. Which armies do you rate?"

Although Casca's expression changed very little upon hearing the question, he was always happy to recount old war stories and be consulted on military matters.

"Well the Gauls were brave whenever they outnumbered us three to one. But they would often also just down swords, like guild members their tools, and surrender. The Greeks seemed more concerned with being well groomed than well trained. Sometimes I think their officers wanted to fuck us rather than kill us, such was their effete manner. I rated the Britons. The gods were right to give those savages their own island, away from everyone else. They can out drink anyone, and out fight most. But by far the greatest, finest army we faced was Pompey's. His legions were well-led, well-equipped and well-disciplined. But

Caesar had Bellona for his mistress it seems. Pharsalus was a close run thing. But quality will always best quantity."

"And what of the Egyptians?"

"The Egyptians? They were more likely to poison us with their cuisine than kill us on the battlefield," the veteran exclaimed, laughing at his own joke.

Oppius and Roscius briefly turned their heads back at the audible cackling of their comrade. The centurion then gazed intently ahead once more, furrowing his brow in concern, or scorn, that the two scouts he sent ahead of the party had not reported back as ordered.

*

Dried blood and tiny blisters of rust stained the blade of Gravius' lieutenant as he held it aloft. Once Gravius gave the word he would swipe his sword downwards, giving the signal for the men hidden in the woods on the opposite side of the road to attack. Their brown and russet tunics camouflaged them well. The overcast sky helped conceal them, too. The gods were on their side, Gravius thought, although he put more stock in himself and his men than any deities.

The orders were clear. Once he had given the signal his men, numbering fifty, would attack the party on both sides simultaneously. A compliment of archers and javelin throwers would launch their missiles before joining the rest of the cohort to race down the grass slopes between the trees and road. The priority was to find and assassinate the boy - but no one was to be spared. The mission called for corpses, not prisoners or witnesses. They would bury the bodies in the forest.

Enobarbus' agents had confirmed that Lucius Oppius was leading the party. He looked forward to doing battle with the famed centurion, who had made his name off the coast of Britain all those years ago. He would need more than the Legionaries' Prayer to keep himself safe now, though. Prayers had done little to help the two scouts that Oppius had sent along the Appian Way. They had duly revealed the proximity of the rest of the party, before Gravius slit their throats.

Gravius first heard the tamp of boots and rumble of wagons on the road, before he spied the party. The menacing centurion gripped the handle of his giant double-bladed axe, a trophy won from a warlord in Long-Haired Gaul. His eyes glinted as brightly as the steel in anticipation of the attack and slaughter.

"Archers at the ready," he instructed, grinning.

"We will soon be in Rome, Lucius."

"Where will you head first once there old friend - the baths or brothels? Just make sure that both are clean. You're itching to get back to Rome it seems. I don't want you itching from some pox when departing from it."

"Fear not, I've got more wits and sesterces than when I was last in Rome. And where will you head to?"

"I can tell you who I won't be visiting."

"Who?"

"My ex-wife."

Roscius tossed his head high and roared with laughter. However Oppius' attention was fixed firmly on the road. He noted the dark marks splattered across the flagstones. Blood rather than rain. Fresh blood. Something was wrong. The centurion's keen eyes darted left and then right. The forest had crept even closer towards the road. Something was amiss. They were in the perfect position for an ambush!

"Defensive positions!"

The bellowed order was soon accompanied by the sound of a flurry of arrows whooshing from bows. A number of javelins also skewered the air. Thanks to their commander's constant drilling the reactions were rapid - second nature. Balbus' men crouched behind their large shields. Without a thought for himself Tiro swiftly moved to cover Caesar with his shield - and thankfully so as an arrow thudded into it.

Gravius cursed the gods that his initial salvo had been blunted by Oppius' good, or lucky, judgement. Yet his anger only spurred him on down the slope to his quarry, his giant axe swinging in his hand.

Oppius ordered his men to close ranks around the baggage carts. If they kept their heads then they may just keep their lives, too.

Whilst the rest of the escort manoeuvred themselves to defend - Oppius and Roscius attacked. The hulking legionary charged up the slope to meet a brace of the brigands. Their war cries turned into screams however as Roscius turned his shield horizontally and rammed into them both. All three of the combatants were floored but the legionary recovered the quickest to stab one in the chest and the other in the throat.

Oppius sped to the crucial point of the ambush to help even the odds - whilst shouting orders to his own men. Shields and swords clashed against each other but still his voice could be heard over the melee.

"Agrippa, get into position on top of the cart. Start shooting the bastards. Cleanthes, to me. Roscius, to Caesar."

After delivering his orders, Lucius got in position to outflank the line of attackers outnumbering the defenders. He efficiently unsheathed and unleashed the two daggers he kept upon his belt. Despite his enemies being side-on, both blades bit into the ribs of their targets and felled them.

Even before the order had been issued, Agrippa raced towards the wagon in front of Octavius' to retrieve his bow. He launched himself on the vehicle. Fear and exhilaration coursed through his body but Agrippa quickly centred himself. He found a target and released the arrow, shooting over the heads of his comrades to plant the shaft into the chest of an attacker.

Octavius had drawn his sword but he resisted not when Tiro instructed him to hide himself beneath the cart. The veteran stood by him, gladius and shield at the ready to protect Caesar. And protect Caesar he would have to, for a trio of the attackers made a bee-line for the prize. Tiro flinched not, despite it being three to one. For Casca it was like being on his training ground again as he parried and lunged to fend off the brigands. Yet his opponents were not as ill-trained and fearful as his students back in Apollonia.

"Give it up old man. It's three against one."

"I hope you count as well as you fight," Roscius exclaimed, slightly breathless from his sprint.

Whilst the trio were distracted by Roscius, Tiro threw his gladius into one of them, having dropped his shield down to leave his chest exposed. He then swiftly grabbed Octavius' sword to, along with Roscius, confront the remaining pair. With vicious yet efficient strokes they soon hacked them down.

Gravius stood with a boot on the dead man's chest as he worked his axe out of the shattered collar bone. Blood spotted his face. He licked his lips, enjoying the familiar metallic taste. Despite the screams and commotion around him, Gravius calmly located and walked towards his prey, smirking wolfishly as he did so. The enemy were well disciplined and accomplished fighters, but his cohort would out-match and outnumber them in the end. Although outnumbered himself, Gravius was confident of out-matching the two legionaries guarding the Caesar who cowered beneath the cart.

"You'll flee if you know what's good for you. Just leave the boy to me. It took two dozen daggers to kill the last Caesar. But it'll take just one axe to send this one to the ferryman."

Recognising a seasoned soldier and brute when he saw one - it takes one to know one - Tiro approached the powerfully built opponent with caution. Roscius continued to guard Octavius. The two men traded blows and insults. In another man's hands the axe would have proved too unwieldy to duel with but Gravius handled his weapon as nimbly as Casca did his sword. Such was the force of one of Gravius' blows that his axe splintered his opponent's shield, at which point Casca pulled Gravius close to him and butted his nose. Yet Gravius absorbed the blow and butted the veteran back. With his opponent slightly disorientated Gravius cleverly lengthened the reach of his weapon by holding the end of the shaft and swiped low, beneath Tiro's shield, to slice him deep into his shins. Before Tiro had the chance to recover his opponent buried the axe-head in his chest, cutting through his leather breastplate as if it were papyrus.

Octavius' face dropped at witnessing the veteran fall. Even if Roscius could best the ferocious brigand he sensed that they could not survive the attack.

Eight of Balbus' men faced close to twenty of the enemy in their ever dwindling shield wall. The ratio was similar on the other side of the road. Such was the attackers' numerical superiority that they could surround and out-flank the shield wall. And that was their plan, as the bandits were ordered to back off from the shield wall before one last, decisive, offensive.

But little did the rogue cohort know that one man stood in the way of victory - albeit he stood behind them. During the fight Oppius had ordered Cleanthes to collect up as many stray swords and pilums as he could. The centurion did the same, despatching a couple more of the enemy whilst doing so. The first javelin thudded into an attacker's back - and its gore-tipped point glistened as it poked out of his sternum. Ere the first man fell Oppius clasped another pilum and, standing twenty metres away, he launched it at the enemy standing next to his first victim. The third turned towards the danger, but still not in time. A sword then twirled through the air and could be seen jutting out of the enemy's shoulder. Confusion and fear infected the enemy line as Oppius, as if he were completing a training exercise, struck his targets. Balbus' men responded and moved forward as many of the enemy suddenly turned their backs to them. The tide of the battle turned within a minute. Oppius continued to methodically attack the line from behind, as Cleanthes handed him his missiles. Yet not all of Gravius' men panicked and found themselves sandwiched between the enemies. The man at the far end of the line, possessing a javelin still, peeled away. If he could bring down the centurion then all would not be lost. Oppius was blind-sided to the assassin- but Cleanthes was not. The pilum briefly whistled through the air before spearing into the tutor's stomach, as he moved himself in front of the centurion. Oppius looked to Cleanthes but the tutor, wincing in pain, gently shook his head to communicate that he was finished, or that Lucius shouldn't worry about him. Oppius drew his sword, already slick with blood, and fixed his storm-filled eye towards his would-be assassin.

The axe-head dug into Roscius' shield. Roscius took his chance to strike at the handle of the weapon. The legionary's blow was powerful enough to crack the shaft and render the axe useless. Gravius grunted, gifted his opponent a nod of respect, and drew his gladius.

"Why do you protect this whelp? Because of his name?"

Gravius pointed his sword towards Octavius. Octavius, desiring revenge for Tiro Casca, had grabbed a nearby gladius and shield - but Roscius beckoned him back. The brigand was too fierce an opponent.

"No, because he's my friend," the legionary calmly replied.

Witnessing that the tide had turned upon one front, Agrippa focused on the other. Although the two rows of combatants were hazardously close together, Agrippa bided his time and sent another wretch to the underworld, shooting him in the face. The scream momentarily curdled the air before the clang and curses of battle drowned out the sound again.

Gravius' lieutenant lunged at Oppius but the centurion deftly avoided the thrust and quickly jabbed his sword up into his enemy's neck, tearing his gladius out sideways rather than backwards. The centurion then ordered for the remainder of Balbus' forces to converge on the remaining enemy.

A cheer soon went up as the bolstered shield wall overcame the remnants of the enemy, routing them.

Gravius was dextrous with his axe against Roscius - but deadly with his sword. Too swift. Too savage. Blood poured from cuts upon the legionary's arm, thigh and hip. Drool fell from his mouth as Gravius stood over his enemy and slit Roscius' throat, the curve of the fatal wound mirroring the grin on the rogue centurion's face.

Tears streamed from Octavius' face - and he gripped his sword as if he would attempt to avenge his friend's death - but a firm hand upon his shoulder stayed any rush of blood.

"Gaius, attend to Cleanthes. I'll attend to this," Oppius said.

At witnessing his tutor behind him, dying, Octavius raced to his side.

"Unfortunately for you, I've killed your two best men," Gravius goadingly remarked.

"Unfortunately for you, I'm better. Marcus, if this bastard tries to run away then stick an arrow so far through the back of his head that it comes out the other side."

Agrippa nodded grimly, as he stood in a horseshoe around the two combatants with his other comrades.

As when two wild stags, with their nostrils flared and haunches up, will butt and shatter the silence of the forest - so too did the centurions clash, their swords and shields striking each other like antlers. Balbus' men cheered their commander on. Agrippa nocked an arrow, deciding that he would unleash the bolt if the enemy looked like he was winning, rather than running.

Cleanthes lay upon the grass on his side, his knees tucked up, his eyes half closed as if he were about to drift off to sleep. His body twitched in pain with each breath he took. Petals of blood bloomed ever outwards upon his tunic. Octavius kneeled before him, clasping his limp hand.

"Stay with us," the youth, partly ordering him, partly pleading, exclaimed. Tears soaked his cheeks.

"It's time to cross over. There's someone waiting for me on the other side I hope," the tutor quietly replied, a contented smile suddenly enlivening his ashen features. With what little strength remaining, Cleanthes squeezed his student's hand.

"When you cross over I'll be waiting for you. I just want to be as proud of you then as I am now."

Octavius thought he heard his friend whisper a woman's name. His grip on his hand - and on life itself - then ebbed away. His serene expression remained however, as the words of Socrates came to him: *Death maybe the greatest of all human blessings.*

Gravius attacked more than his opponent. His blows were forceful, the angles of his strokes diverse. Both men tried to foot swipe, head butt and push each other to the ground but both men were experienced and equal to the tactics. Oppius realised that he would need to come up with something different to penetrate his opponent's defences, else the duel would be one of attrition – and his body was already tiring. He decided he would risk it all - not on the throw of a dice, but rather on the throw of something else.

Although Gravius was adroit and experienced enough to look for Oppius throwing his gladius, he wasn't expecting his opponent to throw his shield at him. The large scutum crashed against Gravius' body and momentarily blinded him. Oppius was quick to take advantage of his opponent's disorientation. He grabbed Gravius' wrist on his sword arm with his now free hand and - with a gap opening up between his round shield and body - the centurion swiftly stabbed his enemy in the stomach. The gladius protruded out of Gravius' back. Oppius made sure to look his opponent in the eye as he slowly twisted his sword, feeling the intestines wrap around the blade.

*

The road was littered with corpses, or wounded who would soon be so. Blood browned the yellow grass. Night descended. The wind howled and caused the rain to slant into mournful faces. Prisoners were tortured - and the enemy confessed to being Roman soldiers - but the secret of who was their paymaster had died with their leader. Neither Oppius nor Octavius regretted his death however. The prisoners were then executed. The young Caesar took the time to thank and praise every soldier individually - and he helped them bury their comrades. The only bodies they took with them were Casca, Roscius and Cleanthes.

31

When the party reached the town of Praeneste, Oppius recruited more men and purchased horses, provisions and equipment. They would now travel in safety - and luxury. Balbus' men were granted a short leave of absence for the evening and following day. Oppius gifted each man a bonus and recommended a couple of establishments at which to spend their bounty.

A joint funeral service was arranged for Roscius, Casca and Cleanthes. They hoped that their three comrades would enter Elysium together - and to jolly them on their way Oppius poured an amphora of Falernian over their bodies. Their companions, after the service, also worked their own way through a measure of the vintage, celebrating and mourning their friends. Oppius spoke for Roscius, Agrippa for Casca, and Caesar for Cleanthes for the funeral orations.

"… Rome has lost a legionary, I have lost a friend. I never had to check to know you were by my side. And even now I would take your ghost and memory over any other soldier to fight alongside me. In death you kept your oath - and therefore your honour - to defend Caesar. As such you fought for Rome till the end…"

"... *My cup will be raised as high as my esteem. Actions always spoke louder than words for you but I hope that you can hear me now, Tiro. In treating me like a man I became a man. In disappointing you I believed I was disappointing myself - for somehow you imparted in your teaching a piece of your Roman soul, as well as your military knowledge. I will abide by your lessons in honour of your memory - and to keep me safe. Oppius gave me your letter. I hope to inherit your courage, as well as your sword. I will sharpen the edge at night - and by day sheathe the blade into the enemies of Rome ...*"

"... *I feel like I have lost another father - and from your will it seems I have inherited another estate. Part of me wishes to venture back to Apollonia and tend to your garden. Yet - and you would be all too conscious of the irony - the seeds of virtue that you helped sow into me means that I must abandon your estate for another. I must tend to Caesar's gardens - and ensure that they are gifted to the public ... Yet far more important is what is unseen that I inherited from you - to recognise man's follies but to not always condemn them. To question, yet not always negate. That goodness should be valued over knowledge - and that philosophy cannot and should not bring faith ... Death will not snuff out your flame. Your teachings will not vanish with the closure of your academy ... I pray my tears do not water down the Falernian. After this night there will be no more tears spilled - just the blood of our enemies.*"

*

Evening. Puteoli.

Cicero, Tiro and Caecilia Attica sat around the dinner table. Braziers heated the chamber. The pungent aroma of oysters still filled the air. Marble busts of Thales and Democritus sat upon the centre of the table. The servants had departed to leave Tiro and Caecilia to their venison - and Cicero to his sweetened porridge.

"It was a shame that you did not get to meet our guest last week, Attica."

"I hear he is honourable," Attica replied with a hint of a question, as much as an assertion, lining her tone.

"Who told you that, my dear?" Cicero's smiling eyes briefly narrowed in curiosity, or suspicion.

"Oh, no one," the woman remarked, shaking her head and dismissing the hearsay - and the "no one" in question.

"What did you think of him, Tiro?" Cicero asked. Having already questioned the secretary about the young Caesar, the conversation was more for their dinner guest's benefit.

"He has a modicum of Caesar's wit - but thankfully only a modicum of Caesar's ambition. But these traits may ripen - or rot - with age. In some ways he seemed to me more studious than ambitious. For instance he would perhaps wish to know about our friend Thales here - and question the sculptor about his methods - rather than just blindly covet the bust because of its rarity and value. Cleanthes said that he wanted Octavius to return to his studies and complete his education. But the tutor owned doubts, as well as hopes, that this would happen."

"And what of his companions? We know all too well of Oppius. All your father's gold Attica could not buy his allegiance - a trait which would prove admirable should he serve our cause. But what of his other lieutenant, this Agrippa?"

The sound of the silver fork falling first clattered on the plate, and then clanged against the tiled floor. Attica, suddenly flustered, nearly dropped her knife, too. Thankfully the blonde curls which fell down the sides of her face concealed her blushes.

"He is steadfastly loyal and has Caesar's ear as much as Balbus I warrant. We should still spend our time courting Salvidienus, or rather we should let Salvidienus court us. His son was close to Octavius on Apollonia but the family are staunch Republicans."

"Alright, continue in that vein. But do not encourage too strong an alliance with the self-regarding would-be optimate. That I have to suffer the man's prose is enough. I do not wish to suffer the man's company. Oh, there are so many throws left in this game of dice, not even Euclid could calculate a winner. Yet if the gods would permit me to load the dice I would still favour Brutus. Did I tell you both what he said to Mark Antony at their meeting after the Ides? Antony joked, 'Have you perchance a dagger under your arm even now?' To which Brutus drily replied, 'Yes - and a large one should you desire too, to be a tyrant.' Now there is a man with a sense of humour and sense of fearlessness for doing what's right. I warrant that it'll be a matter of when rather than if that Brutus musters an army and returns to Rome."

Although somewhat sighing at first when beginning his speech, Cicero beamed with paternal pride by its close. The young woman listened with rapt attention, humouring her host (having heard the anecdote before).

"So what do you think the fate of Rome will be?" Attica asked, partly curious and partly indulging the seasoned statesman.

Figuring that his master may now wax lyrical for some time, Tiro turned his attention to some notes he had to catch up on. Years of service had weakened the secretary's sight - and he squinted over the parchment to decipher his own shorthand.

"Firstly, the fate of Rome equates to the fate of us all. But to the matter. The wish is father of the thought, but Mark Antony and young Octavius will hopefully tear the Caesarian party apart. A house divided cannot stand. As such Mark Antony will not have the strength to defeat the Senate. And the Republic will be restored. Already some of the legions that Antony was relying on are siding with Octavius, or rather the pay rise he's promising them. Our agents have informed us that Antony is even going to have to leave Rome to win back the mutinous regiments. Although he is married to Fulvia - perhaps it's all just an excuse to get out of the house."

The years fell from his wizened countenance as Cicero smiled at his own remark.

"But in all honesty my dear I am unsure as to the future. At my age even the past becomes unclear. We will see what fate has in store for Rome. The hen is the wisest of all the animal creation, because she never cackles until the egg is laid. But let us not talk of politics any longer. We will depress ourselves. Or, it seems, worse - for we have bored Tiro it seems."

At hearing his name uttered Tiro pricked up his ears and turned to Cicero, as if awaiting instruction.

"Instead of admiring your own shorthand I would you look up and, wide-eyed, admire Attica's latest fresco on the wall behind you. The picture, still glistening with wet paint in the firelight, was that of the view of the valley from her bench. Azures, yellow-greens and textured browns brightened up the previously bare wall. Dominating the centre of the image however was a mysterious male figure, gazing out across the valley also.

"You flatter me by saying, my dear, that the figure in the painting is a young version of me. I neither had the stomach for soldiering in my youth, nor a soldierly build like that. Moreover I owned but my wits, rather than this estate, when I was your protagonist's age. But it really is quite an accomplished work. Thank you. Your father could have saved a small fortune in employing yourself, rather than commissioning overpriced Greek artists, to decorate the walls in his own villa."

But the winsome artist was barely listening to the praise of her host as she stared at her own work, lost in thought - thinking about Agrippa; her friend, world. Attica found herself praying to Octavius, to keep him safe. Later that evening she wrapped her blankets tightly around her, closed her eyes and imagined his muscular arm coil itself around her waist. She recalled how his rough hand tenderly caressed her back - and then scrunched up her buttock and pulled her pliant figure even closer. She smiled, mischievously, remembering the sensation, and placed her hand between her silken thighs as she drifted off to sleep. Her body tingled. Tears - of happiness at finding him and fear of losing him - soaked her pillow. She had never felt like this before, because she had never been in love before.

*

Moonbeams poured through the open windows. Brutus closed his eyes and breathed in Porcia's scent - honey and roses. She had finally drifted off to sleep. Her husband however could not sleep. Nor did he wish to, for the ghost of Caesar waited for him there. The quack doctor attending to his burgeoning army had brewed all manner of sleeping draughts - as foul as any nightmare - but to no avail. Brutus quietly slipped out of the bedroom and headed to his study. His eyes had become accustomed to the dark. Where before his night-time reading had been Plato and Sophocles - muster books and quartermaster reports now lay open upon his desk. Philosophical problems had given way to calculating rates of interest. He, Rome, was at the mercy of the money lenders. Would all their fates be decided on who could borrow the most money? He read the letter from Cassius again. Octavius had adopted the name "Caesar" – and was on his way to Rome. Brutus smiled, grimly. Would this Caesar now haunt his waking world, as Julius did his dreams?

32

Morning. A swirling crest of smoke - fuelled by homes, forges and ovens - hung over the sprawling, hilly city in the distance. The white marble of the Palatine still shone through, like coral beneath murky water, however. Indeed a stranger may have mistaken the stately grandeur of Hortensius' villa atop the Palatine as being the estate of a god rather than man, Octavius idly fancied. Hortensius, that famed advocate who proved, for Cleanthes, that "one can be master of the law without serving justice". The party could also discern the Aqua Appia and Aqua Martial wend their way around Rome's towering hills. The Viminal, the Aventine (the people's hill), the Capitoline with ornate temples flowering upon it like a stone garden, the Quirinal, Caelian and the Esquiline - with its senatorial properties lining the crown of the hill and the slums of the Subura littering the bottom, the houses as rickety as the inhabitants' prospects.

The gilded sun was still ascending in a vibrant sky behind Caesar, the sun seemingly appearing like a halo over his head. The evening before bore witness to a comet streaking across the starry firmament, auguring the arrival of good fortune. Aye,

Balbus had been astute in choosing his date for Caesar's arrival. Octavius, riding a white gelding akin to his great-uncle's famed steed, trotted at the head of the party. Agrippa rode alongside his friend, pensiveness etched in both of their faces as they took in some of the tombs of Rome's dead lining the Appian Way. A particularly ornate and original design caught Agrippa's eye and he slowed to read the inscription.

"Stranger, should you stop to admire the beauty of this tomb, know that the woman housed inside was more beautiful still. Helen was her name. We were betrothed, but she passed away before we were married. Although never her husband, I feel like a widower. I will try and live my life as if still inspired by her bright soul, so that in death, I may marry her in the afterlife. And so my sad story may become a happy one."

Agrippa thought of Cleanthes, then Attica.

"So, what do you hope that someone will say on your tomb?" Octavius asked his friend, with half an eye still on the magnificent villa of the Palatine.

"That I died peacefully in my sleep at a ripe old age. And that I did not owe anyone any money. On second thoughts, that I owe a huge amount of money - and to my bitterest enemy."

"I shall make sure that our bitterest enemies are lying in their tombs before us Marcus," Octavius darkly declared, as he thought of those responsible for the deaths of Caesar and Cleanthes. "They must die," Octavius coldly stated, as if a logician were determining their fate.

*

The sound of the breeze whistling through the pillars and effigies of the tombs was soon eclipsed by the murmuring and hubbub of the crowd, ever-increasing in number, which was spilling out of the city to greet Caesar's heir. Balbus had sent letters ahead to loyal Caesarians to arrange a welcome for Octavius. Water vendors and costermongers had set up stalls. Soldiers, citizens, plebs, woman of rank (and their nubile daughters, dressed in their finest stolas and jewellery), merchants and the political classes populated the crowd alike. A few wore the black toga pulla as a mark of respect and mournfulness. Yet many wore their gayest attire. Children were placed on their parents' shoulders to get a better look at the Caesar. Anticipation and expectation rippled through the throng. Many carried placards, articulating their support for the Caesar.

"A Rome without a Caesar would be like the Cyclops without his eye."

"Caesar, save Rome - from itself!"

Agrippa whispered into his horse's ear and stroked his neck to sooth the nervous animal, not used to such scenes.

"Look smart men, eyes front - no matter which wench attracts your attention," Oppius ordered in all seriousness, but with a smile also. In response the infanteers tightened their formation and step and puffed out their chests, like sails billowing in the wind.

"At such times it should be my duty to remind Caesar that he is mortal - so what would you like someone to say about you upon your death?" Agrippa asked.

The clip-clop of hooves and caligae across the flagstones was soon muffled out by the congregation, as an increasing number of people spied the party and cheered. Octavius raised his voice to his friend to make himself heard.

"All the world's a stage - and all the men and women merely players. When I come to the end of my life I just hope I can look back and say that if I have played my part well, clap your hands, and dismiss me with applause from the theatre." Irony and sincerity vied for sovereignty in Caesar's expression as he spoke. "But let us talk no more of our end, my friend. We are all but in Rome - and he who is tired of Rome is tired of life. I want to introduce you to Octavia as soon as possible, Marcus. We shall have dinner - and the food will be as fine as her company."

Octavius warmly smiled, thinking about his sister. The idle fancy crept into his thoughts again that he would like to see his best friend and sister betrothed, to formally make his lieutenant part of his family.

Cheers began to mushroom into jubilant roars and salutations. Petals were strewn across the road ahead. Agrippa slowed his pace a little, allowing Caesar to march at the vanguard of his party alone. Agrippa was content to be the second man of Rome. The scene had an air of a military triumph however - and he was tempted to whisper in Caesar's ear, "Remember you are mortal; remember you are mortal."

Octavius was both touched and amused by the crowd's adoration. He waved imperiously, yet also affectionately - Caesar-like - at the people below him. Women gazed up, almost swooning. Men nodded approvingly, remembering Julius Caesar. Priests and augurs pronounced prayers and blessings, perhaps hoping to be spotted and provided with patronage. As the party passed a segment of the crowd who appeared impoverished, Oppius ordered a number of his men to distribute food and alms. Some raised their hands in gratitude to the Caesar, worshipping him like a god.

Not everyone viewed the young Caesar with such adoration and affection, however. From the city walls a trio of optimate senators looked down with disdain at the interloper from Velitrae. The adopted son had inherited his father's arrogance. The mob was displaying certain atavistic tendencies too - servitude and vulgarity.

"How long do you think the boy will last?"

"About as long as the bread he's handing out. Antony will chew him up and spit him out. He's far too wet behind the ears. An aedile has more influence and could politically outwit him. I look forward to his speeches, too. Will there not be pauses in the oration when the boy has to suck his thumb?"

The self-important senators let out a chorus of laughter, albeit the man who stood close to them, overhearing the exchange, merely raised an eyebrow and the corner of his mouth in a half-smile. Domitius Enobarbus thought to himself how Octavius had inherited Caesar's luck. He knew not the details but the party had somehow survived Gravius' attack. An agent from Praeneste had sent word ahead. It was the very last dispatch that Antony had read before the consul had ventured out to Asculum, to quell the disquiet among the Caesarian legion encamped there.

"I shall deal with the whelp when I return. The boy needs to get used to waiting upon my decisions anyway. This will be good practice for him."

The aristocratic senators beside him laughed again at a jibe, yet Domitius shook his head - in disappointment or amusement. If the reports were true - and Octavius had gleaned the support of both Balbus and Cicero - then the Senators may well now possess a shelf life as long as the bread that Caesar's heir was distributing.

Oppius offered a subtle nod to a brace of fellow centurions who stood with their cohorts on either side of the road. As Octavius passed they saluted in unison and then drew their swords in a guard of honour.

"Caesar, Caesar, Caesar."

The chant swelled, rumbled, like magma inside the belly of a volcano, waiting to explode.

"Caesar, Caesar, Caesar." Citizens soon took up the soldiers' cry.

Balbus and Oppius hadn't informed Octavius of this part of the reception. They wanted Caesar's reaction to be genuine, as the authenticity would add to the performance. Cornelius had also expressed to Oppius, whilst planning the young Caesar's arrival into the city, how Octavius needed to be convinced of his greatness as well as the people.

"Caesar, Caesar, Caesar."

Agrippa soaked up the colourful and jubilant atmosphere. He started to compose in his head what he would later write to Salvidienus, who had begged him for more news on what had happened and what was going to happen. He would posit how

314

they would soon all be debating the future of Rome in the Senate, instead of under a shady tree in an Apollonian field. Agrippa thought of Rufus but briefly however - and he started to compose a letter to someone whose mettle was more attractive.

"In some senses Rome was always more of an idea than place to me - a just, intelligent and magnificent idea. Yet today I witnessed the semi-divine city which housed that idea ... And riding through its gates was Caesar, who embodies the idea of Rome ... But for all its expanse and opulence my mind's eye rested upon a far more just, intelligent and magnificent image ... More than Rome or Caesar I aspire to the idea of you ... I keep your letter by my bedside. I house it in a sealed jar, so as to preserve its perfume ... Every night I drink in your scent and swim in your words ... Oppius asked me if I was drunk the other evening, as he caught me 'grinning like a fool' as I thought of you ... You make me want to be a better man Attica ..."

"Caesar, Caesar, Caesar."

The words thumped out from hundreds of lungs, in tune with his beating heart. Caesar beamed, as brightly as the midday sun. The light spun his fair hair into gold. He waved, warmly and magnanimously - and shook the occasional hand. The people loved Caesar. He was Caesar. Therefore the people loved him. And he would return their love. He would provide food for their stomachs, a sense of glory and worth to fill their hearts - and spectacles and entertainments for their eyes to feast upon. Caesar should be a servant of the people, as much as their master. His client list would be every Roman citizen, equestrian and farrier alike. Laws, libraries and religion would edify. Odours and ordure - and the cacophony of sound - poured out the gates of the city as Octavius approached its entrance. The people's love - and his sense of destiny - bore him upon a cloud. He would become the First Man of Rome. *If Sulla could, why can't I?* - Gaius asked himself, quoting Pompey. Again, irony and sincerity laced the thought. Octavius smiled, mercurially.

"Caesar, Caesar, Caesar, Caesar, Caesar, Caesar."

He had never felt so close to Julius as now. He sensed Caesar's burden, pride and ecstasy - admiring and pitying his great-uncle more as a result. The cheers chimed in his ears, spurring him onwards. The gates sucked him in too, Charybdis-like. Inside, the walls and buildings bred shadows. Agrippa fell behind as the tide of supporters increased between them.

"Caesar, Caesar, Caesar."

The people swarmed around the heir. Some just wanted to touch his cloak.

Endnote

Many of the major characters who feature in Augustus: Son of Rome existed. Much of the narrative adheres to historical events. But Augustus: Son of Rome is very much a novel - so I have made stuff up too. Apologies for any historical inaccuracies, whether they are unwitting or not.

Over the years I have had the chance to meet - and work with - a number of authors whose books proved to be a source of inspiration and information for Augustus: Son of Rome. Tom Holland, Adrian Goldsworthy, Conn Iggulden and Simon Scarrow continue to entertain and educate. I am not alone in also owing a debt to Cicero, Shakespeare, Plutarch and Suetonius - whose works are equally entertaining and educational. In regards to further readinzg about Augustus and his era I can strongly recommend Ronald Syme's The Roman Revolution, Josiah Osgood's Caesar's Legacy and Anthony Everitt's biographies of Cicero and Augustus.

Should you have enjoyed spending time with the characters of Lucius Oppius and Julius Caesar then you may also want to read the novella series, Sword of Rome. The book covers Caesar's invasion of Britain, the Battle of Alesia, the crossing of the Rubicon and the Battle of Pharsalus.

Augustus and Agrippa will return in Augustus: Son of Caesar

Should you have enjoyed Augustus: Son of Rome, or have any questions, please do contact me at richard@endeavourpress.com or at richardforemanauthor.com

Richard Foreman

ENDEAVOUR INK

Endeavour Ink is an imprint of Endeavour Press.

If you enjoyed *Augustus: Son of Rome* check out
Endeavour Press's eBooks here:
www.endeavourpress.com

For weekly updates on our free and discounted eBooks sign up
to our newsletter:
www.endeavourpress.com

Follow us on Twitter:
@EndeavourPress

ENDEAVOUR PRESS